PASSION
FAVORS *The*
BOLD

Other titles by Theresa Romain

Season for Temptation

Season for Surrender

Season for Scandal

Season for Desire

Fortune Favors the Wicked

PASSION FAVORS *The* BOLD

THERESA ROMAIN

ZEBRA BOOKS
KENSINGTON PUBLISHING CORP.
http://www.kensingtonbooks.com

ACKNOWLEDGMENTS

My deepest thankps to my husband and daughter, who make my life good and make my work possible. Thanks to all my family and friends for their support, especially Amanda, CP and carnival-food enabler.

As always, my agent Paige Wheeler has been a wonderful advocate, and my editor Alicia Condon made my work better with her insights. Gratitude and virtual chocolate to you both, with real chocolate to follow in the future!

Many thanks to the team at Kensington Publishing Corp. for turning manuscripts into beautiful books: the copyeditors, production staff, marketing and publicity team, art directors, and those who stay on top of the myriad details involved in shepherding a book through publication. I'm so grateful for your work.

And dear readers, thanks for taking Hugo and Georgette to your hearts when you met them in *Fortune Favors the Wicked.* I hope you love their story.

2-23-17 BT

Chapter One

Late May 1817
London

As one would expect of a young woman raised in a bookshop, Georgette Frost was accustomed to flights of imagination. But not even in her most robust fancies could she have dreamed her present situation.

Not because she was garbed in boys' clothing. Many the blue-blooded heroine of a *conte de fée* had disguised herself to escape the cruel predations of a wicked relative.

True, Georgette's veins ran with the ink of her family's longtime bookshop rather than blue blood. And Cousin Mary was not wicked; merely overwhelmed by the ceaseless demands of the shop and her multitude of children.

Nor was Georgette dismayed to set out on her own, with all her worldly possessions in a small trunk. Freed from the endless shelves of the shop, the constant questions of starched-collar customers, she had felt gloriously unfettered as she sought a coaching house and prepared to join her elder brother on his travels for the first time.

There was only one problem, but that problem was a significant one: six feet tall, hawkish of feature, and stuffy of temperament. Lord Hugo Starling, the youngest son of the Duke of Willingham. Friend of Georgette's elder brother, Benedict. Representative of everything chill and sterile about the life of the mind: study, solitude, and sternness. Every time he had visited Frost's Bookshop, he had demonstrated this anew, curt and exasperated by the world outside of the latest book on which he had his eye.

Unfortunately, Lord Hugo didn't remain confined to bookshops. He had encountered Georgette at the coaching inn before she could take her seat on the stagecoach. After a public spat, which did credit to neither of them—though far less to Lord Hugo, who ought to have kept his high-bridged nose out of her business—Georgette had grudgingly scrambled into his carriage.

She now faced him, glaring, as he settled against the soft velvet squabs. "How can you say what I want is impossible? You *asked* where I wanted to go."

"I asked, yes. But I didn't say I would take you there. It would be wrong to send you to the wilds of Derbyshire."

The wilds. She almost snorted. Likely Derbyshire, all grasses and livestock, *did* seem wild to a London-bred noble with a perfectly knotted cravat. Georgette was London-bred herself, but with an elder brother once in the Royal Navy, she felt she'd seen a bit of the world, if only through his letters.

This carriage, though, came from a world of luxury she'd never known. Unmarred and sleek, the wood shone with lemon-scented oil. Within sparkling-clear glass globes, the wicks of the unlit lamps were trimmed. The velvet squabs were brushed clean and soft.

Her secondhand jacket and cheap boys' shoes had seemed the perfect disguise when she was outdoors. Now she felt shabby and false, her pale blond hair falling in drab strands from beneath the cap.

Rapunzel, back in a different sort of tower. *Cendrillon*, doomed to a new sort of drudgery.

In retrieving her—no! *abducting* her—Lord Hugo had been splashed with mud and cheap liquor, his fine coat stained and reeking. Somehow he still managed to look confident and unbending. Like the carriage, he was tidy and elegant except for his encounter with Georgette.

She set her jaw. "I wish you'd left me alone. I was going to find my brother."

He muttered something that sounded suspiciously like *fool's errand.* "You want to seek the Royal Reward, don't you? Your brother is sure he'll find it, and you want to help him."

She waved a hand. "Of course. Who wouldn't want five thousand pounds?"

For such was the reward offered by the Royal Mint to anyone who located fifty thousand missing gold sovereigns. New coins, not yet circulated, they had been stolen from the Mint in a mysterious and violent rampage some weeks before. Four guards had been killed, and six trunks of the sovereigns stolen. Since then, no evidence of them had been found—until one gold sovereign was spent in a Derbyshire village, drawing the curious and the treasure-mad from all corners of England.

That village—called Strawfield—was where Benedict

had gone as soon as he returned to England from his latest voyage. And so that was where Georgette would go to find him, and her fortune.

"Until I can write your brother, I shall take you to stay with my mother," Lord Hugo decided. "You shall be the guest of the Duchess of Willingham. Won't that be . . . er, nice?"

She could almost hear the gears of his mind grinding. *Smile! Present single option as though it were appealing while giving no choice!*

"No." She folded her arms. Rude, yes; but he had been rude in taking Georgette away from her coaching stop. Her ticket, purchased with scraped-together savings from her salary at the bookshop, was now money wasted. "None of your behavior has been nice at all. I cannot *believe* you told a crowd of strangers that I was your criminal nephew who had stolen silver from my dying mother."

Instead of looking chastened, the cursed man shot her a grim smile. "Turnabout is fair play. You told them I was drunk. *And* you told your own cousins at the bookshop that you'd been invited to stay with my family. Won't it be agreeable to convert one of your lies into the truth?"

"Certainly. You have my permission to get drunk. As soon as you return to me the price of my wasted ticket, that is."

He scrubbed a hand over his face, then sank back against the squabs with apparent weariness. "I took you up, Miss Frost, because your brother would want you to be safe. And that is the end of the discussion."

"Oh, good! Then you agree with me." She bared her teeth in a grin. "You should let me go to Benedict."

"I can't let you go alone, Miss Frost," he replied. "It

wouldn't be right. A woman alone . . . there are those who would hurt you."

Thus my disguise as a boy. She rolled her eyes. "If your conscience won't permit me to travel alone, you may accompany me to Derbyshire."

"Out of the question. My business holds me in London."

"What business?"

"Endless business. Only today, I have a meeting at Somerset House with the president of the Royal Society. Then I must review a new treatise on infection at the Royal College of Physicians."

"Say 'royal' once more."

His dark blue gaze snapped to meet hers, suspicious. "Why?"

"Because I hadn't got it into my brain that you're a lord who moves in exalted circles and can do whatever he likes."

The carriage rocked on its well-oiled springs, swallowing the roughness of London's roads. Twisting and cornering. Taking her away from the coaching inn. Was she closer to Derbyshire now, or farther away?

Farther. Definitely farther.

She sighed. "Lord Hugo, I don't want to stay with your mother. I want to go to my own family. Surely you can understand that."

He lifted a brow. "Such a wish is unfathomable to me. But then, my family is ashamed of me."

Dark suppositions about hidden chambers and monstrous deeds flooded her mind. Now it was her turn to ask, with some suspicion, "Why is that?"

"Because I went to medical college instead of into the clergy. Because I call upon ill people and sometimes perform surgeries."

Georgette released a caught breath. "How terrible. I can understand why they are disgusted by you."

He winced, then tried to cover it by adjusting his starched white cuffs.

Oh, dear. "I'm *teasing*, Lord Hugo. I can understand nothing of the sort. To me, such behavior seems . . ." She cast about for the right word. "Acceptable."

"Acceptable," he repeated drily. The carriage gave a sway, and he steadied himself with a broad hand against the fabric-softened ceiling.

"Is that why you're going to all those royal locations? To learn something about patient care?"

"Nothing so admirable. I'm looking for a patron for a private hospital." He lowered his hand, regarding her narrowly. "You're about to ask why again, aren't you?"

"I would never intrude into a matter that was no business of mine." She fired a pointed stare at him.

"Right. I'm sure you wouldn't." The curve of his mouth was distant and haughty, the sort of not-quite smile worn by classical statues. "Surgeons with little knowledge cut and operate, while the physicians with the most medical training drone and profess and hardly ever see patients. I think the best of both roles should be blended. I intend to see that it is."

"So your meetings are to ask important people to give you money because your family will not support your scheme?"

"Indeed. Honesty is the most expedient way of getting what one wants."

"When one is dealing with the elite?" She hooted. "Not likely. I've changed my mind. Take me along with you. I want to watch this."

"Ah—well. No. This is a delicate matter. If I hope to persuade them this time—"

"*This* time? You've asked before?"

His gaze slid away. "Twice."

"So you'll batter them with arguments and proposals they've already rejected. Twice."

"Because they are *wrong*."

"Say no more. That would convince me."

"I ought to put you out of the carriage right now," he muttered.

"If you'll give me coach fare to Strawfield village in Derbyshire, I'll be on my way."

It wouldn't be the first time she'd left right before being evicted. After Georgette and Benedict's parents died, Benedict had inherited the bookshop—and sold it to Cousin Mary and her husband with the understanding that they would house Georgette until she turned twenty-one. But in the cramped family quarters above, Mary needed another day maid much more than she needed a cousin who served as bookstore clerk. And Georgette's wages, meager though they were, would easily hire Mary the help she needed.

Better to leave now than to find herself cast out— with kindness and apology—in a few more weeks. Better to descend from Lord Hugo's carriage before she found herself in a world she knew not at all.

She had raised her hand, prepared to rap on the ceiling and bring the carriage to a halt, when Lord Hugo spoke: "Wait. Please."

She glared at him.

"Miss Frost. Please do not make yourself unsafe."

His tone was stern, but not unkind. How odd. She let her hand fall to her lap, fingers twisting together.

"My lord, I don't wish to be unsafe. I wish to go to my brother."

This observation seemed to strike the high-handed man in the solar plexus. "I am trying to *help* your brother. And you. Why do you think I visited Frost's Bookshop so often?"

"Because you wanted books."

"I could buy books anywhere."

Her mouth opened—and then closed again.

He turned aside, working at the latch on the carriage window. "Warm day," he grunted. "Some air would be— *ah.* There. Isn't that pleasant?"

The gruff tone of his voice had gone tentative.

In fact, the air was humid and close outside as well as in. With the window open, smuts wafted in like a sprinkling of black snow, making him blink.

If his expression were always thus—a little weary, a little befuddled—he would be quite handsome.

Digging her split-seamed shoe into the mat cushioning the floor of the carriage, she looked down. "Thank you for your concern."

"If you were my sister, there is no way in heaven I'd let you run off and seek treasure."

As quickly as that, the moment was spoiled. Her head snapped up. "Let, let, let. Just *stop.* If I were your sister, I wouldn't need the money, so the point is moot. If I were your sister, I'd have been raised on clouds of spun sugar and dined off dishes made of carved diamond."

"That is ridiculous. Diamond is far too hard to carve for use as crockery. Too small as well." He considered. "However, my sisters-in-law are remarkably fond of spun sugar."

"Hugo." She used his name without the honorific for the first time, and his brows lifted—displaying surprise, but not, she thought, displeasure. "You asked where I wanted to go. Besides the cousins I have left behind, my brother is the only close family I have in the world. I do not know him well, and I do not know what his life is like. But I know being in his company would be better than being alone."

And then an idea struck her. A marvelous, wonderful idea, worthy of a heroine in a fairy tale. "You really could come with me," she said. "Leave your business with Royal This and That behind and try something new. Pursue the Royal Reward instead."

Impossible. Illogical. Yet as Hugo turned the suggestion over in his mind, it did not seem inconceivable.

He bought himself a moment to think. "Not while you're wearing those ridiculous boys' clothes. I can't imagine how you fooled anyone."

She shrugged. "People see what they want to. I couldn't have deceived Benedict, of course."

This was undoubtedly true. Her brother had lost his sight due to a tropical illness during his stint in the Royal Navy. Ever since, Benedict had navigated the world—including medical college alongside Hugo—through hearing and touch, and there was little nuance that escaped his notice.

"There's an idea," she went on, sounding pleased. "If you don't like my boys' costume, I can change my garb and travel as your sister."

"I never said I would travel with—"

"It's *perfect*." She leaned forward, eyes wide with enthusiasm. The already precarious cap tumbled from her head, allowing all that fairy-pale hair to fall. Down about her shoulders; down, down, to her waist. "If you help me, I will take the reward and you may take all the credit. You can use the popular notoriety to gain acceptance for your pet project."

Hugo bridled. "'Pet project' is hardly the way one ought to refer to a private hospital with the potential to save many lives. And why should I not set off on my own and have both the acclaim and the reward?"

"Because that would be horrid of you. And if you have the acclaim, you won't need the reward."

His brows lifted. "So you say. Another thing I won't need is the scandal of being thought to have abducted an ungrateful whelp."

"I give you my word, I won't tell a crowd of strangers you're trying to abduct me. As long as you don't try to abduct me," she added. "Again."

Abduction. *God.* This was his thanks for rescuing her from a crowd that, if they recognized her as a gently bred young woman rather than a scrubby youth, would have turned on her in every way imaginable.

"If you accompany me to Strawfield," Georgette added, "I shall behave properly."

Feigning docility, she lowered her eyes. Light eyes, like the pale of a summer sky. Pale hair and skin, too. Seeing her among the mazelike shelves of Frost's Bookshop, Hugo had always thought she looked as though she were half faded into the pages of a story.

A fanciful observation. Most uncharacteristic of him. Especially since, as his visits to the bookshop stacked in number, he saw how hard and how prosaically she worked. Because Hugo had befriended her brother during their medical studies in Edinburgh,

Georgette seemed not to regard the duke's son with the formality she would a stranger. In his presence, she carried garments for the laundress, scooped up her cousin's wayward toddlers, marked accounts, stacked books—and so on, in ceaseless motion.

"Do you want to search for your brother, Miss Frost? Or for the stolen coins?"

She considered. "First the second thing. Then the first thing second."

"I should have guessed," he murmured. "Do explain to me. My family already disapproves, and my would-be patrons have already declined. How would notoriety for finding stolen sovereigns increase my credibility in medical circles? And better still, how would it translate into financial support for my hospital?"

"Finding the sovereigns would make you tonnish. Then everything you said and did would be acceptable to people of influence." She spoke matter-of-factly, as though this were obvious.

And maybe it should have been. These people of influence—of which his father was one, and of whom his family was constantly aware—were unimpressed by the carefully constructed appeals to logic on which Hugo prided himself. By accounts of the increased productivity of fields when tenants were fit and healthy. By evidence of the opposite, too: tales of infection, of suppuration, of dirty wards, of lives that should have been saved.

Accompany me to Strawfield: the words painted a lovely picture such as he had not seen for years. A wide sky, absent the caustic smell of chloride of lime and the heavy odor of ill bodies, often beyond help. People who listened to him simply because they thought him worth listening to. Not because they *had* to, because his father was a duke. Not dismissing him, either, as a younger son with wild ideas that trespassed against the upper class's notions of suitability.

When influenza broke out among the dukedom's tenants, Hugo's own father, the Duke of Willingham, had called Hugo mad to quarantine ill tenants away from their healthy relatives. Everyone knew that influenza came from an imbalance of humors, said his father, so what use would a quarantine be? But when the spread of illness was halted and the outbreak ended almost as soon as it began, the duke granted that perhaps Hugo had been right.

Not right enough to support his other medical ideas, though. Not right enough to grant that Hugo's chosen field was a worthwhile way to spend one's life.

They hadn't spoken in quite some time. It was better that way.

"Think of all the people you could help with your hospital," Georgette coaxed.

Hugo folded his arms. "You are thinking of one. You."

She beamed. "You only fold your arms when you're about to change your mind."

"I do not." He unfolded his arms, but they snapped back into a cradle about his midsection. "How did you—why . . ."

"I learned such signals working in the family bookshop. When to push someone harder. When a bit more persuasion would help me to make the sale."

She had sorted him out, that was true enough—though he wasn't prepared to tell her he'd give in. Despite himself, his mouth curved up at one corner. "All that fluffy blond hair covers a diabolical mind."

Her brows knit. "What is diabolical about both of us getting what we want?"

To this, he had no answer: only a question. In this agreement, would he be the devil, or poor Faust, who sold his soul?

Chapter Two

"You'll have to stay in here," Hugo decided.

Georgette Frost was improper from head to toe, from tumbled-down wavy hair to falling-apart shoes. There was no place for her in Somerset House.

Through the carriage window, he eyed the familiar, immense structure. The headquarters of the Royal Society was a great pale pile of columns and arches, of story upon story that gobbled a great stretch of the Strand as if space was no matter and money no object.

Lord Hugo Starling did not make mistakes. He acted with calm and logic, following analysis and forethought. But if he *did* make mistakes, bringing Georgette Frost with him to Somerset House would have been one of them.

It was the only way he could attend his planned meeting with the Royal Society's president, though. So. Analysis. Forethought.

When he reached for the carriage door, Georgette spoke up. "Wait. I have an idea."

Hugo halted, half arisen from the squabs, hand outstretched. "You strike fear into my heart."

"I should come in with you. I can be a good distraction from your . . ." She motioned at his upper body.

"From my stinking, stained, formerly fashionable coat that I owe to my last attempt to intervene on your behalf?" Reluctantly, he settled back onto the squabs. "Any more of your *help*, Miss Frost, and I'll find myself in Bedlam."

She looked amused. "First, that was *your* help, not mine. And I didn't ask for it or want it. When I help *you*—well, your coat won't miraculously come clean, but I think your meeting will go far more smoothly."

"Is there to be a second point?"

"Yes. Second, you may call me Georgette. You've bought enough books and seen me carry enough laundry that we ought to be more informal."

"And I've seen you in breeches with your hair down."

"Oh, right. You'd better not call me Georgette at the moment." Starting at the ends, she began twisting her hair into a tight coil. "While I'm dressed as a boy, you ought to call me . . . Bone-box."

She looked as if she were enjoying herself. "I'm not calling you Bone-box," he said.

"'Course not. I don't know you, guv. How could you know my name?"

"*Guv?*" Hugo regretted not opening the carriage door and flinging himself through it when he had the chance.

"I can't call you 'my lord,' because we've only just met. How could I know how blue-blooded you are?"

"Your feigned uncertainty is not my greatest reservation about this suggestion of yours."

"This is going to be effective. Trust me." Georgette finished twisting up her hair, then yanked her cap over the mass. "What would make more sense than for you to bring in the sort of urchin who would be helped by the new sort of hospital you have planned?"

"Many things. Many things in the world would make more sense than that." The air was humid and close, the open window providing no breeze.

"You still regret your coat, don't you? You mustn't worry about it. If men always went home when they smelled of liquor, all society balls would end before ten o'clock."

She had a point there.

Even so: "Why are you so suspiciously helpful all of a sudden?"

"Because you're so delightful and handsome that I can't stay away from you for so much as a minute?" Before he had time to take this in, she continued, "Perhaps not. Perhaps it's because I am sorry your coat was ruined. And because I believe you need all the help you can get, determined as you are to berate a man who has already told you no three times."

"The first reason was much better," Hugo grumbled. "And it was only twice, not three times. Though both rejections were from Latham at the Royal College of Physicians. This is my first approach to Banks."

"Is it? Then you're assured of success with me at your side."

Damn the woman; he was about to fold his arms again. He clenched his fists, forcing his elbows to remain straight. "What sort of plan do you have in mind?"

"Don't trouble yourself, Hugo. You'll come out smelling like roses." She sniffed, wrinkling her nose at

the sour odor of his rotgut-stained coat. "Figuratively."
And then she grinned.

It was the grin that won him over, as though they
were coconspirators. Hugo couldn't recall the last
time someone other than a shopkeeper had offered to
help him. Not since his brother Matthew's death fourteen years before had someone taken his part.

"All right," he said. "I believe you're sincere. You
may come to the meeting with me, but only because
you begged."

It wasn't a mistake to say yes. It was reasonable. She
said she would help. The unexpected ringing in his
ears of *you're so delightful and handsome*—spoken in
jest—was decidedly *not* reasonable. But that did not
matter; it didn't influence his decision.

From beneath the squabs, he fetched his hospital
plans, rolled up in a long leather case. Then at last, he
opened the door. His coachman had descended, waiting for the carriage's occupants to emerge, and the
man let the steps down at once. Hugo clambered out,
then extended a hand to help Georgette.

"I'm not a lady," she said in a gruff semblance of a
stripling's voice, ignoring his hand and hopping down
on her own. "I'm Bone-box, the horrid urchin you
plucked from the gutter."

"The gutter, you say. Of the Strand." Hugo squinted
down the bustling length of the wide, tonnish street.
"Right. Let's be on with it, Bone-box."

As the coachman closed the door behind them,
she fell into step at Hugo's side. Tallish for a woman,
she had a long and determined stride, and they made
their swift way to the main entrance.

Though not a member of the Royal Society, Hugo
had been to Somerset House any number of times

before. Besides the quarters of the scientists, it housed
public offices and the Royal Academy of Arts, which,
during Hugo's youth, had inflicted upon him many a
dull afternoon of regarding paintings at his mother's
side.

The sound of their footsteps was gentle on the
floor; the air seemed cooler in the great open space.
The entry hall of Somerset House was designed to im-
press, with a painted ceiling two stories above and long
arcades of windows taller than a man. Hugo led Georgette to the spiral staircase, which took them to the
story on which Sir Joseph Banks kept his office. This
required a complex navigation through smaller chambers and corridors that bumped this way and that. As
they walked, Hugo nodded greetings to the curious
faces he passed by.

"They're looking at you, Bone-box," he muttered.
"Give the good people a wave."

She ignored him. "It's so grand in here," she
breathed. "It's lovely and tall and airy."

Today Somerset House seemed to Hugo no more
than a nut that needed to be cracked. But to someone
who had spent her days in a bookshop where empty
space meant income lost, the vertical portions of the
building granted to each department must have
seemed, to borrow Georgette's understatement, *acceptable.*

Outside the door to Banks's chamber, Hugo paused.
"Remember, you promised you'd be helpful. Behave
yourself."

"I will behave *like* myself," she replied. "Only better."

"Better? Have I come upon the Royal Reward already?"

"Better suited for this situation, I mean." She stuffed

her hands into her pockets, adopting the slouching posture of a reluctant youth.

He regarded her with narrowed eyes. Would her disguise fool Banks? Was this a fool's errand entirely? A lock of her hair had loosened from its coil beneath the cap, slipping in a loop over one ear. Clean and long, it was unmistakably the hair of a lady.

With his thumb, Hugo caught the edge and stroked the treacherous lock back under the cap. He had acted without thought—but her hair was smooth, and her skin was soft. As of their own accord, his fingertips lingered on each.

The tender sensations took him aback, and he jerked away his hand. "Sorry," he said. "You had— there was this—that is, I saw a hair coming loose."

Her hand lifted to her cheek, her expression puzzled. "Thanks. Right."

"In we go." Hugo hoisted his long leather case under one arm, remembering this time to precede the supposed Bone-box through the doorway.

"Lord Hugo! Greetings to you," called the old man behind the huge desk.

Sir Joseph Banks, president of the Royal Society for longer than Hugo had been alive, had created himself a scholarly nest in one of the chambers given to the use of his organization. Fireplace and desk, massive chair and pillowed lap desk, books and books, more books and yet more. The grate was unlit, the curtains opened to draw in wistful daylight.

At the center of it all, the baronet sat in a great wheeled chair. "Gout," he grunted, gesturing to his chair. "It's dreadful today; couldn't take a step. Forgive me for not rising, Lord Hugo. And whom have you brought with you?" Sir Joseph's face was like a turtle's, fierce and forward and with shrewd eyes. They lingered over the rumpled bits of Hugo's appearance, the unlikely presence of Georgette at his side.

In for a penny, in for a potential patronage. "This rapscallion darted in front of my carriage and spooked the horses. My coachman collared him."

"I didn't want to steal them," said Georgette in her gruff boy's voice, sounding as though she had wanted nothing more in the world. Her tidy accent had slipped into the brasher cadence of the rookeries. "I weren't going to use my knife to cut the harness."

"This nameless young urchin—"

"Bone-box!"

"—is," Hugo hurried on, "exactly the sort of Londoner who currently receives indifferent care from indifferently trained caregivers at one of the city's public hospitals."

"Coo, no I don't," said the professed Bone-box. "I wouldn't go to a hospital 'less I wanted to die of somethin' worse than what I went in for."

She wasn't the only one who held this opinion. The city's public hospitals were short of staff, overcrowded, undersupplied. Too often, they were a place where the ill and weak went to become more so, not to be healed.

"As I mentioned in my correspondence arranging this meeting," Hugo said, "I seek patronage for a different sort of hospital. One in which the patients wouldn't die."

Banks gave a bark of laughter. "You have such power?"

"I have such skill and vision," Hugo replied. What was the purpose of false modesty?

Georgette made a noise he would have previously

thought impossible from the throat of a respectable woman.

Opening his leather case, Hugo extracted his precious plans and unrolled them before the baronet. Banks spread them flat, centering them before him on the large desk. "Why have you applied to me here, my lord? Why not the Royal College of Physicians?"

Hugo chose his words carefully. "They lack the vision required for such a project."

"Turned you down flat, eh?" Banks looked pleased. Though not a student of medicine himself, he was known to nurture competition with the Royal College of Physicians. The stocks of medicinal plants grown by the Royal Society surpassed those of any other organization in England.

"They tossed the rotgut on him, like," said Georgette. "When he was there earlier. Saw it happen m'self."

"Now, really, er, Bone-box." Hugo tried to sound as though he were covering for a true statement rather than a ridiculous lie. "We needn't speak of that. Our business is with Sir Joseph."

The baronet looked gratified. "The Royal College allows members who aren't proper gentlemen," he tutted. "Surgeons in the mix; apothecaries, too. Not true men of science." He peered more closely at the architectural drawing atop the stack of plans.

Hugo's opinion of surgeons and apothecaries was more favorable, but he pressed on, choosing his words carefully. "I intend that men of learning and skill will administer the proposed hospital. You see that I have accounted for separation between patients with various illnesses, as well as rooms for surgeries, treatments, and convalescence. Complete care until the patient has recovered."

"Any ideas about gout?" Banks asked.

"Drink lemon juice," said the ruffian at Hugo's side. "As much as ever you can get your hands on. Or if that costs more rag than you can get—"

"Thank you, I think Sir Joseph can locate lemons if he wishes." Hugo shot her a threatening glare. "And . . . Sir Joseph, that is not a terrible suggestion, if you wish to try it."

"Me mam had gout. I been stealing lemons for her since ever I could walk," Georgette confided with alarming smoothness. "Or should I not say that? I mean, me brother was."

Hugo cleared his throat. "Never mind the lemons. These plans were drawn to my specification by an engineer; then I made corrections and alterations for maximum efficiency."

"And used a purse-full of ten-pound words," hooted Georgette.

Most young women would have quailed at the glare Hugo shot her. She only blinked back at him, all innocence.

"Hmm." Oblivious, Banks looked over the carefully measured and drawn diagrams and plans, the lists and recommendations. "Uh-hmm." He peered through a glass, scrutinizing some details more closely. Taking pages from the top and setting them aside. Sometimes flipping one back over again for a second look.

Hugo fought the urge to tap his foot.

At last, the old man straightened in his chair. "These are ambitious plans."

"Thank you," said Hugo.

The baronet shook his head. "Too ambitious. I'm a naturalist by training, not a physician like you, but I speak with confidence that people want to be treated in their homes."

"That wastes the medical man's time," Hugo protested. "Think how many more people he could help with all his patients at hand."

"People are not bolts of cloth, to be woven into shape and sent out into the world in identical fashion."

"I am not saying they would receive *identical* treatment. They would receive *excellent* treatment."

The elderly baronet sighed. "The most excellent treatment is that denied to one's inferiors—or so many believe. Medicine is exclusive, Lord Hugo, and I mean that literally. Certain portions of society are excluded from receiving it."

"Oh, aye," said Georgette. "You know it's not the best unless most people can't afford it."

"Well . . . yes," said Banks. "Lord Hugo did state he wished to establish a *private* hospital."

Damn. "That's not what I meant by private," said Hugo. "I called it private because the funding would be drawn from—"

"You don't know it's a good hospital," pressed Bonebox, "unless it's too good for the likes of me."

Banks folded his hands atop his desk, looking like a judge rendering a verdict. "Yes, that's so. Do recall, Lord Hugo, that private hospitals aplenty already exist. Not only for the physically ill, but for lunatics. And the ill who can't afford private treatment may enter workhouses and poorhouses and prisons."

"Ooh, that's like choosing between three heavens," scoffed Georgette, causing the baronet to scowl.

Hugo hadn't considered the stubbornness of those at the edges of high society. But then again, they hadn't considered *his* stubbornness. "No one ever regained his health in a workhouse or a poorhouse or a prison. The hospital I propose will provide better care than any other available. The comforts of home, but with more constant medical attention."

Banks looked prepared to argue—but before he could speak, Georgette hopped up to sit on the edge of his desk. "This be bigger than my whole house. Though it's not so much a house as it be a room. Well, it's a room if a bit of tin across a hole makes a roof."

"Do get off my desk. Get off at once." Banks pressed himself back in his great chair. "You live in a *hole*?"

"No!" Georgette sounded offended. "There's a *hole* in the *roof*." She slid from the desk and began to prowl about the room, touching everything she could. "All these books would make a fine glimmer in that empty grate. D'you ever pitch one in to watch it blaze up?"

With a pained look, the elderly man said, "Lord Hugo, does the boy carry lice?"

"Coo, who doesn't?" said Georgette as she pulled a leather-bound volume from a shelf, then stuffed it back askew. "You probably have lice under that wig of yours."

"It's not a wig!" Banks barked.

"Then why does it look like that?"

Banks was red, practically choking. "It—I—It is not!—I—"

Hugo was not going to smile. He really was not. "Dreadful boy," he said. "Apologize to the baronet, then leave the room at once."

Brilliant woman. Absolutely brilliant. She had distracted Sir Joseph before he could decline further discussion. Then she made herself so obnoxious that Hugo and the baronet could unite against her.

Once Georgette had obeyed Hugo and left the chamber with seeming bad grace, he faced the baronet across the desk in taut silence.

"I beg your pardon," he said to the older man. "What an abominable youth. Some people have no idea how to behave in good company."

Sir Joseph grunted his agreement, slightly mollified.

"But," Hugo added, "they still deserve medical care. As do sons of dukes, and baronets with gout, and—"

"I take your meaning." The baronet lifted a quelling hand. "But I cannot agree to invest the resources of the Royal Society in an untried scheme. Now . . ." His dark eyes glittered. "If someone of influence supported the plan—someone such as your father, for example— then it would have the social cachet needed to draw financial backing."

If I had my father's support, I wouldn't need financial backing. "Thank you for your time." Hugo reached for the plans, beginning to roll them again. "Unfortunately, the Duke of Willingham and I do not speak. It will not be possible to gain his support."

The baronet put a broad, gnarled hand on the papers, halting Hugo. "It's a good plan, Lord Hugo. But at this time, it's not practical."

And what had *practical* ever done for Hugo? *Practical* would have bound him to London, never to visit his cottage in Edinburgh or study medicine there.

Practical had been his behavior when Matthew grew ill, when conventional treatments dictated by an absent physician failed.

He pressed a hand to the pocket of his waistcoat, feeling the familiar weight of his watch. "I understand, Sir Joseph."

"But if you get the duke's investment . . ."

"Right. I take your meaning. If it comes to pass"—
if the sun falls and the mountains crumble—"be assured
that I will notify you." He finished gathering his plans,
then returned them to their case. Bowing a farewell,
he exited the office.

Georgette had been leaning against the wall, scuff-
ing her broken shoe against the floor. She darted up
to Hugo as soon as he emerged from the room, then
drew up short. "You look like you want to scowl."

"I don't want to scowl."

"Frown, then."

"Maybe." He told her what had passed since she was
evicted from the room. "You were right, Bone-box. You
did help. Without your dreadful behavior, the meeting
would have been terminated more quickly. Instead,
now there's a slim chance of success." Very slim. Too
slim for his liking.

The plans he carried were light, too fragile to bear
the many hopes Hugo laid upon them.

For he wasn't hoping only on his own behalf. For
the past fourteen years, he had been hoping—and
acting, and learning, and working—for two.

"What do we do now?" Georgette asked. "Guv."

Hugo smiled thinly. "Let me consider."

They retraced their path through the building. By
the time they emerged into daylight, leaving the sweep-
ing Palladian structure behind, logic and forethought
had led Hugo to one inevitable conclusion.

"We'll have to give the appointment at the Royal
College of Physicians a miss," he told Georgette.
"There's somewhere else we need to go, and it'll be
even more of a knife-edge of negotiation than this
meeting was."

Sometimes he hated logic and forethought.

Georgette looked pleased at the use of the word *we*, and she climbed into the waiting crested carriage with a leap. "Bone-box is ready for the task, whatever it might be."

"Yes, well, that's going to be a problem." As he followed her into the carriage, soot made him blink. For a moment, it seemed the sun had fallen. "We're going to pay a call on the Duke of Willingham."

Chapter Three

Thus it was time for Bone-box, the irreverent youth, to be transformed back into the proper Miss Frost. The coachman retrieved Georgette's trunk, from which she removed her favorite gown and the other necessaries.

Then she looked around with some doubt. A private room failed to spring into existence on the Strand. "Where can I change my clothing?"

Hugo hefted the trunk and helped the coachman stow it again. "In the carriage. Where else? We can spare five minutes."

"Five minutes?"

"Too long?" His dark brows knit. "That's fine. The sooner we reach Willingham House, the better for all of us."

Honestly. "Obviously you have never tried to put on women's clothing without the help of a maid." She shoved the bundle into the carriage and climbed in after it.

"In this, you are correct." Hugo held the edge of the door, preparing to shut her in.

"All right, all right. I'll change as quickly as I can. In the carriage." In front of Somerset House! And the carriage had only the sheerest of window shades; she might as well sell tickets to passersby. "Could you— stand in front of the carriage window?"

He raised his brows. "To what do I owe the honor, Bone-box?"

Her cheeks went instantly red. "I don't mean that I want you to look *into* the carriage. I mean . . . blocking the window is—is what I mean."

He was kind enough to ignore her stammering. "Miss Frost, you may trust me to be a gentleman." And he closed the door.

She crouched on the floor of the carriage, all elbows and knees struggling to free herself from breeches and tight jacket. Through the thin shade, she could see the outline of his head and shoulders. It was the back of his head—so yes, he was turned away.

Well. She *had* trusted him to be a gentleman. But what good was a gentleman? Rapunzel would never have escaped the tower if the prince had been a gentleman, listening respectfully to her singing from a distance—then walking away without a word since he had not been formally introduced to the lady.

Georgette had avoided the scholarly tomes that so captivated her parents, feasting instead on fantastical stories. Stories in which a castle was always around the next corner, and a peddler was as likely to be a prince as a pauper. Stories in which animals could speak; in which a lonely, impoverished young woman always made her fortune and found someone to love her.

They were only stories, she knew. But the fanciful promises of stories were better than having nothing to dream about at all.

Shadows passed before the window; Hugo was lifting his arm to shade his eyes, maybe. As Georgette scrabbled into her stockings and gown, she was slightly disappointed that he didn't even *try* to peek. Which meant, perhaps, that he regarded her as a horrid rapscallion like Bone-box in truth. Or as no more than a duty he hoped to discharge quickly.

She had few enough people who were glad to be around her. Since she had left the family bookshop—could that have been only earlier today?—maybe she could count on none at all.

But that was to be expected. It was greedy for a faded-looking girl with scarcely a coin to her name to hope for others to notice her at all.

So. That was why she had to make her own fortune, like the heroines of her favorite stories. She'd learned from childhood, she couldn't rely on others to see to her interests. Especially not her parents, living with their noses in books, learning fact after fact instead of noticing when their own daughter was hungry or hadn't a candle to call her own.

Quickly as she could, she rolled up the boys' clothing and pinned up her hair in a simple knot. She knocked at the carriage door, and Hugo opened it at once, looking up at her with reproach. "That was far longer than five minutes."

"It was such a delight changing my garments in this enclosed space that I decided to prolong the experience."

"Have you finished?"

"As well as I can without the help of a maid." For her boys' garb, she had bound her chest tightly. She had left the binding on in place of her stays, which fastened up the back and would require a servant to lace them.

The bodice of her gown also buttoned up the back, and there was no help for it. She couldn't call on a duke with the top half of her gown drooping. "I need you to do up these buttons. I can't reach them."

Her own face grew hot. Again. Hugo only looked amused. "Now I am become a lady's maid. This day has taken any number of unexpected turns, hasn't it?"

"If you were truly a lady's maid, I'd have you do something with my hair. I've never met a duke, and . . ." Her hands flailed, the universal gesture for *I would like to look more elegant, but this is the best I can do without a glass or the help of another pair of hands.*

If that wasn't a universal gesture, it should be.

"It'll be fine." Hugo halted on the carriage step. "You'll be with my mother. If she doesn't like you, it won't be because of your hair."

"Is that meant to be comforting?"

"Not particularly. Why? Are you comforted?"

"*No.*" If she hadn't needed him to do up her buttons, she would have been sorely tempted to sock him. "And why are we going to your parents' town house? I told you I didn't want to stay as your mother's guest."

"We're not going for that reason. I hope to avoid a likely fruitless search for stolen coins, and to make a request that is slightly less likely to be fruitless." He paused. "That's what I have to do, that is. You can . . . I don't know. Drink tea, or whatever it is ladies do in their free hours."

"I wouldn't know. I didn't have free hours at the bookshop." He meant well, so she managed a smile. Though she'd never thought of her birth as low—her parents were educated, and at some point a generation or two ago, the family had owned land—she felt the gulf between her station and Lord Hugo's keenly at the moment. Nothing could have knit a man of such rarefied status in friendship with her brother Benedict except, of course, for books and study.

He made a sound under his breath that might have been a curse. "You're right. I'm sorry. Here, turn about and I'll fasten you up."

He hoisted himself into the carriage and sat on the squabs beside her. Hitching up one leg, he turned toward her on the cushioned seat. With hands that were tentative, even gentle, he caught her shoulders and turned her away from him. "Buttons, buttons," he said. "How impractical."

"No one in the history of England ever said women's fashions were practical." Sharply, she folded her legs to the side, presenting him with more of her back. "Don't think I didn't notice, by the bye, that you said you wanted to avoid the search for coins. I didn't agree to that."

"I know. And I don't expect that of you. Whether or not my request is granted, I'll see you safely to your brother. You two can hunt together, if you choose."

Georgette had been preparing for a splendid, indignant rant. But . . . "Oh." Now that the need for it was stripped away, a lump caught in her throat.

At her back, light movements marked Hugo's progress with the buttons, tiny circles of horn that marched from her nape to the high waist of the gown. The bodice grew more and more snug with each one fastened, making her short of breath in a way she could not remember ever being before in this gown.

"That's done, then," he said. When she touched the back of the bodice at her nape, feeling for the top button, her fingers brushed against his. Her breath pulled in short and sharp, as though she'd been startled.

Maybe she had been startled, at that.

When she faced forward again, Hugo at once flung himself across the carriage to the other seat.

"How dramatic," Georgette said. "Are you all right?"

"Quite all right." But his dark blue gaze traced her in ways unfamiliar and unfathomable, as if she were a room in his hospital plans that he could not remember having designed, and for which he could not imagine the purpose.

Georgette forgot this oddness when the carriage pulled up before Willingham House. For that matter, she almost forgot her own name.

A duke and duchess who bore a grudge against one of their sons would, in a proper tale, inhabit an isolated stone castle where the weather always stormed. But a mansion in London was even more impressive, and when a butler opened the door to Hugo and herself, she gawked at the broad, elegant stone building as she had at Somerset House.

"This is beautiful," she whispered to Hugo once a butler admitted them to the entry hall. "I was certain it'd be dour and dark. One of those melancholy Gothic piles of chipped stone and portraits with long noses."

He smirked. "That's all on the second story."

He opened the door to the drawing room, which looked exactly like society papers had led Georgette to expect. The ceilings were high, the windows tall and sparkling, the plasterwork intricate and snowy. Everything was spacious and clean, with no musty stacks of books and not a speck of dust anywhere. Certainly no laundry to be folded or packages to be stowed.

No, instead there was a small flock of richly dressed women sitting on velvet-covered chairs. As one, they turned to look at the intruders. Some froze with teacups raised halfway to their lips. The effect was one of genteel shock.

Amidst the elegant splendor, one woman spoke. "Lord Hugo. What a delightful surprise."

"Mother." He bowed.

So this was a duchess. Tall and well-dressed, grayhaired and brittle, with careful posture and an expression of determined calm.

"It has been too long since your last visit, Hugo." The duchess shifted her posture in a graceful flutter: of hands, of shawls, of the faded curls that hung in careful arrangements about her ears. "Are you here to apologize to your father?" Her Grace set down a teacup, and that was fluttery too, the china cup rattling against its frail saucer. "With your coat in that state?"

"It's not his fault, Your Grace," Georgette said, remembering to curtsy as she spoke. "A horrid street urchin threw cheap liquor on him when he was trying to help. The boy was in trouble, you see."

Hugo slanted a sharp look at her. "I'm pleased to hear you say so, Miss Frost. That is exactly how I viewed the incident as well."

The duchess regarded them each in turn, then asked, "Who is your companion, Hugo? I was not expecting callers at this hour."

It was impossible to ignore the presence of five other women in the room. *Not expecting callers*, it was clear, meant *not expecting someone like this*. Georgette's favorite gown of pale yellow appeared plain and cheap next to the rich silk hangings on the walls, the cut velvet of the upholstery on which was seated the duchess. Again, she experienced that jarring sense of being pulled into a world she did not understand.

But Hugo introduced Georgette politely around the room, and she gave a creditable curtsy to each of the noblewomen. "It is my pleasure to meet you, Your Grace," she told the duchess. "Your son is helping me locate my brother."

"Is he indeed, Miss Frost?" the duchess said, as a servant brought in yet another tea tray molded of enough silver to entice the beleaguered Royal Mint. "I have been curious about Lord Hugo's acquaintances from his medical years. Your brother is fortunate in his friendships."

"A *medical* acquaintance? How intriguing." A woman with lovely blond curls and a sweet, fatigued smile selected a tiny cake from the tray of delicacies. "Miss Frost, I have never encountered a medical woman. Is your gown a sort of . . . of academic costume?"

Hugo flipped her a wave. "Oh, hullo, Tess. Heard you and Loftus were expecting again. Congratulations."

The blond woman's smile slipped. "The *marquess* and I are not discussing such a matter at present, *Hugo*."

"That's my sister-in-law," Hugo told Georgette. "Which you doubtless gathered from our use of Christian names."

"And the fact that he was remarkably indiscreet," added the marchioness.

"Pleased to meet you, my lady," Georgette said. "I

have no medical training myself." She looked at her gown. "Nor do I have a fashionable modiste."

"Not at all, not at all," hastened the marchioness. "I was merely curious about—that is, one meets such a lot of different people in London."

"And how," the duchess broke in, "did you meet my son, Miss Frost, if not in the course of his medical studies?"

"When he came to my family's bookshop. Frost's?"

"I have never been there," the duchess said, "but the name is not unfamiliar."

"It's a small place," Georgette admitted. "As much a sleuthing agency as a bookshop. My cousins, as did my parents before them, pride themselves on research-ing and locating any desired book or manuscript." And if no one had tasked them with a mission, her par-ents indulged their own scholarly curiosity.

"Hugo, what was it you wanted the bookshop to find?" The duchess sounded curious.

"I don't recall." Hugo looked as if he wanted to be anywhere else in the world.

Though Georgette still felt too plain for comfort, the determined politeness of the duchess and her callers was reassuring. No, she didn't belong here, but they'd surely wait until she had left the room before picking her apart.

So, she might as well enjoy herself. "You don't recall, Lord Hugo? Yet the day you first walked into the shop was one of the finest of my life." Georgette warmed to her story, rocking on her toes. "Your Grace, when Lord Hugo opened the door, the bell was like the call of an angel's trumpet. When he asked whether I could help him locate a folio copy of *De humani corporis fabrica*, I thought my heart would pound out of my body, like the woodcut dissections in the book."

At her side, Hugo kicked at a fat red rose in the carpet pattern. "Miss Frost, you are reaching new heights of absurdity."

The duchess's brow puckered. "Is that not true, Miss Frost? I could wish everyone thought so well of my youngest."

Oh, dear. She had touched on a mother's finer feelings—feelings with which she was wholly unfamiliar. Carefully, she formed her reply. "My words were overblown, Your Grace, but not dishonest. Your son has been most kind to me. And he *did* request a copy of the Vesalius, which my cousin purchased on his behalf within the month."

Hugo made an impatient noise. "Enough of all this. I haven't been kind, I've been sensible. And Mother, you're going to embarrass the girl."

"I'll probably embarrass myself," said Georgette. "Her Grace need not go to any special effort on my account."

Her Grace's expression turned considering. "Would you two care to join us for tea? Hugo, here are your favorite ginger cakes."

"That is thoughtful of you, Mother, but time is short and my business is urgent. Miss Frost is of an adventurous nature, so will you keep her shackled while I write to her brother? Then I need to speak to the duke, and we'll be off."

The duchess lifted a sculpted brow, a look of skepticism that reminded Georgette very much of her son's. "You wish to speak to the duke? Your words are like the call of an angel's trumpet."

Georgette swallowed a laugh.

"Shackling one's guest is not the done thing this season," Her Grace added. "But if you will allow me to propose an alternative, Benton can show her to a guest chamber where she might freshen up."

"A guest chamber?" Georgette frowned at Hugo, hoping he would interpret the expression as *I have told you time and again that I want to be on my way to Derbyshire.* "I am sure that will not be necessary. And Lord Hugo, what do you intend to write to my brother?"

"The truth, God help you," Hugo said. "For now, go with the butler." That silent figure—Benton, apparently—gave a bow from the doorway.

As they made their way toward him, the duchess called after them, "Come back if you wish for a ginger cake, Hugo." A pause. "Or ring for them, of course. You—needn't come back down."

Georgette looked back, made curious by the halt in the duchess's speech. The noblewoman was twisting her hands together in the tassels of her shawl, looking fluttery again as conversation at once began to ripple through the room.

Georgette could not put a word to the emotion traced upon the older woman's features before the ornate painted-wood door closed her into the drawing room. Then the butler led her to a twirling staircase, all wide marble treads and lacy ironwork, and Hugo gave her a little wave and headed in a different direction altogether.

For a moment, she hesitated between them, caught between the familiar and the unknown. She did not want to see Hugo go; she did not want to climb the stairs.

Yet climb them she must. And they were beautiful

stairs, of the sort one only had the opportunity to ascend when one was fortunate in one's friendships.

She followed the butler, step by step—and soon enough, Georgette realized which emotion had crossed the duchess's proud face. It was the same one that clutched at her own heart, more tightly with each step.

As soon as others turned away, she was lonely.

The duke was not in his study. The duke was not in the library. The duke was not in the music room, or the yellow parlor, or the rose room, or any of the other usual places one might find a duke in late-afternoon.

While in the rose room, Hugo stripped off his troublesome coat and hung it over a chair at a writing desk, then scribbled what he hoped would be a reassuring note to Benedict. *Sister retrieved, staying with duchess.* Et cetera. Once he sealed it and gave it to a servant for posting, he resumed his search.

Hugo finally happened upon his father in the ballroom on the mansion's second floor. The draperies were flung open, letting the late-afternoon sunlight flood the great space. The floor shone with wax and lemon oil, the fragrance of citrus mixing with the musty odor that crept into a long-unused room. It was empty now, save for a headless, armless figure hanging from a pole, and for the Duke of Willingham, who was stabbing it with a foil.

So. His father was fencing with a tailor's dummy.

When the duke saw Hugo, he let the foil fall with a clatter, where it rolled to bump another like it. Heedless of his white fencing jacket, he used a forearm to shove back his disarranged hair—now more gray than black—and crossed the distance between them.

The Duke of Willingham had always been a sturdy barrel of a man, but he had used to be a much smaller barrel. The years had made him stout and slow. Slow to change, that is. Quick as ever to judge.

Breathing hard from exertion, he flicked an icy gaze over Hugo. "No coat? What is this disrespect?"

"Believe me, it would have been worse if I'd worn it," Hugo said. "I'll find another coat sometime, but until then, the world will continue turning."

The duke grunted—then stepped back, heavy on his feet, to stand beside the foils again. "I thought we weren't speaking to each other anymore. So you told me—what was it, fifteen months ago?"

It was a small triumph that his father had been the one to speak first, even if it *had* been about the cursed coat. Hugo gestured toward the dummy. "For that matter, I thought one fenced with another human if one wanted to gain skill."

"Sometimes one just wants to stab things."

"In that case, give me the foil for a few minutes."

The duke made a *be my guest* gesture, and Hugo crossed to the weapon and picked it up. It was light in his hand, but an unfamiliar form. Hugo had never bothered with pugilism or swordplay, the aggressive arts that so fascinated many of his peers. He had always preferred to take his exercise outdoors, climbing trees to observe animals or picking his way up tor after tor to collect geological samples. If he were ever called upon to defend himself, he had a perfectly good pair of fists at his disposal.

But there was something to be said for a sword in one's hand, for the pleasant *swish* of honed metal through sluggish air. Whipping the foil forward,

Hugo sank its buttonless tip into the figure of cloth and batting. *Pfsss.*

"You are right." He drew the foil free. "Sometimes one needs to stab a tailor's dummy."

"It's not the most satisfying thing to stab, but it has the advantage of being legal."

Hugo gave the foil a little toss from his right hand to his left, then offered it back to the duke. "What has you feeling so stabby today?"

The duke waved it off, picking up the second foil from the floor. "Fifteen months ago, one of my sons said he wouldn't talk to me."

"Good attempt, Duke, but I don't believe you for a moment. What was it really?"

The duke adopted what Hugo supposed was a fencing stance, legs bent and left hand held up fussily. "What is it not?" With a smooth gesture, he struck out—not quite at the dummy, not quite at Hugo. "Parliament is a mess, the servants are neglecting their duties and wearing your mother to a thread, and your eldest brother has asked for funds to repair his town house now that his wife is expecting their fourth child."

"I thought she was," Hugo said. "Tess didn't seem to want to talk about it, though." Four children already; good Lord. She and Loftus had only been wed six years earlier.

"And," the duke added, "my gout has been dreadful of late. Though not today, which is why I seized the chance to stab."

"Drink lemon juice. It might help with the pain." Even Bone-box knew that much, a thought that made Hugo smile.

Only for a second, though. The duke gave the foil a

swish, a flick of impatience. "I see what's about. You're here to discuss your ridiculous scheme of a hospital again. I won't fund it, Hugo. It's too impractical."

This wasn't the most opportune time to approach Willingham, clearly, but it had to be done. "I'm not asking you for that."

The duke stepped back. Turning toward the dummy, he took up a fencing stance. "So this is not about the hospital?"

Poor dummy. About to be stabbed again. "Well . . . it is, yes. But," he rushed on, "I'm not asking you to contribute anything from your pocket. Not so much as a farthing."

"Oh?"

"Only send a note stating your approval of the plan to the Royal Society, and I believe that institution will support it."

"Out of the question." *Lunge. Stab.*

"No, it's not. I could even write it for you. You'd only need to sign and seal it."

The duke turned his foil toward Hugo, pointing it at him. "A man's good name is worth even more than his purse. I would be more likely to give you the money anonymously than attach my name to such a wild project."

Each word was punctuated with a flick of the foil. Out of reflex, Hugo lifted his own in a tight grip, ready to parry. "I've no objection to that. Give me the money anonymously, then."

"I don't want to support such a scheme. The spectacle of it bothers me."

The duke's face had gone ruddy—with exertion, maybe, and with irritation. "If you would be *considerate* of this family for once." He swung his foil in a wild arc, clashing with the sword in Hugo's hand. The blow reverberated up Hugo's arm. "Think of the notoriety you take upon yourself in caring for the dregs of society."

Feet planted, Hugo let his fencing weapon fall to the floor. It was a fine sword, but he didn't want it. "Why?"

That one word, one syllable, was the essential difference between father and son. Willingham had not yet accepted that Hugo always had, did still, and always would ask this question. That he had long ago stopped accepting that what others said was right was, in fact, so.

"Pick up your foil." The duke was breathing hard, an enraged bull. "Let's have this out."

Hugo laughed. "Not like this. I'd be a fool to fight on another man's terms, with another man's weapons."

The duke's foil slashed raggedly across the cotton torso of the dummy, thin blade winking in the slanting afternoon light. "You ought to have gone into the clergy. Yet I accepted your wish to become a physician because I thought it respectable. I even tolerated your pursuit of education in Edinburgh, though it falls at the far edge of civilization."

"I liked it there," Hugo said. "The accents were instructive."

From an uncle, he had been deeded a cottage in Edinburgh; that was his excuse for studying so far north. But in all honesty, he wanted to get away from London, from England entirely. To learn in a place that had not been sullied by loss.

Slash. "Edinburgh," the duke bit off, "gave you *ideas*. Not satisfied with helping your peers, you must dirty your hands with the blood and gore of surgeries, with treating the unwashed."

"I always had ideas." Hugo followed the pour of sunlight across the glossy floors, lining up the toes of his boots against one sunbeam. "And who is peer to a duke's son?"

"What?" Willingham wiped at his forehead again with the sleeve of his jacket. "What are you getting at?"

"I remember my station. But that doesn't mean I'm defined by it. If I only dealt with people like me—"

"Are there more people like you? God help us."

"—then my circle of acquaintance would be tiny and dull. And I don't seek out blood and gore. But if I must be bloodied to help someone in pain, so I shall be." It was an old, deep argument; a heart-deep feeling. He had to laugh, hollowly, to soothe the pain of it. "Getting a little blood on my hands feels like the opposite, in truth. Like I'm making up for harm done."

"For the harm *I* did, you mean. You think the blood is on *my* hands."

The duke's voice was so raw that Hugo flinched, stepping away from the hopeful sunbeam. "You said it. Not I."

"I only said what has lain between us for years."

This was true. Since Matthew died, this resentment had distanced them. Unspoken, a wound unlanced, it poisoned their every interaction.

"You could never forgive me after Matthew died, yet I did everything possible to save him. I hired the best physician money could arrange." The duke's tone was bitter.

"He was the most expensive. He wasn't the best. Just because he bled my brother into a silver bowl doesn't mean bleeding was the right treatment."

"For poisoning of the blood, it was surely right."

"But where did the poison come from?" *Why* was the question. His father never asked *why*, and so Matthew had died. "Treating the cause could have helped. Bleeding him only made him weaker."

Hugo remembered every detail of those waning days. The fever, the cough that worsened hour upon hour. His brother's nails and lips tinged with blue as he fought for every breath. The only treatment that brought Matthew relief was when the housekeeper dosed him with a tea of mullein and honey.

For which the woman had lost her position for interfering with the medical treatment of a duke's son.

"We've talked about this time and again." The duke circled the dummy, as though looking for a spot he hadn't yet slashed. "It was fourteen years ago, Hugo. He's been dead almost as long as he was alive. When are you going to forgive?"

The sharpness of the duke's tone brought out the same from Hugo. "After fourteen years, you can't look at me when you ask that? When will you forgive me for having his face?"

After Matthew's death, neither his father nor mother had wanted to look at the copy of the son they had lost. Hugo's very existence was a reminder, refreshing their grief anew.

"I'm not speaking of him." Fierce and sudden, the duke hacked at the side of the figure of batting. "I am asking you to consider *reputation*, Hugo."

Words coming tersely between labored breaths, he added, "Think of how your behavior reflects on this family. What would you have to sacrifice to bring your plan to fruition? And is it worth the sacrifice?"

Back where they began, then. As ever. "What more

could I sacrifice than what I already have, Your Grace? I lost my twin, the other half of myself."

Willingham turned toward the slow-slanting sun, his back to Hugo. His hand gripped the weapon fiercely— a sword that looked far too small to have caused such damage. The tailor's dummy was all flayed cloth and oozing batting.

Slowly, Hugo shook his head. "You may cut that figure to ribbons," he said. "But you'll never win your fight."

The duke walked away, standing framed before one of the tall windows. The streets in which dwelled London's elite embraced him; the heart of the *ton* beat around him. That was the closeness he most desired.

Since there was nothing more to say, Hugo nudged the fallen foil with his foot, sending it spinning toward the duke. Then he left the ballroom.

To look for Georgette.

He found her standing in the corridor of the guest wing. She looked soft and faded, studying an old portrait his parents had hung up here so they wouldn't have to look at it.

She was bound to find out about Matthew sooner or later. He tried not to sound too grumpy as he spoke. "It was too much to ask, I suppose, that you would stay in your chamber like a docile houseguest."

"It was," she said. "I've never been in a mansion before. I wanted to look about."

She pointed to the portrait: one of the ducal family, made about fifteen years before. "You were painted twice here. I can tell it's you because of the nose."

"The Willingham nose. God help me."

"Why is that? I know your brothers from the society papers. They look much the same now as well.

Here is the marquess—Loftus? And here your second brother."

"Lord Hilary, yes. I always considered myself fortunate not to have had that name foisted on me."

"Haven't you an embarrassing middle name?"

"No, my parents were less creative by the time I was born. I'm a plain lord with a plain name." He gestured toward the painting, less a wave of the hand than a shove of a shoulder toward the face that matched his own. "So was Matthew."

He could tell the moment when understanding dawned. "It's not you painted in double? You had a twin?"

"I had a twin." Hugo paused, mustering the always difficult words. "He died of pneumonia when we were eighteen."

Her eyes went wide—then filled with an emotion so pure, so sincere, that he had to look away from her. "Oh, Hugo, I didn't know."

"There was no reason you should."

"That's why—you—the hospital? Why did you not tell Sir Joseph Banks about this?"

Hugo leaned against the wall and bumped the heel of his boot against the baseboard. "Because it's a personal matter. It's not relevant to my pursuit of hospital funding."

"He was unmoved by logic and evidence. The personal is all that *is* relevant."

He ventured a glance at her and immediately wished he had not. "See? This. This is why I don't tell people. They treat me differently. Your expression has gone all melty."

"How can I not treat you differently? I think better

of you now. You are acting not out of obstinacy, but out of the deepest desires of your heart."

"Don't be so certain about the obstinacy," he muttered. "Look. Miss Frost."

"Georgette."

"Fine. Georgette. Do you still want to find your brother? Get the Royal Reward?" Abrupt, yes, but some subjects had been spoken of enough for the day.

Her mouth opened, as though she were on the verge of speech—then slowly she nodded.

"Then don't allow the servants to unpack your things," he said. "We will leave for Derbyshire by the next mail coach."

Chapter Four

Georgette had traveled by hackney within London. She had taken a stagecoach to the environs of the city a time or two. Thanks to Lord Hugo, she even had been stuffed into a ducal carriage. But never before had she traveled in a Royal Mail coach.

Excitement, anticipation, eagerness—all of these bubbled in Georgette's veins. Even the name of the coaching inn was fascinating: The Swan with Two Necks. The inn, with its two stories of galleries and a gabled roof atop, enclosed a bustling courtyard on three sides.

The archway leading into the courtyard was constantly threaded by one conveyance or another. Coach after coach pulled up and pulled out; mail bags were loaded up or tossed down; luggage was stacked and strapped; people clambered atop the coach or spilled from within.

Sunset colored the sky in jewel-bright reds and oranges and golds, a warm smile over the busy travelers. How strange it seemed to set off on a journey near nightfall—but so it was, Hugo had explained, when one traveled by Mail. Speed was of the essence for the nation's post, and lantern-lit coaches made far better time on empty nighttime roads than on the bustling thoroughfares of daylight hours.

"'The setting sun,'" Georgette quoted, "'and music at the close, as the last taste of sweets, is sweetest last, writ in remembrance more than things long past.'"

"Music at the . . . what?" At her side, Hugo frowned down at her. "What *are* you talking about? No one is playing music."

"It's Shakespeare," said Georgette. "I'd have been kicked out of the bookshop long ago if I hadn't known Shakespeare's work."

"Shakespeare," he scoffed. "Only a determined romantic could think of verse at a time like this, when we're surrounded by horse droppings."

He was not wrong about this. The scent of horses, of manure and sweat, pervaded the courtyard. "When is verse more needed than when one is surrounded by horse droppings?"

He stared at her as if she'd spoken an unfamiliar language—but then his mouth curved. "'A hit, a very palpable hit.' If it makes you forget the droppings, Madam Bookworm, quote all the Shakespeare you like."

She looked about the courtyard for their coach, hopping on her toes. At Willingham House, Georgette had traded her bulky, ancient trunk for a smaller leather valise a servant found in the attics. Hugo—now wearing a fresh coat and a caped greatcoat, having stopped at his bachelor apartments in a hotel—had brought the same sort of luggage, along with the long leather case that held his precious hospital plans.

"Do try not to tread upon my feet," Hugo said. "You

appear to be under the impression that this is a noble quest. It is not. It is an errand, albeit a long one."

"You may call it what you like, and I may think of it as I choose." She craned her neck. Was that the right coach, with its four chestnuts ready to spring? No, that one was to go southeast.

They held tickets for the Manchester coach, which would slip through the towns of Derbyshire—including the infamous Strawfield, from which her brother, Benedict, had sent his most recent letter. At four pence the mile, the tickets had cost a sobering three pounds each.

"It's of no consequence," Hugo had said, and paid for her ticket as well as his. "Don't be top-lofty; I owe you a ticket. You've told me so today at least a hundred times."

She had no intention of being top-lofty when a sum such as three pounds was involved. Her small store of money, tucked inside her reticule and knotted into a pocket of her gown, would soon be exhausted otherwise.

At last they spotted the coach to Manchester. Four horses stood ready to set off, a mismatched quartet by color but all equally eager. Their ears were pricked and their hooves danced as trunk after trunk and parcel after parcel was loaded atop and behind the coach. Passengers with cheaper tickets climbed onto the outside of the coach wherever they could find space.

Georgette clambered inside and took a front-facing seat. Hugo sat across from her, carrying the long case for his papers.

Theirs was not a noble quest, maybe, but it was more than an errand. Perhaps it was an adventure? How odd that earlier today she had thought Lord Hugo Starling had brought an end to her travels, her plans to secure her own future. Now he was thoroughly a part of both.

Odd, indeed. Yet not uncomfortably so.

Not for the first time today were they alone in a carriage, but this time they seemed far more alone than before. The bustle outside made of the clean but spare interior a cocoon. The opposite seat was very close, and Lord Hugo somehow seemed closer still—as though he owned the air around him. Every time Georgette breathed, she borrowed that air, and it traced her face and body, gentle and warm. It was good not to be alone.

It was good to be alone with him.

She drew back her feet. Hesitated. What ought she to say? *Thank you for not being as stuffy and stubborn as I thought? For being . . . rather nice? And not at all bad-looking?*

She had better say nothing at all.

"You should have a maid." Hugo was turning this way and that on his seat, looking for a place to stash his leather case. "We should have brought a maid along."

"Nonsense," Georgette said. "We didn't have the time to argue your parents into letting one accompany us. And we'll end in meeting my brother, which means you're traveling in his stead." He looked skeptical, but she added gamely, "So really, you're like family. For this journey."

"That doesn't make sense at all." Hugo gave up on stowing his case and held it lengthwise across his lap. "I'm thinking of your reputation."

"Not as much as I must," she said drily. "Didn't you say I might trust you to act as a gentleman, though?"

He searched her with eyes made dark by the fading

light of the setting sun. "Yes," he finally said. "You can. Though I can't promise the same for other travelers."

"I wouldn't expect you to promise anything on behalf of others." Was she disappointed or reassured?

She was a fool, that's what she was. She needed to remember her purpose, which was to find stolen coins, then her brother. The means of independence; the only remaining person who might be presumed to care about her.

Her purpose was certainly *not* to evaluate the attractiveness of the man across from her.

"Never mind that," she blurted in response to her own thoughts. "Let's think of what we *can* rely on instead. Have you a sheet of paper and something to write with?"

He drew both from his leather case, then handed them to her. She spread the creased foolscap across her knees, flat as she could, and began writing dates with the stub of a pencil. "Today is the twenty-ninth of May. That leaves little more than a month until the first of July, when the gold sovereigns are released. If the money has not been found by then, the Royal Mint will withdraw the proffered reward."

"Fine. I ought not to be away from London even that long."

"But how long before . . ." She scribbled a few more notes. "About, say, seven miles the hour . . . we'll arrive in . . . hmm."

"Do show me what you're writing," he said. "Calculations accompanied by muttering are alarming for the observer."

She switched seats, took up the leather case on his lap, and gave him her paper and pencil as she slid onto the squabs next to him. "I was trying to determine how many days are left for searching. See?"

"You must account for the time wasted on travel."

"I've tried to. Though travel time needn't be a waste."

"Needn't it? The coins are not in this coach." He took back his leather case, then rested her paper atop it and skimmed the numbers.

"It's not a waste if you're doing something you enjoy." For example, she enjoyed sitting next to him now that his clothing was clean. He smelled of shaving soap and starch, and the angles of his body were determined and stern. She didn't mind the sternness as much as she'd thought, though, tempered as it was by flashes of humor.

Hugo gave the paper back to her. "I'll have to trust your calculations. It's too dim for me to make out the numbers. I'd need my spectacles."

"You wear spectacles?"

"Sometimes. When reading. They are a common accessory among those who study by candlelight for years on end." He offered the pencil back to her. "So. Thirty-three days from today, the gold sovereigns are released. No later than that date, I will return to London."

"But—"

He held up one finger. "First, we'll find your brother." Another digit. "Next, we'll find out what he has learned about the stolen coins in Derbyshire. Third, I'll join his search."

Georgette folded her arms.

"Oh, God. You always fold your arms when you're about to disagree with me. What is it?"

"*You'll* join his search? It was my idea, Hugo. I'm not to be abandoned at this point."

"You won't be abandoned. You'll be with your brother. I'm seeing you to him, as I promised."

"Bullheaded man." How had she thought he was pleasant to look upon? He would be pleasant to kick in the shin. "That's not a promise I sought nor extracted. I intended to arrange my own travel, to pursue my own aims."

"You can. Only now I'm helping you."

"Yes, but on your terms, not mine. I never asked for your help, and I don't want it."

He looked bewildered. "Everyone wants help."

Not if you ask for it, time and again, and it isn't given.

She hardly knew her elder brother. Benedict had gone to sea when she was only three years old and he twelve, and his returns home had been no more than occasional. For years, then, it was just Georgette and her parents. Her mother and father were little more than an outgrowth of their books; both expected their daughter to be the same. To have no human needs, no hunger, no fatigue. No desire for friendships other than those to be found within the pages of a book.

She had met their expectations less well than they wished, but better than she ought to have. Ah, well. A child would do anything to get her parents' notice and affection, even pretend she didn't covet it. Still her parents gave her up for their own ends: not for leaves of rampion, as Rapunzel's did, but for leaves of paper, printed and bound.

"I don't need help," she repeated. "And I'm going to keep traveling, chasing the gold, until the last second. I don't want to go back the way I came."

He blinked, long lashes softening a hard look. "But you can't flit around rootless. You need a purpose."

"Finding the stolen gold *is* my purpose."

"But by the first of July, the hunt will be over one way or the other. Then what will you do?"

"More than a month away. Surely I'll have another purpose in mind by the time we attain that date." She kept her tone flippant.

"That's not how a purpose works," he argued. "You can't *decide* to have one without caring what it is, and then—"

"Not everyone goes through life like you, Lord Hugo, with a gold signet and a bespoke leather case of bespoke-er plans." Her fist clenched on the pencil. "I said I wanted to find the stolen sovereigns. My brother is a means to that end. But if I can find the sovereigns without finding him, then that's what I'd want. More than the other way 'round."

He only looked at her, as though deciding something. She wished she had roused his temper; had baited him into displaying an emotion toward her other than patient exasperation.

"You always worked so hard," he said. "In the bookshop, I mean. I never took you for the sort that didn't concern herself with other people."

His tone was patient now, but not exasperated. He sounded as though he were truly curious.

So she answered, this time without flippancy. "I wasn't that sort until recently. My parents are dead, the family shop sold. My traveling brother returned to England without visiting me. On my twenty-first birthday, I will become homeless and impoverished. I chose to leave before then so I could have the dignity of leaving before being booted out. I'm not entirely without resources, but no one is concerned about me."

He drew back, brows knit. "Georgette, that cannot be—"

"It is. And once I realized that, what had I to lose? Why *not* put on breeches and set off on my own? Why not lay aside what and who I'd been, if being Georgette Frost wouldn't help me in future? I can't live on companionship and promises. I have to secure my own future."

He let her finish without another word. Then he smiled—an expression both awkward and sweet. "You have been wanting to say that for a long time."

"I have." She felt like a balloon, punctured after it had been tested beyond its strength.

"I . . ." He hesitated.

"Don't say anything trite or pitying. Please. If you do, I will have to stab you with this pencil, and I'll be sent to jail, and that would prevent me from finding the stolen coins."

"Maybe you can stab me in July, then," he murmured—distracted, of a sudden.

Georgette followed the turn of his head, only to see that they were about to have company in the coach. Two women, middle-aged and in the neat dress of the middle class, were stowing odds and ends in their baggage. They clutched their belongings tightly, clambering into the coach one after the other.

"Oh, isn't this nice!" said the thinner one in the feather-trimmed bonnet, settling herself with a hamper on her lap. "I never traveled inside before."

"It's not so bad being a widow, is it now?" The second woman, who had rosy cheeks and a bonnet trimmed in bright silk flowers, shoved her bag along the floor against the far side of the coach. "You get what the mister left you in his will and you spend it how you wish."

With a huff and a heave, she settled onto the seat beside her companion, and the carriage door was closed behind her. "Well! Edna, look. We're to have company for the journey! This is pleasant, I must say."

"How do you do?" Hugo said politely. "I—"

"Have you ever traveled inside before? We were saying—well, you heard us saying, I'd wager! Yes, it's such a treat to have the shelter of the coach. A body can't catch a wink of sleep riding atop the carriage."

"Quite so," said Hugo. "I—"

"I'm Mrs. Drupe," went on the rosy-cheeked woman merrily. Through the wall, Georgette heard a whip crack and a quick clamor of voices, and the coach lurched into motion. "And this is my sister Mrs. Brundadge."

Hugo didn't speak this time—certain, no doubt, that he'd be interrupted once more. A pity. Watching a duke's son be silenced time and again was the funniest thing Georgette had seen this evening. She knew she shouldn't laugh, and with a heroic effort, she managed to stay silent. But she couldn't keep her sides from quivering.

Hugo must have felt this, for he elbowed her in the ribs.

Possibly it was an accident, caused by the movement of the coach. But probably not.

"We're both widows," said the thinner sister. "Having the time of our lives! We're off to visit our sister—for we've another one—actually, two others, but we don't speak to the youngest, because she—"

"Edna," clucked the first to speak. "We mustn't be talking our friends' ears off! What will they think of us?"

Georgette would have paid half the money to her name for an engraving of the look on Hugo's face when the woman called him "friend." She elbowed him in the ribs right back. It was not an accident.

"They're not thinking of us at all." The thinner sister dimpled. "All wrapped in each other, aren't they? Look at how they sit so closely! You are newly-weds, yes?"

Hugo pressed himself against the far side of the carriage seat, quick as a blink. "Not. Newlyweds."

He didn't have to sound so *offended* by the notion. Before Georgette could do more than open her mouth, Hugo said, "No, no. I am Mr. Hugo Lark, and this is my cousin Miss Snow." He shot a dark look at her. "Ah—my *mute* cousin."

Her mouth fell open. His dark look shifted to her elbow.

That rat. He had elbowed her first.

She opened her mouth again to speak, prepared to put the lie to *mute cousin.*

"If she ever were to speak," Hugo added, "it would mean she had a brain fever and should not be paid any heed."

"Oh! What a pity," said Mrs. Drupe. "She's mute, you say? Tut! Well, you can't think of wedding her, then, can you? Poor dear! But I do love a newly wed pair. So happy! Not that I'm not happy in my widow-hood. Why, I . . ."

Brain fever indeed. As the woman spoke on, enter-taining herself and her sister with a shared memory, Georgette turned over the sheet of foolscap. With the bit of pencil in her fist, she scrawled *I'll get you for this.*

In nice big letters, so he could read it without his spectacles. The pencil tip broke with the force of her writing.

With a sweet smile, she thrust the paper back at him.

"What did she write, Mr. Lark?" Mrs. Drupe was all curiosity.

"My cousin writes that she is most pleased to make your acquaintance." He did not look at Georgette as he said this. Wise man.

"Isn't she a dear!" Mrs. Brundadge twinkled at her. "Would you like an apple from my hamper, Miss Snow?"

As a matter of fact, Georgette would. Today's travel had taken priority over food, and she realized she hadn't had a real meal since breakfast. She offered her most thankful smile to the older woman.

As she sat back and crunched through the apple's red skin, Hugo took the broken-tipped pencil from her hand. Rummaging through his leather case again, he pulled forth a folding knife.

"Oh!" The plump Mrs. Drupe choked back a little shriek. "A knife, sister! He has a knife!"

"Never you fear." Mrs. Brundadge snatched back the hamper and rooted through it. "I have one too. I shall protect us. Here, Mr. Lark!" With a flourish, she pulled forth . . . a fork.

Hugo had begun shaving bits off the pencil end, and he looked up blankly at her. "I beg your pardon? Do you want me to have that fork?"

"Heavens! No, no." Looking about in some desperation, she finally handed her sister the fork. "It's here somewhere. . . ." Next she pulled forth a pie, another apple, and a packet of cold chicken; these too were piled into her sister's lap. "Only wait, Mr. Lark, and I shall find it."

"I am all eagerness." Hugo held up the pencil, squinted at it, then trimmed off a few more slivers of wood.

"Here it is! Oh—no, that is the bone from the chicken we ate earlier. Sister, did I leave the knife in the—ah!" Mrs. Brundadge pulled forth a knife from the depths of the hamper. "There, Mr. Lark! You see?"

Georgette had not seen such entertainment since her last outing in Vauxhall Gardens. By now, Hugo had stowed his penknife again and carefully disposed of the wood shavings out the carriage window. When he shut it again and looked back at his traveling companions, Mrs. Brundadge thrust the knife toward him. "Ha!"

"Oh, thank you. How kind." Hugo took the knife from her nerveless fingers, then took the apple from Georgette and cut off a sliver. Returning both knife and apple, he then popped the slice into his mouth. "That's a fine apple, Mrs. Brundadge. Thank you for sharing it."

Georgette kicked at his foot.

"And thank you, Miss Snow," he added. "Also for sharing it."

"Oh!" The widow regarded the knife replaced in her hand as if she were not sure where it had come from. "That is—you are welcome, I'm sure."

"You don't intend to threaten us?" Mrs. Drupe sounded disappointed. "Not even to try? I assure you, we could protect ourselves."

Georgette smiled. This woman had, she guessed, read as many storybooks as Georgette herself.

"I would be a fool to attempt it," said Hugo. "And a villain, after you fed my cousin so nicely."

With that, all, it seemed, was forgiven. "Now, isn't

that kind?" Mrs. Brundadge eyed the contents of the hamper, all spilled out in her sister's lap. "Would you two like some of this pie? It's made from the same apples you like so much. Ah—I'll do the cutting, if you don't mind."

The kindly, if agitated, widows shared out a sweet, flaky-crusted pie, then sliced into the remaining chicken. From his surprisingly capacious leather case, Hugo found a packet of roasted almonds and handed them around. Georgette alone had nothing to contribute, yet they let her partake all the same.

So she looked her gratitude at them all—though more toward the sisters. And she enjoyed the spectacle of Lord Hugo Starling making awkward chatter with two middle-aged ladies. He'd thought to make his journey easier by muting her, but . . . what was the saying? *Hoist with his own petard.* Yes, Georgette had learned her Shakespeare.

The miles unrolled outside, and the sun slipped away like a lost gold sovereign. As the sky darkened, the waxing half-moon took its place in cool silver. The coach lamps winked outside, like fireflies bobbing alongside the travelers.

When the food was eaten and the refuse packed away, when night blanketed the coach, Georgette began to drowse and droop. She fought it for a time, holding herself up straight and clenching her jaw against yawn after yawn. The widowed sisters had fallen asleep already, their heads lolling toward each other as if their conversation continued even now.

She didn't hide her fatigue as well as she intended, for Hugo chuckled. "Tired, are you, *cousin?* It's been a long day and will be a longer night."

In the dim silver light, she saw him ease out of his greatcoat, then fold it carefully. He wedged the thick garment between himself and Georgette, up his side and atop his shoulder. "Sleep," he then murmured. "I've got you. Sleep as long as you like."

She folded her arms of habit—but at this hour of night, she could not disagree for long. She curled into the thick wool of the greatcoat, her head supported by the solid breadth of his shoulder beneath. The carriage swayed, and Hugo was solid and silent, and within minutes she was asleep.

In her dream, she lived in a tidy cottage, and she grew a garden of rampion that was lush and green. Whenever she wished, she plucked the leaves, and nothing was lost when she did.

In her dream, she was home, and she was safe. And when she opened the door to the cottage, someone who loved her greeted her from within.

Chapter Five

I'll get you for this, she had written.

And, Hugo thought, she certainly had. Through the ink-dark hours of night, Georgette had pillowed her head on his coat. She had rested on his shoulder for hours on end. She had slumped against him, a tender weight gone peaceful and slack. The floral scent of her hair had teased his nose; the line of her thigh had pressed his.

Such trust was beguiling.

Of all this, she was unaware. Innocent in sleep. Yet he *was* beguiled—and this was most annoying, for he had no time to be beguiled.

He drifted off himself, but awoke each time the mail coach stopped during the night. These were quick halts, lasting only for the amount of time it took to toss bags down and receive new bags from the coaching inn. For Hugo, the night progressed in fits and starts. By half six in the morning, the other travelers were waking. The sun had risen more than an hour before, and the sky was a fresh, tentative blue. When the coach stopped in Northampton for a rest and change of horses, Hugo and Georgette and the most talkative sisters in the world piled out.

Inside the coaching inn, he saw to his more urgent bodily needs, washed his hands and gritty-eyed face, then bought a pair of meat pasties from the innkeeper. He searched for Georgette, finding her at last to one side of the bustling courtyard. She was flicking through a newspaper with the sort of eager look he was directing toward his meat pie.

"Breakfast," he said, handing her one of the steaming pies. It was a fat, fragrant semicircle of golden-baked crust. When he bit into his own, he found it full of pleasantly spiced beef, potato, and onion. Hot and savory, it silenced his querulous belly, and he gobbled it in greedy bites.

The distraction of hunger eliminated, he turned his attention back to Georgette. She was chewing at her pasty, but her attention remained on the paper.

"Hugo," she said. "I don't think we ought to continue on to Derbyshire. Look at this!" She extended the paper toward him. "A maid has been arrested in Doncaster for possessing gold jewelry. It's crude and heavy, and she says it's ancient jewelry she dug up by chance. But surely she stole it. So says the local magistrate."

He squinted at the page, finding the article in question. "And?"

"'Or,' I think, is a better one-word question. Or, she had it created out of other gold. No one in the area has reported missing jewelry, according to the article."

He folded the paper and handed it back. She dusted the last crumbs of pastry crust from her fingers and took it from him. "You look puzzled," she said.

"Not at all. I always look like this at half six in the morning when I'm surrounded by carriage traffic and Doncaster is unexpectedly mentioned." He looked over his shoulder, locating their coach among the early-morning flurry of vehicles and vendors. No, their driver wasn't back at his seat yet; they had a few minutes before the coach left.

"That explains it, then. And I shall explain what I mean. I think some of the stolen gold coins have been taken north."

"But one has been spent in Strawfield. Derbyshire. Where we're going."

"That doesn't mean all the coins are there. Six chests were stolen, correct? Fifty thousand sovereigns? They could have been sent in fifty thousand different directions."

"That would do no one any good."

"Well, they could have been taken to more than one place. And this bracelet? It's made from the sovereigns. It *has* to be."

He must have looked his doubt, for she flapped the paper at him, forestalling his interruption. "Hugo! Only think. If I had murdered a great number of people and stolen a fortune in gold coins, I should melt it down."

"Ought I to be alarmed by how readily you enter into the criminal mind-set?"

"I hoped for impressed."

"Fine. I'm impressed." This wasn't entirely false. He had not considered that the coins might be melted down rather than hidden away. "How would you melt it, then, you criminal woman?"

"With a . . . however one melts coins. Probably a blacksmith's forge could do it."

"And what would you do with great chunks of gold bars?"

She tossed the newspaper into the basket of a maid walking by, startling the woman. "Live the life of a spendthrift wastrel."

"How foolish of me not to guess." He wished he'd filled a flask with coffee while he was inside the inn. "Do consider, though: it would draw attention, a formerly poor person with a newfound fortune in recast gold. Especially with the theft from the Royal Mint known."

"Exactly. It would. Thus the existence of this article about the maid in Doncaster." She bit her lip, looking after the retreating newspaper. "It didn't *say* anything about the stolen sovereigns, but we can't be the only people to make the connection. If we don't follow the trail at once, others will beat us to it."

"We? No. Leave me out of this," Hugo grumbled. "The notion doesn't make financial sense. If the sovereigns were worked into jewelry and pawned, a pawnbroker wouldn't give the thieves nearly what the gold was worth."

"But they would get more than nothing. Which is the amount of gold they can spend in the form of sovereigns for the next month."

This, he had to grant. But. "There's a significant flaw in your hypothesis. The four thieves who stole the trunks from the Royal Mint were male. Not maids." A call sounded from behind them; their coachman was climbing onto his box. "Georgette, we haven't time for this. We must get back to the coach."

"There's one more thing." She leaned closer to him, a confidential whisper. "That man over there? The one in the odd sort of slouching hat?"

He followed the direction of her gaze. "I see him, yes." The broad-brimmed hat was the only feature that distinguished the man. Average in coloring, height, and build, he had the sort of appearance that slid from memory as soon as it was not before one's eyes.

"I think he's a Bow Street Runner. He had one of those newspapers too, and he was questioning one of the servants about her pay."

"Oh, good. Intrigue. We've fallen into a gothic novel." He pulled his watch from his waistcoat pocket. "Or there's a simpler explanation: he wants to hire a servant."

"Or maybe he's wondering whether he's found a clue to the stolen gold."

Time was ticking; the talkative sisters were clambering back into the coach. "We've got to go, Georgette," he said, stuffing the watch back into its pocket. "No matter where the coins are, this is the way to find your brother."

She folded her arms. He groaned. "No. You are not disagreeing with me right now."

"I want to go to Doncaster. Remember: I said first coins, then brother."

"The coins are *with* your brother."

"One coin, yes, and it might be no more than a decoy. And half of England is looking around Straw-field for the reward. But if we go north right now, we might be the only ones to follow that trail."

This woman would be the death of him, or at least the death of his sanity. "You are proposing a gamble. I haven't time to calculate the odds, but they're too long for this to be a worthwhile pursuit."

"Don't call it a gamble, then. Call it a leap of faith." A slight smile curved her lips. "Even if only one trunk was taken north, it's worth pursuing. A trunk in the hand is worth six that aren't found before the public release of the sovereigns, thus negating the Royal Reward. Or so goes the old saying."

"That's not an old saying." He grabbed her wrist. "Come *on*. Our luggage is leaving on this coach, whether we do or not."

"Then we'd best take it off the coach." Tugging free of his grip, she darted toward the coach as if it had been her idea all along.

He strode after her. When they reached the coach, he caught the driver's eye and flipped him a shilling— then held up a finger. *Wait.*

Grudgingly, the man nodded.

Georgette was already calling up to one of the women sitting atop the coach, pointing toward her bag.

Hugo joined her. "If the merry widows inside the carriage hear you speaking, Miss Snow, you will destroy their faith in humanity."

"I'm not the one who lied to them and said I was mute." She gestured up at the woman again. "Yes! That's the bag. Thank you."

"Leave it there," Hugo called up. "She doesn't need it. We're getting into the coach."

"He's teasing," Georgette shouted back. "He loves to tease strangers at inopportune times. Toss it down, please." She crouched—and when the woman tossed her valise down, she caught it neatly with a little *oof.* "There, Hugo, it's too late. We're staying."

"This is recklessness, Georgette. Come, get back into the—"

"I'll get your bag, too," she said sweetly. "You'd best retrieve your hospital plans from inside the carriage, unless you want Mrs. Drupe to put them in her hamper."

His plans! She was right; he'd left them within. With a curse, he growled, "You force my hand, Miss Frost."

Wrenching open the carriage door, he blurted a quick explanation to the startled sisters within. His words made no sense, even to him, so he grabbed his case and bowed out as swiftly as he could. When he turned around, a man smacked into him, hard, then reeled away with a slurred apology.

Wasn't that delightful. It was his fate this week to be assailed by drunkards.

He returned to Georgette, brushing off the sleeves of his greatcoat as he did. "All right. Here I am. With my plans. Are you buoyed by triumph?"

"Moderately so." She held out his valise. "You don't want to continue to Derbyshire? You're certain?"

"To the contrary. I'm certain that I *do* want to continue to Derbyshire."

"You can, you know."

"The time for me to abandon you to your solitary fate was two minutes ago." He shaded his eyes, watching ruefully as the driver cracked his whip and pulled the coach into motion. "Damnation. That's more than half the fare wasted."

"I thought you accounted the fare of no consequence."

"I thought you were mute." Had the coach driven that quickly when they were inside it? Already it was nearly out of sight around the bend of the dew-damp road. "This hell-bent impulse of yours has left us stranded. And on what evidence? Nothing. The evidence is all leaving us behind and traveling to Strawfield."

"Maybe, but we have intuition drawn from the piecing together of unforeseen bits of information." She scuffed a boot against the ground. "Or I have. *You* have a plan, and once you formulate it, you want only to follow it inflexibly. But the story about the maid, and the presence of the man in the slouchy hat—that's evidence too."

"It is a fancy, that is all." He watched the carriage disappear entirely. "And I change my hospital plans all the time. When a better idea presents itself."

"Ideas don't *present* themselves. You have to snap them out of the air and stitch them together."

"Ideas are not cobwebs," he muttered. He knew she was being figurative, but he was feeling determinedly, rootedly literal. Not even the dust of the carriage's wheels remained, his purse was considerably lighter, and he'd no idea in which direction this troublesome young woman would drag him next.

"Hugo." All was silence for a moment; then she scuffed her boot again. "Hugo?"

He turned to look at her. "Is your vaunted intuition telling you nothing of my current mood?"

"It is, but if I waited for you to be cheerful and pleasant before speaking, I'd be your mute companion in truth."

"I don't see the problem with that."

She waved this off. "I am sorry that you are missing the chance to visit my brother. You wanted to, didn't you?"

What he wanted didn't matter. "I said I would go with you. I'll go with you."

Setting her valise down at her feet, she tied the trailing strings of her bonnet in a neat bow beneath her chin. "I don't think that's what you said at all. I think you said you'd take me to your mother, and then you said you'd take me to my brother."

"I say a lot of things to which no one pays heed. And yes, I did want to visit my friend again. Also to meet the people with whom he's staying, the Reverend Perry and his wife. Mrs. Perry is one of the finest translators of ancient Greek with whom I've corresponded."

Georgette laughed. "This implies that you have corresponded with more than one."

"Of course."

She stuffed a few trailing strands of hair under her bonnet. "There's no 'of course' to such matters, Hugo. Most people can't be bothered with dead languages."

"Most people can't be bothered with anything outside of the everyday," he said. "But I don't think that describes you, Miss Bone-box Gothic Novel."

"Ah, that was almost a compliment. Then you had to go and spoil it."

"It was not a compliment. Only an—"

"An observation. Right, right." She squinted up at the sky. "It's good to be out of that coach for a few minutes. At what hour do you think the mail leaves for Doncaster?"

"I've no idea. I haven't a *Pocket Gazette* with me." Of habit, he felt for his watch to check the time.

His waistcoat pocket was empty.

Was it in one of his other coat pockets? He patted them all, coat and greatcoat. No, it wasn't there, either. He looked about on the ground for the familiar gold case.

"You have suddenly gone into a frenzy," Georgette observed.

"I'm looking for my watch. I just had it—I *know* I put it back in my pocket. . . ." He had stepped that way to retrieve his case from the coach . . . he had turned . . . "That man! That drunken man!" He scanned the courtyard.

"Where?" Georgette followed his gaze.

He gritted his teeth against a curse. "I don't see him now. Though I wouldn't know him by sight; only by the smell of inebriation. He bumped into me. I thought it an accident, but he must have done it intentionally to steal my watch." Now he *did* curse. What was he to do without his watch?

"That's unfortunate. But we can inquire after the time inside the inn."

"I *want* my *watch.*" His fingers scrabbled at his pocket again, as if they might find the watch within it this time.

Georgette blinked at him.

How petulant he must sound. With an effort, he drew in a deep breath and spoke evenly. "It's not merely a watch to me, Georgette. It's one of a pair that my father gave to Matthew and me on our eighteenth birthdays." Matthew's last birthday. The case was chased in both their initials; two watches engraved identically, since, as the duke liked to joke, there was no difference to speak of between the two sons.

At the time, they had both found the statement annoying. Now Hugo liked turning it over in his mind, one of a precious and dwindling store of memories involving his twin.

Georgette grabbed his arm. "Shhh," she murmured. "You're too loud. The Runner is looking this way. Shh, don't make a fuss."

"If he is a Runner, then he's exactly the person I want to talk to." He shook off her hand, ready to stride in the direction of the slouch-hatted man.

"You can't," she insisted. "You'd have to tell him who you are, and then he'd want to know who I am. And either it would come out that you were traveling with an unmarried woman, which would ruin me, or we would have to be wed, which would ruin us both."

But his *watch*. He took another step toward the possible Runner.

"Hugo. Please. Don't talk to him. Don't draw attention. Oh! And take off your signet."

If only he had climbed into the coach and continued on his way to Strawfield. He'd have his watch, and he wouldn't have Georgette Frost tugging on his arm, and he wouldn't feel so torn about what was the right thing to do—which was something he rarely, if ever, doubted.

He looked at his leather case of hospital plans. He looked at Georgette's face: imploring and wide-eyed. With her features framed by the pale-blue lining of her bonnet, she looked young and fragile, though he knew she was certainly not the latter.

But her pleading look plucked a string of loyalty within him, setting it to sounding through his body. He was here to protect her, wasn't he? That's what one should do. That—and his hospital plans—and so many other pieces of his life—were his atonement. His distraction. His response to a bone-deep grief.

Whatever word one wanted to put to it.

He tugged the gold signet ring from his finger and

put it into his watch's place, in his waistcoat pocket. "You are a hard woman."

"I'm not this way because I chose to be. I'm this way because I've had to be. Left to my own devices, I would be calm and delightful and would never be involved in melodramatic situations."

"I doubt all of that," he said drily. Well, maybe not the "delightful" part. Her resourcefulness was becoming— how had she once put the matter? Acceptable.

She glanced across the courtyard. "The Runner is still here. See? Now he's talking to that maid to whom I gave the newspa—oh, *no*. He's looking at us again. Hugo, he's coming toward us!"

Yes. He was definitely right about melodramatic situations following her about. "What would you like me to do about it? Shall I shoot him?"

"Do you have a pistol?"

"*No*. Good Lord, Georgette."

She bit her lip. "I think we shall need false identities again. But *don't* make me mute this time. Or say that I am given to brain fevers."

"I'm not going to lie to an Officer of the Police. If that's who he is."

"Then I will instead. We're traveling together without servants or chaperones, so we'll have to be siblings or married." Narrowing her eyes, she looked him up and down. "It'll never do."

"What?" He stepped back, not liking her scrutiny. At least, not liking it when it brought on that look of doubt.

"Siblings. We don't look a bit alike. He won't believe it. Plus, I don't know enough about your family nor you about mine, in case he questions us."

"I thought you wanted to lie to him."

"It's hard to remember a great lot of lies." She looked abashed. "Er . . . or so I've heard. No, best to stick as close as possible to the truth." She glanced over her shoulder again, then fairly hissed, "We're newly wed. We eloped. You're madly in love with me."

"*What?* No. No, I'm not doing this."

"How sweet! Our first argument as a married couple." She tucked her arm through his. "You ought to embrace me."

"You're lucky I'm such a gentleman," he said, "or I should dunk you in the rain barrel over there."

She looked him straight in the eye. "Embrace me, Hugo, unless you want our journey to end right now."

"I do, rather."

But he didn't. Not really. Returning to London right now wouldn't bring him success. He needed this journey, the promise of this reward, to bring the plans for his hospital to fruition.

His hands moved, uncertain. He couldn't just *touch* her. She was a lady. Under his protection. The sister of his friend.

"Hugo," she hissed again. "Pretend you like me. Pretend . . . I'm your hospital plans."

"If you insist." Dropping his leather case, he shook free of her arm and grabbed her around the waist. She squeaked. Then he swept her off her feet, still holding her about the middle, and carried her a few steps. "Happy? Did you love that?"

"You are a strange man."

He dropped her.

Oh, not *dropped* dropped. She had her footing; he only let go of her abruptly.

"*Ugh.*" She stood straight. "He's almost here. We

can't run off now. He saw me seeing him. Look, I know you have a second brain in place of a heart—"

"A biological impossibility."

"—and I don't expect you to make believe well."

This stung. Everyone always expected the best from Hugo, and he prided himself on surpassing their expectations. So what was different about her? Why was she unimpressed?

"But I can." She smiled up at him—and her face changed. It was warm, it was bright, and her eyes crinkled as though the mere sight of him brought her joy.

His mouth fell open. He swayed on his feet, tugged toward her by the longing in her look.

"Begging your pardon?"

The bland figure in the odd hat had reached them. With a tip of that hat, he looked at them each in turn. "Everything all right over here? I noticed you left your coach in a hurry. Then you were arguing."

Georgette turned toward the man, seeming to blink away her soppy expression with an effort. "Oh, no! Not at all. We are newly wed. It's too soon for us to argue."

Bah. They'd been arguing since the moment they met. Every bit of her statement was a lie.

Hugo straightened up, trying to look as if he agreed.

"Newly wed?" The man looked skeptical. "Have your parents' permission, do you? You look young to be wed."

"Not particularly," Hugo said. "I was thirty-two in spring."

"I meant the lady."

"I'm twenty-one," said Georgette. Another lie. "Of age to marry. We're honeymooning. Going north, where my uncle has promised us work."

"What sort of work? Where are you going?"

Georgette looked beseechingly up at Hugo. "Oh, don't tell him, my love! He wants to follow us and try to peep in our carriage windows!"

The man in the odd hat set his jaw. Gritting his teeth, likely. It was an urge with which Hugo had become very familiar in the past day. "Callum Jenks, Officer of the Police. I have my reasons for asking, you may be sure, and they don't include peeping."

"You are a Bow Street Runner!" Georgette sidled next to Hugo. None too gently, she elbowed him. Again. Wonderful. Now she'd crow about being right about spotting Runners along their path.

"Officer of the Police, if you please," Jenks replied. "I noticed you taking off a ring, sir. Mind if I have a look at it?"

This was not, of course, a question. Hugo took the ring from his pocket and handed it over.

Jenks took a quizzing glass from his pocket and held up the ring before it. There wouldn't be much detail for the man to see. The band was finely worked, but the ring was simple, with no stones in it.

"Too old," grunted the Runner, and handed it back. "The design's been worn down."

"I'm sorry my family heirloom doesn't meet with your approval," Hugo said. Naturally, Georgette elbowed him again.

"I'm not looking for family heirlooms." Tucking away his quizzing glass, Jenks said, "Either of you heard of the theft from the Royal Mint?"

Another elbow to his side. He was going to pay her back for this. "Indeed," Hugo wheezed, easing his ring back on. "Surely everyone in Europe has."

"I've been commissioned by the Mint to look into the matter."

"Good luck to you, then," Hugo said.

"Hmm." Jenks looked them up and down. "Perhaps we'll see each other again on the road north. I never forget a face. Or a name, for that matter. And what are yours?"

"Crowe," said Georgette. "Mr. and Mrs. Crowe."

"A murder of Crowes, are you?" For the first time, the Runner looked amused instead of suspicious.

"Give me time," Hugo muttered. "I've only just wed the lady."

Yes. She elbowed him again.

"Right," said Jenks. "Well, as long as there's been no law broken, I wish you a pleasant journey." Again, he looked them up and down. "Crowe. He and she. Thirty-two and twenty-one. Black hair. Blond hair. Six feet. Five feet . . . say, five inches."

"Five feet, six inches," sniffed Georgette.

"If you say so." With a tip of his hat, Jenks strode back the way he'd come, then entered the coaching inn.

"How delightful," said Hugo. "We have been added to the mental catalogue of a Bow Street Runner. I can't thank you enough for removing us from our nice, safe, calm mail coach."

"Good. You *ought* to be thanking me." She beamed up at Hugo. "Didn't you hear? He's following the stolen gold, and he's traveling north. We made the right decision."

Except that now they would be traveling as a married couple. Under false names. Under the eye of a suspicious officer.

None of that seemed at all like *protecting Georgette* or *avoiding scandal*.

"*You* made the decision," he said. "I agree only

under duress to continue on this journey. And by duress, I mean the threat of another elbowing."

In truth, his heart had taken up a quick, excited rhythm. He had felt the curve of her waist; he had been smiled upon as though he delighted her. She had taken his arm, a gesture of casual affection that caught him unawares, with his defenses down.

No, he wasn't going with her under duress. That was a lie. But how many times today had a lie been preferable to the truth?

Chapter Six

Georgette almost felt guilty about wasting the remaining fare to Strawfield. Almost. But when one had the chance to plunge into a bathtub full of hot water, scrub clean of the past day's travel dirt, and change into fresh clothing, it was difficult to feel much of anything but contentment.

Hugo had bidden Georgette go into the inn and make herself comfortable while he determined their options for traveling northward. Probably by *comfortable*, he hadn't meant *order a bath brought to a guest chamber*, but she didn't intend to waste the opportunity. Once she had bathed, the innkeeper's wife helped her dress and pin up her hair. Georgette then placed a few orders with that good lady and went downstairs in search of Hugo.

He was planted in the entryway of the inn, arguing with a beefy man in a high-crowned hat and a long, drab-colored greatcoat with four capes. The man looked like a dandy gone to seed, his every garment once fashionable and expensive but now worn and dingy.

"Fine, fine. We'll split the difference," Georgette heard Hugo say. He and the other man shook hands, neither one looking particularly pleased.

Hugo turned, catching sight of her. "Ah. My dear." He looked weary, but a wry smile tugged at the corner of his mouth. "How good of you to make an appearance. You are a treasure spit down from heaven."

"Heaven's spittle? My darling, you flatter me. You are a pearl excreted from an oyster's unspeakable bits," she responded sweetly. "What have you been arranging?"

"This is Mr. Seckington." Hugo introduced the large man at his side, who gave a courteous bow. "He maintains a private carriage for hire and has agreed to drive us northward."

"Only I'd be missing days and days of fares," commented that man with a hangdog look, "so I couldn't take you two up unless your man paid me for all the time I was gone from home."

"A fare you estimated outrageously," pointed out Hugo.

"A body never knows when he'll be given the best fares of his life," said Seckington. "I have to think of the future. I'm a family man and all. You'll understand soon enough, newly wed as you are."

Hugo looked as if he wanted to argue, so Georgette interrupted to thank the man. "I am ready to leave at any moment," she said.

"Generous of you to say so," said Hugo, "considering you've had time for a bath."

Hmm. Apparently she hadn't got her hair as dry as she thought.

"You'll be glad of how clean I am when you have to

sit in close quarters with me," she replied. "I smell of rainbows and delightfulness."

"I have no doubt." He rubbed at the stubble darkening his chin. "Would that I had time for a shave, but we'd best be on our way. Mr. Seckington, have our bags taken to the coach, then toss the lady in as well. I'll see to a hamper."

"It's already done," said Georgette. "The innkeeper's wife is packing it now."

"What?"

"I ordered one." She shrugged. "Mrs. Brundadge's hamper of food was a good companion last night. I thought we'd like our own. I ordered you a quart of strong hot coffee, too."

For the first time this morning, Hugo looked pleased. "Did you really?"

"I really did. I'm not so cruel as to promise a man coffee and not provide it."

"Oh." His brows knit—and then he smiled. It was a tight, awkward twist of the mouth, as though he were embarrassed to express happiness. "Thank you. That was thoughtful of you."

The rarity of his smile made it too sweet to look upon. Georgette felt as if she were standing before a bakery window, determined not to look at cakes she could not afford.

"It's of no consequence," she muttered, looking at the toes of her boots. They were neat and brown, the same shade as the wooden floor on which she stood. She would have faded into it if she could; anything to avoid the gentle scrutiny of his gaze.

Soon enough, they were bundled into Seckington's carriage, valises and hospital plans and hamper and coffee and all.

Compared to the ducal carriage in which she'd been transported semi-involuntarily the day before, this was a worn vehicle. She guessed it had once belonged to a noble family, but like its driver, it had come down in the world. The outline of a crest showed through the dull black paint on the door, and the once-crimson spokes were flaked, showing patches of bare wood. Inside, the thick velvet nap remained at the edges of the squabs, with derriere-shaped worn spots and sags at their centers.

"I like it," Georgette decided. "It suits me."

"It's merely a conveyance. It doesn't suit you any more or less than the Willingham carriage I used yesterday, or than the mail coach did." Hugo was seated across from her. From his valise, he took a small shagreen case.

"Well, I *feel* like it suits me." She inhaled deeply. "What's that smell coming from the fabric of the squabs? Snuff?"

Hugo opened the little case and withdrew a pair of gold-framed spectacles. "I think it is. One of the maids can clean the insides of the doors before we set off."

"I like it."

"You cannot convince me that you like snuff."

"Not exactly, no. But I like that it's not perfect. Perfection is . . . intimidating."

"I wouldn't know." Unfolding the spectacles, he put them on.

As the midmorning light slanted through the carriage window, the gold wink of the spectacles' frames softened the sternness of his features. Oh, how she wanted to trace the lines of his face, to see whether he had changed or whether she was only seeing him differently. When he began searching through his valise again, the gesture was so unconcerned, so domestic, that it clutched at something vulnerable within her. With an intensity almost painful, she wished . . . wished that this was real, and that he truly thought her *dear* and wasn't only traveling with her out of obligation.

She wished that she were different too. More irresistible. More lovable. Or else more independent; so independent that she didn't care what others thought of her, or whether they were around her at all.

"Oh, please," she grumbled. "That's all you are: perfect perfect perfect. Perfect carriage, perfect plans, perfectly prepared for whatever comes your way."

"Clearly I have you completely fooled." He drew forth a book. "I'm not going to argue with such a flattering perception. Here, if you're ready, we'll set off."

She agreed, and he stretched up to knock at the ceiling of the carriage. Seckington chivvied his team into motion, and with a pleasant crunch of wheels over gravel, they turned north out of the courtyard.

"How much is the hire of this carriage going to cost?" Georgette asked. "I should have asked that earlier."

"You needn't have, and you shouldn't ask it now." He flipped open the book and held it up before him. The bit of her who'd lived in a bookshop all her life awoke, stretched, and took note. The volume was octavo-sized, bound in red calf. A diamond pattern was diced across the binding, the title tooled in gold on the spine. *The Elements of Chemistry, III.* A sturdy binding; elegant but not showy.

She would have preferred it had been levant morocco, polished to a sheen and plaque-stamped in gold all over. The people who liked books with that sort of binding were easy not to like: they bought their books for show, not for reading.

"What do I owe you, Hugo?" she tried again.

He lowered the book. The lenses of his spectacles magnified his eyes slightly. "Just your safety. Not another thing in the world."

"But—"

"If you are determined to press for a total, then fine. Seckington is charging a shilling per mile."

"Oh my God." A shilling per mile? The journey to Doncaster would cost more than she earned in a year.

A flicker of a smile tugged at his lips. "Suffice to say I don't owe you a coach ticket anymore."

"I shall have to find the stolen gold, if only so I can pay back all that I owe you."

He closed the book, holding his place with one finger, and looked out the window. "Please don't trouble yourself about it. Your brother would do the same for me, without question."

Would he? Would Benedict do the same for Georgette? Her brother meant well, but that didn't mean he *did* well. Now here was Hugo, treating her with kindness and generosity, but for reasons she didn't quite like.

"I don't want you to think of me only as Benedict's sister," she ventured. As soon as she spoke the words, heat rose in her cheeks. "I don't mean it like . . ." She cut herself off. Like what? Like a demand? Like a flirtation?

"Believe me, I don't," he replied. "I also think of you as Bone-box, as Miss Snow, as Mrs. Crowe, and as the cause of my favorite coat's ruin."

Well. That was something. "Should I be honored?"

"Probably not." Without another word, he flipped open his book again and resumed reading.

Georgette looked out the window, watching yellow-green spring grass roll by. The land was gently swelling, dotted with trees here and there, sometimes divided by hedges or tidy fences. It was beautiful. Peaceful. Wholly unlike anything she'd seen in London.

With nothing to do but stare in silence, she was bored within five minutes.

That wouldn't do. There must be so many things she'd not seen before. She would be more observant. "A flock of sheep," she said. "How many of them there are."

Hugo grunted an acknowledgment that she had spoken.

"I won't count them or I'll fall asleep. Ah, there's a cow."

Grunt.

"A stone cottage with a thatched roof. I haven't seen one of those outside of a storybook."

Grunt.

Not once did his gaze leave the page of his book. In the intensity of his focus, there was something dreadfully attractive. Georgette could not help but wonder what it would be like to have all that attention, all that interest, turned her way.

"Look, Hugo," she said. "A witch shoving a child into an oven."

His head snapped up. "What?"

"Ha. You were listening."

"I heard every word you said, yes. But don't you have anything to do to amuse yourself while we drive?"

"Yes. I'm doing it. This is the farthest I've ever been

from London, and I like seeing the land for real. Not just in a book."

"Could you see it for real without speaking?"

"I could. But I would prefer you not try to silence me all the time."

Her arched brow made him pause before replying. "It is not gracious of me. I am sorry. I'm a grumpy old loon who is unaccustomed to traveling in company."

She huffed. "See? Perfect perfect perfect. How am I to stay annoyed with you when you take blame upon yourself so readily?"

"I promise you, I don't mind if you are not annoyed with me."

This she ignored. "Sometimes I think everything I know of the world comes from a book rather than my own experience."

"Surely not everything."

"Not quite. No, not quite. Today I have managed an adventure of my own." When she hesitated, he turned his attention back to his book.

"Did you bring any novels with you?" she asked.

With a sigh, Hugo looked up from his book. "Did I what?"

"Grumpy old loon. Did you bring novels? Or any type of story. Anything except scholarly books."

"Certainly not."

Unfortunate. She didn't feel like paging through *The Elements of Chemistry, I* or *II.* "Did you never read fairy stories at all?"

"If I did, I had too much sense to credit them."

"What is there of nonsense in such stories? They tell about the dark deeds that hide within human hearts. Widows who remarry men who wish to cook their

children. Witches who prey on families in desperate
need. They're about people, only . . . more so."

"If I want to read about people, I shall study history.
Then I could learn something as I read."

Ugh. Scholars. Years of experience with her parents'
dust-dry studies and uninterested care should have
prepared her for an answer such as this.

But this journey would be far too long if Georgette
and Hugo rode in silence. She could not allow him to
abandon her for his book; not yet. "Fine." She leaned
back against the squabs, wiggling against the ham-
mocked seat until she found a comfortable spot. "Tell
me what you like reading about."

He shut his book again, looking ruefully at the
cover. "At the moment, the characteristics of vegetable
acids."

"You like reading about vegetable acids. Really."

He adjusted one of the gold stems of his spectacles.
"I don't know that anyone feels strong enthusiasm for
such things. But I don't know much about vegetable
acids, so I'm learning about them."

"To what end?"

"To know something I didn't know before."

"So people will say how intelligent and well-read
you are?"

He opened his mouth, then closed it again. His
brows knit. Then he cleared his throat and said, "No
one minds hearing such things, certainly."

"I wonder what else you might like to hear."

"At the moment, I would love to hear nothing at
all so that I could concentrate on my book. But it
would not be gracious to say so, so I never would."

She snorted. "Would you not? Oh, what fun we'll

have traveling to Doncaster together. What will it take? Two full days?"

"More, since we didn't set off from Northampton until midmorning." Marking his place, he set aside his book and pressed at his temples. "You want a story, do you?"

"Um. Something about that question sounds foreboding."

He extended his legs, bumping the opposite squab where Georgette sat. "Once upon a time"—he removed his spectacles—"there was a terrible maiden with hair lighter than flax and eyes paler than the morning sky."

"Already I don't like the direction of your story."

"Please don't interrupt. It is severe upon the creative temperament." Folding the stems of his spectacles, he tucked them back into their case. "A handsome and intelligent prince came upon her once while she was carrying books. 'I love books,' he said. 'I love to learn things I don't know.'

"'What about me?' she asked.

"'I have no idea what you love,' he said. So she flew into an almighty rage and pushed him down the stairs, where he would have broken his neck had he not possessed magical healing abilities. The end."

Hugo tucked his shagreen case back into his valise, then looked at Georgette expectantly.

That fiend. That ridiculous fiend. She tried to glare at him—but laughter seized her, bubbling forth like wine uncorked. "And here I thought you didn't care for fiction."

"Did you think that was fictional? I thought it was about real people. Only more so." So soberly, he spoke these words, but in his eyes there was a wicked twinkle.

She nudged his foot with hers. "Tell me more about your magical healing abilities."

"Another time. Don't you have a book with you? Or letters to write?"

"I have no correspondents except my brother, and you already wrote to him. And I don't own any books of my own. Everything I read belonged to the family bookshop."

"You own no books?" He looked horrified.

"Correct," she said. "And I don't mind that. I like books, but sometimes I hate them too."

"Hate books?" His expression of horror deepened.

"Sometimes. Yes. You see, they were my parents' favorite. My parents chose acquiring more and more books over everything. Over allotting money to improve our living quarters, over expanding the shop, over spending time with their daughter."

"That can't be true." He shot a guilty look at the book that lay beside him.

"It shouldn't have been true. But it was." Finding a loose thread in the stitching of the squabs, she picked at it with her fingernail. "I think that's why Benedict went to sea so young. But girls cannot go to sea, so in the bookshop I stayed."

The loose thread was as long as her thumb before he replied. "I am sorry for that."

The quiet, simple words were a knife to her composure. Quickly, she whipped her face toward the window, blinking back tears. "Oh look," she choked out. "A . . . something or another."

"Georgette."

"What?"

"Georgette."

Reluctantly, she turned toward him. He had pulled

back his feet and was leaning forward, elbows braced
on his knees. Had she thought she wanted to be the
object of his focus? It was unnerving in its intensity, as
if by looking at her he might determine her true
nature, her deepest secrets. She shied away, not wanting to be seen so clearly.

"Georgette, I came to the shop to buy books. But I
bought them at your family's shop because of you."

Her heart paused. Her stomach gave a nervous twist.
"I . . . I don't understand."

"I visited Frost's Bookshop because I wanted to know
whether you were all right."

She swallowed. "How could you determine whether
I was all right? I know you value evidence, as a man of
science."

Now it was his turn to lean back, to look away as if
hunting an answer in the landscape through which
they rolled. "Well . . . if you were there, and moving
about, and—you know, clothed and clean—then you
were all right."

"Did it seem so?" God, she was tired of a sudden.
"Did that mean you were all right after your brother
died? Being dressed and walking around?"

His jaw tightened. "How *can* you compare?"

The loose thread in her seat beckoned her. She
gave it another tug, another pick. Something to do to
busy her hands. "I lost my parents. I lost my home—if
it ever was such a thing. I have hardly seen my brother
in years." When she looked up, he was again regarding
her with that curious focus. "I cannot fathom what it is
like to lose a twin. But I do know what loss is like,
nonetheless."

Leaning forward, he took up one of her hands and

gave it a quick squeeze. His touch made her fingers shake, and she pulled free at once.

He sat back again. "We both know a little more than what we've read in books. We merely read different books."

"I have no doubt that we have," she said drily. "You read to learn. I read to experience." To see young women finding love. To know their finest qualities were appreciated. To feel, as she read, a flutter of hope that such things might one day be real for her too.

Such sentiments would mean nothing to Hugo.

"But you do learn, don't you?" asked Hugo. "I have recently been informed that one can learn a great deal from *contes de fée* about the darkness of the human heart."

She snorted.

"And I read to experience too, you know. Just now, I am experiencing an increased level of knowledge about the structure of vegetable acids."

He didn't understand. Scholars never did. Somehow it always came back to books and facts with them. That was even worse than the darkness of the human heart, sometimes: a heart that was, quite simply, indifferent.

She managed a smile. "You must go back to your reading, then," she said. "I'm sorry I bothered you. I'll look at the sheep."

"So you shall." He knocked at the carriage ceiling, signaling the driver to bring the vehicle to a halt.

As the carriage slowed, Georgette put her hands flat on the squabs. She felt as though she needed to brace for a sudden impact, but instead, they only rolled gently to a stop. "What are you doing? Why did you stop the carriage?"

"Go," Hugo said. "Get out and pet a sheep. Obviously you are fascinated by sheep. Go indulge your curiosity."

"Is any of that a euphemism?"

His nostrils flared. "Of course not. Go on, now."

They had halted beside a fenced-in field dotted with Leicester sheep: rangy and long-legged, their curious heads lifted to regard the unexpected creature on four wheels.

It *would* be interesting to pet a sheep. "What are you planning to do?"

"I'm going to stay in here and read."

"You're going to drive away without me."

"My dear Miss Frost, if I wished to drive away without you—no, let me rephrase. If I thought it *right* to drive away without you, I would never have come looking for you in London in the first place."

Exasperated Hugo was a more familiar Hugo. Exasperated Hugo made her smile. "I don't believe you," she said, just to make him twitch. "Come with me, or I won't go."

"That's not how favors work."

"Is this a favor? I thought it was a bargain."

He muttered something under his breath, then eased by her to open the carriage door. Jumping to the ground, he held up a hand to assist her down. "Happy now?"

"I don't know. I haven't petted a sheep yet."

As soon as she walked up to the fence, some of the sheep came to investigate. They looked to be ewes, tall at the withers, and their spring lambs were already sturdy and well-grown. Their wool was long about the body, twisted like snipped-off yarn. With their bare heads and necks and legs, each sheep looked like it was wearing a hooked rug.

She laughed.

When more sheep collected at the fence, a sheep-dog trotted over to see what was fascinating its flock. It was shaggy and auburn, with pricked ears and a lolling tongue. Georgette reached over the waist-high fence and extended her hand, back up, for the dog to sniff. For the ewes to bump. They were all warm creatures, strong and lively, soft-furred and friendly, nudging at her. The wool was oily and coarse to the touch, smelling of animal and earth.

Hugo stood at Georgette's side, the image of patient tolerance.

"Thank you," said Georgette. "Let us stop more often. And waste time in traveling."

His brows lifted. "I did say that, didn't I?"

"We were in a desperate hurry at the time." When they set off by mail coach, the number of days between the present and the first of July had seemed too short. Now Georgette wondered what fuller use might be made of them. "Do you truly think traveling a waste of time?"

He looked out over the green land, the yarn-wooled sheep. Then he breathed in deeply, pulling the crisp air into his lungs, and he smiled. A real smile this time, without hesitation. "No. It's not if we enjoy it."

"I think I enjoy it," she said, and he turned his smile toward her. Her heart in her throat, she reached for his hand. When her fingers laced with his, he did not tug away.

Chapter Seven

Since they were now agreed that the process of travel need not be horrid, Georgette asked that they pause at every coaching inn along the road to Doncaster.

"I'll collect gossip from the servants each time we stop," she said. "And comb through newspapers, if they're available. That way we'll be sure of doing the right thing."

"That's not what will make me sure." As the day wore on, Hugo had grown quiet. More than once, Georgette saw him reach for the pocket in which his watch had been, only to remember anew its loss.

She tried to distract him. "Would you care to propose an alternative means of collecting information?"

"Such as?" He had turned upon the squabs, leaning against the side of the carriage, his boots up along the seat. His hospital plans were on the floor, nudging the hamper.

"Oh, something very logical." Georgette sat primly, uncertain how much space she ought to take up. She had reached for Hugo's hand, but he did not seem to want to be reached now. "You might map all the possible vectors from Strawfield and Doncaster, then note where the lines intersect."

"You mentioned vectors," Hugo said. "Very nice. But no, it wouldn't be fair to pit that method against your plan to collect gossip."

"Ah, because you know your map would fall short. But Hugo, you're under an insurmountable disadvantage already. I've worked in a bookshop. I know far more about the ways of the world than you do."

"No, I meant that it wouldn't be fair because I've studied . . ." He trailed off. With a double *thump*, his boots hit the floor of the carriage, and he turned to face her again. "Curse it, Georgette. You're baiting me, aren't you? Traveling with you consists of continuous violations of my dignity."

"You love it," she said. "You think it's entertaining and delightful."

"Don't be so sure." But he was almost smiling. Wasn't he?

"I know you value evidence," Georgette said. "I do too. That's good sense. But in this matter, gossip is as close to evidence as we'll get unless we stumble over the stolen trunks."

As the afternoon wore on, they unpacked the hamper and shared out the coffee. A light rain began to fall, tracing idle, winding lines down the carriage windows. The inside of the coach became smaller and smaller, until Georgette felt Hugo could, if he wished, idly reach into her mind and pluck forth every one of her plans and ideas.

At each coaching stop, she had more ideas and fewer plans. And each stop brought the inevitable end of the journey closer. She did not know what she would do when it came, and when the day no longer began and ended in the company of Lord Hugo Starling. Confronted by the towering organization of his plans—those perfect perfect perfect plans—she was more and more unsure.

She could not permit herself to be unsure. She could not afford to rely on help that would soon, inevitably, be withdrawn—or on the heart of a scholar who thought someone was *all right* if she but walked around in a world that mystified her.

As the day went on, gossip guided them north. Blobby bits of gold had been used to pay for items as distant as Northumberland, someone's sister's cousin's friend had heard. Another distant connection had heard that the Doncaster maid had been freed, and that she had fled north instead of returning to her post.

The Bow Street Runner had been seen at some inns, for the servants remembered his questions, but at others Jenks must have passed by without stopping. Always, he inquired about income, rumor, locations to the north. Maybe as far as Doncaster; maybe even beyond.

There was more trail to follow; the journey wouldn't end yet. Not for a few more days. At least that.

When the light faded to a sunset of pink and gold, Hugo agreed with Georgette that the next coaching inn would be their resting spot for the night. For the first time, Georgette thought beyond the immediate implications of her lie to Jenks: that they were a married couple.

Oh. No. No, she couldn't share a room with Hugo.

Not that she doubted he would act as a gentleman ought. No, she only doubted that she'd be able to get her mind in order again. To think of him in the proper way, which was . . . whatever it was. Her brother's friend, her cousin's bookshop customer.

Her own partner in adventure, recently.

"We needn't keep to our story about being a married couple," she said as Seckington turned his carriage into the courtyard of the White Lion, about forty miles from Northampton. They'd made decent progress considering their number of stops. Doncaster lay northward, another day and a half of travel before them. And beyond that, who knew? "Here we could be siblings. That would be wiser, don't you think?"

"It probably would." Hugo was peering through the window, scanning the travelers arriving at the inn for a night's rest. "Except that I see Mr. Jenks in the inn's entryway, questioning everyone as they arrive."

Yes. Jenks, the Bow Street Runner, had recognized them. Hugo had known he would, after the careful scrutiny with which he'd regarded them. The Runner greeted them by their supposed names, Mr. and Mrs. Crowe.

Damnation.

Was that suspicion glinting in his eyes?

Damnation again.

Then he twitted them about wanting a room for the night, a newly wed couple such as themselves.

Damnation to the third power. Exponential damnation.

"We require a room," beamed Georgette. "I always welcome the chance to be with my darling, handsome, wonderful husband."

He was reminded of her falsely effusive praise of him before the Duchess of Willingham. *Is any of that true, Miss Frost? I could wish everyone thought so well of my youngest.*

Sometimes no compliment was to be preferred.

"Forgive my bride," he told Jenks. "She's tipsy. Been enjoying some wine along the way."

"Apprehensive about that job from her uncle?"

"The what?"

Jenks looked at him blandly. "The job for which you're traveling north."

Georgette was going to elbow him again as soon as she got the chance. "Of course I knew what you meant," Hugo replied. "I was only distracted by the use of the term 'apprehensive,' for never in her life has my wife been apprehensive."

"You will put me to the blush, my delight," Georgette said with a most un-Georgette-like titter. "And where are you off to, Mr. Jenks?"

"Northward. Same as you."

"Do you know my uncle, then?" Her voice was all innocence.

Jenks was not impressed. "Unlikely, unless your uncle is Sir Frederic Chapple."

Georgette's eyes went saucer-round. "But this is incredible! What are the odds, my love?"

Hugo recognized his cue. "I cannot begin to fathom them. My love." Chapple . . . Chapple . . . he scrolled through his memories of *Debrett's Peerage*. He had never studied it closely, as had his mother and sisters-in-law, and couldn't place the name. "And is Sir Frederic still living at . . . ah, what was the name of that charming house of his, my angel of distress?"

Georgette glared at him for a second, then added sweetly, "I never thought of it as anything but home."

Jenks was following their conversation with a look

of polite uninterest. "Did you? Interesting, that, since he's only been baronet for a few months."

"I meant before that," Georgette covered. "Of course, now that he is baronet, everything will be different. I hope he will still have time for a mere niece! Will he even remember me, my paragon?" Hugo could tell she was enjoying herself, just as she had when playing Bone-box.

"Let me guess," Jenks said. "He might not know you at all. Because of the baronetcy having gone to his head, or something of that sort."

"Oh, you are familiar with his ways," Georgette cooed. "He is remarkably forgetful, sometimes, though at other times he is not. It all depends. But then, you must know that."

"I'll find out soon enough," Jenks said. "If you'll excuse me."

Once the Runner moved off, Hugo arranged with the innkeeper for a supper and a night's lodging. And for the innkeeper's wife to help Mrs. Crowe with her clothes and hair. And for extra bedcovers, as the night might be cold.

In truth, he planned to use them to create a pallet on the floor for himself. In case Jenks might still be listening or observing, he thought that wiser than arranging for two separate bedchambers.

By the time they had eaten and were established in their room, the sun had turned in for the night. Hugo carried a taper and a branch of candles into the chamber, finding a pleasant fire already lit. The room held the familiar scent of coal.

Their chamber was on the second floor, tucked under the attics. The courtyard was a long look down, lit by lanterns carried by servants and swinging on arriving coaches. This far above, it all seemed small and far away. Those other travelers had no notion that up above, Lord Hugo Starling had found himself in a dreadfully compromising position with a respectable young lady.

Not that he would let it become so. Lighting every candle he could, he brought the room into view. It was not unusual: a bed, a desk with an oil lamp on it, a privacy screen, a washstand. He would be able to shave in the morning.

For now, he set his leather case atop the desk and lit the oil lamp with a taper. The innkeeper's wife had followed Georgette in, and that lady helped unfasten her stays—or so Hugo surmised—behind the privacy screen.

Hugo didn't know, didn't care, wasn't interested, wasn't even *thinking* about it. He wasn't. He seated himself at the desk and unrolled his hospital plans, looking them over for the hundredth time. The thousandth. There was always something more to add, to make sure the building was prepared for every eventuality.

A soft laugh and unintelligible conversation sounded from behind the screen. Not that he was listening.

The hospital walls ought to be thicker. Walls could never be too thick, too sturdy. He drew in a pencil line indicating the alteration, then turned over the paper to add the date and a description of the alteration to his ongoing list. As he wrote, a *whssssh* caught Hugo's notice; out of reflex, he looked for the source.

Georgette's gown had been flung over the top of the privacy screen. It looked frail and thin, the pale fabric no more than a suggestion of a person's shape.

With this, she had covered herself today. It was not much of a barrier between her body and the world. And now there was no barrier between them at all, save for the privacy screen and whatever she might have been wearing beneath her gown.

Which was *not* what he was thinking about. He was thinking about the ink-drawn pages before him.

He squeezed his eyes shut. Spectacles. He needed his spectacles. Then he could read his plans better—though he knew their every line by heart—and make the needed alterations. To the windows, maybe. Should the windows be smaller, the better to keep out negative humors from the outside? Or ought they to be large? Would fresh air be beneficial?

He flipped the architectural plan over to its front and turned his attention to these questions with a determination he had seldom before adopted. Or if not exactly determination, then focus. Intense focus. After a few minutes, the innkeeper's wife bade them a good night, and Georgette emerged from behind the screen, and in all that time Hugo had done little more than squint at the paper and not know what to do next.

"We learned quite a lot from Jenks," she commented. "Now we know where we must go. That is, we will once we discover where Sir Frederic Chapple makes his home."

The Runner hadn't been fooled by anything they said, Hugo was certain. But the man saw no harm in them following him.

Or perhaps he wanted them to, suspicious as he'd initially seemed. Perhaps he was drawing them along after him. And how far would they end in going?

"This journey will beggar me," he said.

"Because of the travel expenses?" Her question was halting.

It was ungentlemanly for him to imply that Georgette's schemes were burdensome. Especially when, though he could hardly credit it, her decision to follow Jenks had been the right one. "No, not that. It is only that Seckington demanded a room of his own instead of sleeping in the stables."

"I had no idea hiring out a carriage was so lucrative. When the hunt for the Royal Reward is done, I shall see about taking up the profession."

Soft footsteps—*bare* footsteps—crossed the room to stop behind him. Hugo dragged his hands through his hair; rubbed at his face; settled his spectacles straight across his nose.

"You are upset? I am sorry," Georgette said. "Being without funds is a dreadful prospect. I have money saved. It would be right for me to cover my expenses."

Oh, excellent. Now he'd made her feel guilty. "No, no. Please don't worry about it." He mentally totted up the amount he'd laid out so far. "I was complaining about Seckington; I didn't intend to complain about you. Besides which, duke's sons aren't ever really beggared." Another quarter's income was never more than ninety days away. Hugo's purse wasn't empty yet, and at the end of June his accounts would be replenished.

"It must be good to be the son of a duke," she said lightly.

"It bears privilege, to be sure." He smoothed the papers before him; plans for a hospital that no one believed in but himself. "Though sometimes, not enough."

The sons of dukes were equipped with a quiverful of fine schooling, but society prevented them from firing off their expensive education in any useful direction. A gentleman didn't have to work. A gentleman didn't *choose* to work.

What good was a gentleman, then? Younger sons

such as Hugo had no land, no promise of a title. Of people to watch out for, to care for.

Hugo would find a way to do so all the same. If he could get some damned money.

"Poor Lord Hugo," said Georgette. "Poor Mr. Crowe. He's handsome and healthy and has all kinds of money, yet sometimes the world dares thwart him."

"You are mocking me."

"It was not mockery. It was merely an observation."

"You are *definitely* mocking me."

Her voice was farther away now. She must be standing before the window. He would not turn, though; not until she said he might.

Or until his head burst from all he confined within it. So many plans and wishes and musts and need-tos. So many wonderings and denials. So many unexpected twists to an unexpected journey. It was all too much for one brain to hold.

"I need a drink," he said.

"No, come look out the window."

He shoved back his chair. "I need a drink," he repeated.

"But it's snowing!"

"In late May? Impossible." He stood. Removing and folding his spectacles as he crossed the room, he stood by Georgette and looked out at the night sky. "It *is* impossible. That is not snow, Miss Frost. Do you need to borrow my spectacles? That is rain."

"I know that. But you were going to ignore me forever unless I said something unexpected."

"You *could* say, 'Hugo, I want attention.'"

"That sounds so needy. No. I don't want attention. I just don't want to be ignored."

Ha. If only she knew: when she thought he was ignoring her, she was most occupying his thoughts.

When he could not look at her, it was because he saw her in his mind's eye; too clear, too painfully clear. When he did not speak to her, it was because he did not want to say the wrong thing.

"I am not ignoring you." For the first time since she'd walked from behind the screen, he looked at her with more than a squint. She stood at his side, heavily clad in a white dressing robe tied about the waist. At the neck, he glimpsed the lace edge of what must be her shift. She was not less covered than she had been all day by her gown. Strange, then, that it seemed so intimate, standing beside her in this night-dimmed room.

"I won't ignore you either, then," she said. "So don't feel you have to beg for my notice. It's beneath you, such begging."

"I never—"

"Only teasing." She smiled up at him, her nose scrunched with mischief—then gestured toward the window. "And look, I called you over for a reason even better than snow. In the courtyard, they are dancing in the mist."

Hugo peered down in the direction she indicated. The fine rain was still falling, making halos about the lanterns that starred the courtyard. In the shifting light, a maid and an ostler—both of whom ought to be worn and exhausted from the day's labor—had caught hands and were twirling in the stable yard. A laugh drifted up through the quieting night air.

"I wonder why they are dancing," he said.

"I shall guess. She has nursed a passion for him for years," said Georgette. "But he never noticed her until today, when she dropped a bucket of oats on his head."

"That would certainly gain *my* notice." Hugo studied

the pair, tiny and dim at this distance. "I cannot guess how they met."

"Oh, you can guess. It probably won't be right, but what does that matter?"

"Fine. They met here at the coaching inn. And they are dancing because he asked her to dance."

"He observes the letter of the game, but not the spirit," sighed Georgette. She crowded close, her arm brushing his side. "How do you think she knows the steps? I always wondered that about Cinderella. She was so busy working, she would never have had time to learn a reel or a country dance. So how did she know what to do when she went to the ball?"

She was very near, and she smelled of floral soap. The braided coronet of her hair looked soft as silk thread, and he couldn't collect his thoughts to understand what she asked.

She tapped at the small-paned window. "Maybe true royalty always knows the right way to behave."

"The Prince Regent should be example enough to prove that hypothesis false."

"You said 'hypothesis.' I am weak in the knees."

Hugo cleared his throat. "I'm going to see you safely back to your brother, Benedict," he croaked. "Soon. As soon as ever I can."

"If it pleases you to think so, go right ahead." She pressed her nose against the glass. "Ah, here comes Jenks. He is making them stop dancing. Why should he care about that?"

"There must be some law against it. Or a petty rule in this establishment."

"Maybe." She straightened up, leaving a palm flat against the cold glass. "I think he doesn't like anything unexpected."

Who does? thought Hugo, though he suspected Georgette would answer in the affirmative. But the unexpected had taken so much from Hugo, he would never be caught unawares by it again. Thus the plans, the plans; more and more plans.

"I'm going to get a drink," he said. "I still need one." With a herculean effort, he stepped away from all that sweet-scented impertinence.

"I'll make a second bed with the bedclothes before you come back." She let the draperies fall back over the window. "Be of good cheer, Hugo. We know now that we are on the right path."

"Are we?" said Hugo.

Tonight he could not hold her while she slept, as he had in the mail coach. As right as he knew that was, it also seemed wrong.

This was only the thirtieth of May. They might be in each other's company for another month. He needed to maintain a sense of what was proper.

He really, really needed a drink.

On his way out of the room, he glanced once more at the hospital plans. This time, the answer was clear. The hospital's windows ought to be larger.

And maybe the walls didn't need to be *quite* that thick.

He penciled a note to that effect, then left to consume an unexpected, illogical amount of brandy.

Chapter Eight

The sixth of June. The first Friday of the month. Five o'clock in the afternoon.

Since Sir Frederic Chapple had ascended to the baronetcy three months before, he'd come to dislike these first Fridays. They were a relic he'd inherited from his elderly cousin, along with a scattering of tenants and this manor house, Raeburn Hall, in a remote bit of coastal Northumberland. On the first Friday of the month—and *only* on the first Friday—the baronet was traditionally at home to his tenants, hearing their problems as a landowner and as the High Sheriff of the county.

Freddie had only presided over three first Fridays so far, but already he saw problems with the custom. First, he would never get acquainted with his tenants if he saw them only once a month. Maybe this had sufficed for his cousin, born to the title, but Freddie had enjoyed a far more social life in London. In his fifty-two years, he'd been a barrister, organized a ragged school for children in poverty, and joined every gentleman's club he could. What was he to do for the other twenty-nine days of the month with no one to *talk* to? No, this custom would have to change.

The second problem with Freddie's new role was Callum Jenks.

As High Sheriff, Freddie was the principal officer of the law in the county—which meant he had to follow it to the letter, and therefore he was never again to enjoy smuggled cigars or chocolates from the Continent. That alone would dampen a man's spirits, but in the past two days a new storm cloud had appeared on Freddie's horizon in the form of Jenks, an Officer of the Police.

Jenks had traveled the length of England searching for gold coins stolen from the Royal Mint, and somehow he had convinced himself that a trail of evidence led onto Freddie's land. Since arriving two days before, he'd done nothing but ask questions and make a nuisance of himself. Some of the tenants, Freddie was sure, thought he and Jenks were investigating together. Heaven forbid! He didn't want anyone prying into his every affair, and he extended the same courtesy to the rest of the world.

For the moment, though, he had a reprieve from Jenks—if one could call the Keelings a reprieve.

After escorting Mrs. Keeling to the door, Freddie blotted his perspiring forehead with a handkerchief. "Send in Mr. Keeling, if you would," he said to the butler, then settled behind the desk in the study he had not yet come to think of as his own.

Poor Mrs. Keeling. She complained about everything from the spring rains to the cold wind. Nothing that Freddie could help with. She didn't ask about the one thing he might have been able to assist with, the one thing in which he suspected her dissatisfaction was rooted: the presence in her home of a woman hired by her husband for farmwork. A *bondager*, such women were called hereabouts. Instead of complaining about the bondager, Mrs. Keeling cloaked her anger in the most querulous of queries.

Querulous queries. That was a nice phrase. He made a note of it in his pocketbook. Perhaps he'd work it into a poem later, if he had time. Since he'd become a baronet, most of Freddie's little notes never became anything else.

He set aside the pocketbook when Mr. Keeling entered the study, hat in hands. "Sir Frederic, you wanted to meet with me?"

"Sit, sit. Yes, yes."

Gingerly, Keeling seated himself on the leather-upholstered chair across the desk. "I can't think why. I've been meeting my obligations, haven't I? Doing everything ye ask of me?"

"Your help has been more than satisfactory. Yes. You've been hired anew this spring, and I don't intend to back out of our contract."

Some of the wariness left Keeling's features.

"But," the baronet continued, "you've a contract of your own with Linton. And it only binds her to you for farmwork. If you take my meaning."

"Ah. So that's your problem, like." Keeling's tone was mild, but his eyes had gone hard. The grizzled farmer was probably no more than thirty-five, but the sun had bleached his hair colorless and carved lines into his face.

Farming in Northumberland was no easy prospect. Spring was marked by cold winds and drought, and rocky hills broke the arable land into the tiniest of parcels. The north of England was more beautiful and more wild than Freddie could ever have imagined from his home in London.

Here near the coast, the weather was milder, but no family could eke out a living from the land without help. Thus the bondager system. It had been entirely unfamiliar to Freddie when he took up residence, and it still seemed odd and immoral. As the landowner, he hired farmworkers—hinds—like Keeling, paying them in a portion of the crops and animals they raised. With the land too large and the work too dispersed for villages to cluster, hinds lived in tiny houses on Freddie's land, sometimes sharing their lodging with livestock. And to help with the work? They hired bondagers. Unmarried women who lived with the family, working for a tiny cash wage.

A new bondager had joined the Keeling household a few weeks before. Linton, her name was. She was young. And pretty. And Freddie was certain Keeling had seduced her.

"Mr. Keeling." Freddie hesitated, considering how best to word his admonishment. "We're both men of the world, are we not?"

"I am, aye. I can't say as I know what you get up to behind a closed door."

"Er—yes. I am too. But. When I have formed a business relationship—such as I have with you—then I do not allow personal matters to complicate it. Or endanger it."

Keeling squinted at Freddie. "What'ud ye have me do, then? Linton's a canny worker. We can't get by without her. But she lives in me house, like." He scratched his head, repeating, "What'ud ye have me do?"

Poor Mrs. Keeling, Freddie thought again. He'd taken steps to better the situation of the baronetcy, but little of the benefit seemed to be reaching the laborers' families. "Are your children not old enough to help in Linton's place?"

"Me oldest bairn is twelve. She'll be a bondager soon, but not soon enough to do me no good."

Not soon enough indeed. The cold summer of the previous year had brought poor harvests across England. As soon as he took up residence at Raeburn Hall, Freddie had heard enough from Keeling and his other hinds to realize that the always-poor farmers had fallen into desperate straits.

"I'm doing my best to help you," said Freddie. "You know that. For your part, I need you to be more cautious. Only hold out, and we'll be much better off soon. The weather is turning, and the growing season about to begin."

"Good advice, like. But a little late, sir." Keeling leaned forward, his voice dropping low and confidential. "Between ye and me, Linton thinks she's fallen with child. So if the piper's been paid, why stop the dancing?"

That was a nice little turn of speech. Freddie would write it in his pocketbook—later. "*Has* the piper been paid? Are you certain?"

"She's sure as she can be without having a doctor look at her, like."

Right, right. There was no doctor for miles; only an apothecary in the nearest village. No lodging house, either. Little work for the young men of the area besides farming, mining, fishing. Living off a land that decided on a whim to turn on its inhabitants. Some of the young men had left a few months ago, but they had recently come back. Northumberland got into the blood, it seemed.

Freddie wasn't one of these men, and he never would be. But he would see to their welfare with a will of iron. Maybe Keeling thought Freddie had no right to chastise him—but Keeling relied on him, and Linton relied on Keeling. And Keeling's pleasure might not be Linton's. And Mrs. Keeling and her four children relied on both of them to work the land, and . . . God, what a tangle.

He blotted his forehead again. Why could Keeling not keep his tackle to himself? "If there is a babe, then what—"

"Sir Frederic." Without a knock, without a beg pardon, a man poked his head into the study. "I need a word."

It was Jenks, of course.

"But I'm speaking with Mr. Keeling," Freddie replied.

"I'll take a word with Mr. Keeling, too." Average in every way save for his doggedness, Jenks shouldered into the study without waiting for a by-your-leave. He looked about at the damask-hung walls, the polished wood furnishings. "You've done well for yourself, Sir Frederic. Must cost a pretty penny to keep up a place like this."

"It doesn't. It's amazingly economical." That wasn't true. But if Jenks asked whether his name was Frederic, Freddie would deny it until his head fell off. He'd had to offer house-room to the Runner, since there wasn't a lodging house for miles. At dinner the first afternoon, Jenks had gulped a twenty-year-old port as though it were cider. Freddie had had to blot his forehead rather a lot after that. Jenks's brusque manner hadn't endeared him since.

The Runner trailed a hand over the smooth edge of

Freddie's desk, then turned a dark gaze upon him. "Still insist you know nothing about the stolen gold?"

"I never said that. I know gold was stolen, and that you think it's on my land. Other than that . . ." Freddie spread his hands in a gesture of hopeless ignorance.

"And you, Mr. Keeling?"

The hind leaned back in his chair. "I *know* about it, aye. Everyone *knows* about it."

"Did you *know*," said Jenks to Keeling, "that your bondager had a bit of gold in her pocket this morning?"

"That I didn't." Keeling stretched out his legs as though he'd all the time in the world. "But if Linton came across some gold, why would she look to see where it came from? She'd pick it up and put it in her pocket, like, and move along. Who wouldn't?"

"I wouldn't," said Jenks. "Because I would know it wasn't mine."

Keeling's expression turned shrewd. "How do ye know what was in her pockets? Have ye a habit of looking through a woman's clothes?"

Jenks's brows lifted. "I am *in the habit* of pursuing my investigation by any means I see necessary. I thought it justified to search Miss Linton. My search was rewarded."

"Aye, I'd say so." Keeling waggled his brows.

"I did not touch Miss Linton in an inappropriate manner, if that is what you're implying."

"Sure, sure." Keeling winked broadly at Freddie. "We're all men of the world, like."

Jenks sighed. "I am a Runner first and foremost, Mr. Keeling. Do not presume that your own sluttish manners apply to others."

Keeling snapped upright, his face going red.

Freddie lifted his hands. "Now, see here. There's no need—"

"Where did she get the gold, Keeling?" Jenks pressed. "Did you give it to her?"

Keeling stood, fists clenched, facing the Runner over the corner of the desk. "I pay her what she's owed. What that be, and how much, is no business of yours." Almost nose to nose, the men stood. Which would back down first?

Neither would. They were both stubborn. If Freddie didn't intervene, they would all have to live like this forever.

"There are mines all around," he offered by way of truce. "For minerals and . . . and things. Surely she discovered the gold by chance."

"Mines." Jenks leveled a skeptical look at Freddie. "Gold mines. In England."

"To be sure." In truth, they were for coal and lead— but lead was next to gold, or so said generations of alchemists. So it was not much of a lie.

"I doubt it," said Jenks. "I know that gold came from somewhere."

Freddie adopted a bland mien. "Everything comes from *somewhere*. You came from London, for one. So did I."

"Yes, and so did someone else, I'll warrant." Jenks took a step back, turning toward Freddie. "Any travelers arriving recently? Within the last two weeks? Three?"

"I can't say," Freddie said vaguely. "Rather, I can't say who *hasn't* come and gone. Throughout the spring, hinds flit from master to new master." Only in May had all the hiring been complete, the laborers again pinned to Freddie's land. Since inheriting in March,

Freddie hadn't always stayed in Northumberland himself.

Every question Jenks asked raised so many more. So Freddie posed one of his own. "Why are you so certain you're going to find the answers you seek here?"

"I'm glad you asked," Jenks said. Sitting on the edge of the newly polished desk—Freddie groaned—Jenks held up a finger. "First, because three empty, scorched trunks from the Royal Mint were found north of Doncaster. Second, because a Doncaster maid with a crude new gold bracelet fled north."

"So go to Doncaster." Keeling dropped back into the chair with an air of utter unconcern.

"Third"—Jenks ignored this interruption, counting off a third finger—"rumor had it that gold was found near the coast. *This* coast. And there's never been gold here before."

"First time for everything," muttered Keeling.

"And finally"—Jenks held up his little finger—"a suspicious couple has been traveling northward from Northampton. Following the same road as me. Had something valuable stolen, but wouldn't report the theft to me. Now, why would that be?"

"Because they didn't like you," said Keeling. Freddie would have to offer him a drink when Jenks left. Maybe even the twenty-year-old port.

"*Because*," Jenks said with a glare, "they were up to no good, and they couldn't afford the scrutiny of an investigation."

"It happens," said Freddie. "There are many no-good-doers in England. Just because some of them were traveling north doesn't mean they have anything to do with—"

"It means *exactly* that they have—"

"Beg pardon, Sir Frederic." The butler, Hawes, had appeared in the open study doorway. "Your niece and nephew have arrived."

"My . . . what did you say?" Freddie had no idea of whom the man was speaking.

A blond woman whom Freddie had never seen before in his life darted into the study. "Uncle!" she cried. "How good it is to see you!" Circling around his desk, she flung herself into his arms where he sat. "Please," she whispered. "Play along, and I shall explain all when I can."

Freddie looked toward the doorway, where a stern-looking man with black hair stood with arms folded. His supposed nephew?

And then he looked at Jenks, who wore an expression of great annoyance.

Jenks's annoyance decided it. Freddie gave the woman a pat on the shoulder. "There, there, dear. So nice to see you. How good of you to come all this way to see your old uncle." With a speaking look of thanks, she stood. Freddie did too, gesturing to offer her his chair.

Jenks looked at them narrowly. "What's her name? If she's truly your niece, you'll know it."

"I always called her Petunia when she was little," Freddie said soppily. "There, I shouldn't have told you that. Now she'll be embarrassed."

"You could never embarrass me, Uncle." Her pale eyes lit with mischief. "But I go by Georgette now. That is—Mrs. Crowe. You won't have met my husband before, but you're going to *love* each other."

Freddie shot a look at Jenks. "Is this the suspicious pair of which you spoke, Mr. Jenks? How you wound me, speaking slightingly of my relatives. How you lack the proper family feeling!"

The Runner's jaw hardened. "That's something I don't lack at all, Sir Frederic. If you'll excuse me." Turning on his heel, he stalked from the study.

Keeling stood. "Eee, you've a houseful now. I'll be off, if we've done?"

Freddie took a step forward. "But the matter of Linton . . ." They'd settled nothing.

"I know ye mean kindly, sir. But mebbies ye be too different from us, like. The old ways have done for a long, long time." With a bow, the laborer left.

Freddie watched him go, torn. An insubordinate hind couldn't be trusted. But all the others looked up to Keeling; relied on him. No, Freddie would have to keep his word and honor Keeling's contract.

They would all breathe more easily in a few weeks, when they could begin harvesting the fruits of their labor.

The dark-haired man posing as Freddie's nephew stepped into the room and shut the door behind him. "Thank you . . . ah . . ."

"Sir Frederic Chapple—or Uncle Freddie, if you like. This is Raeburn Hall. Northumberland."

"Well, I *knew* we were in Northumberland," said the blond woman. "And I really am called Georgette. But my last name's—"

"Don't tell me. Don't say another word. If I don't know anything else, I can't be convinced to tattle on you." Freddie smiled. "I don't know who you are, but your arrival irked Jenks to no end, so I'm pleased to host you."

"We're neither murderers nor thieves," said the

woman. "And Jenks has irked us for a week now, as we traveled north in his wake. Or he in ours."

"He does have that effect."

"I'm a physician," said the man. "Hugo . . . Crowe. We told Jenks you would give me a job. I don't need one, but I do need a reason to be here for a time."

"And what is that? No, don't tell me. You've gold dust in your eyes, both of you. But it doesn't matter. Mr. Crowe, you're my physician now."

Freddie turned to Georgette. "And you? What do you do?" He was foolhardy, he knew, to welcome perfect strangers into his home. But he'd done so with Jenks, and already he liked this pair far better. They had, for lack of a better word, bollocks.

The young woman unfolded from his chair. "I am a frippery sort of creature with no practical skills. Though I can carry a lot of things if I need to. My specialties are stacks of books, heaps of laundry, and children of small to middling size."

Freddie considered. "In that case, I've an idea. If you two have no objection, I shall put you to work tomorrow."

The pair locked eyes. An entire conversation seemed to pass between them in a single glance. For the first time this afternoon, Freddie felt as though he were witness to something too personal for discussion.

"We've no objection," said the man.

"Very well." Pleased, Freddie pulled open the study door again. "The butler will show you to a room." Once more, he studied them. "You *do* look travel-worn. Settle in, and I will have a supper sent up later."

This would be entertaining, housing guests so suspicious of each other. Maybe life in Northumberland didn't have to be lonely after all.

* * *

"You are shivering," Hugo pointed out.

Curse the man. He noticed all the wrong things. "That's because the room is cold," Georgette said.

It wasn't, though. It was lovely and warm, with a cheerful fire in the hearth, a desk at one side, and a dressing room at the other. A carpet on the floor and a woven tapestry on the wall softened the dark wood paneling, and a large bed stood in the center of the room.

A single. Large. Bed.

Not again.

For the past week, night by night, Hugo and Georgette had made do. If they caught up to Jenks, they had to pose as the married Crowes; if he was nowhere around when they stopped for the night, they introduced themselves as siblings and took separate chambers.

Those nights were infinitely easier for Georgette. She could bid Hugo a proper good-night without questioning her every movement, every word she spoke or left unsaid. There was no way to misunderstand *good night*, even in one's own mind.

Otherwise, there were innumerable ways to talk oneself into a state of confused . . . oh, better call it infatuation. That was as good a word as any for the feeling digging its claws into Georgette. It was a nuisance, this feeling that made her pleased to look upon him and made her wish for him when he wasn't there. A desire to be close to him, to touch him.

Such feelings were bound, always, with fear. Fear that in the morning she'd awake and he'd have gone— or even that she'd smile at him sometime, and he would

turn away and retreat behind a book. All the better to
learn something he hadn't known before, as if that
pursuit were worthwhile in itself.

As if she were not.

If the driver, Seckington, wondered at the true state
of affairs between Hugo and Georgette, he was paid
well enough to keep such questions to himself. Already he was on his way back to Northampton with a
purse considerably fuller, leaving Hugo's lighter.

And she and Hugo were alone together again, with
one room and one bed. Georgette hardly knew where
to look. She couldn't look at the bed; she couldn't look
at Hugo. She settled on staring defiantly at the tapestry hanging opposite the fireplace.

Taller than Georgette, and as wide as she could
stretch out her arms, it showed a forest. But not a
sweet fairy-tale forest; no, this one was dark and pat-
terned and detailed and vivid. In front, a cut-off stump
stretched up one lone remaining twig. The earth
foamed like water about the trees, blue green and
angry.

A bird was perched at the edge of the stump, looking down at the heaving earth. The only other living
creature was a paler, smaller, bird, but maybe braver
for all that, for it was perched upon a roll of land at the
base of a tree. Its wings were outstretched for balance;
its head was turned toward the brighter bird. The
other bird seemed not to know it was there.

All this bird did was look, and look, and try to
spread its wings. Fool of a bird. It could fly off at any
moment if it would only stop trying to catch the notice
of the first.

"This is awkward, being put into the same chamber," said Hugo, not sounding the slightest bit awkward.

Georgette turned from the foolish bird to face him where he stood by the fireplace. "You never mean that when you say it, but it *is* awkward. I was willing to throw myself on the mercy of a stranger, but I must stop at deceiving him."

"What are we to do, then? Tell our kind host that he was mistaken? If we are honest with him about who we are, you'll have to marry me."

Her mouth fell open. "No."

"It's true."

"No," she said again. The words were too heavy for Georgette's ears to take them in right away. She looked at him, heart overfull of unfinished feelings.

He looked back at her, a look longer than those Georgette was used to. She could not read his expression. Hugo was frank, sometimes painfully so, but that did not mean he told her everything.

"I suppose," Georgette ventured, "that this is no more nor less than our nights spent as the Crowes in coaching inns. Isn't it? And so—so we needn't be forced into anything."

Yes, and each of those nights had left her more puzzled, less able to sleep. Did she want . . . him? What did she want of him? He had never done more than hold her hand, and she had lived on the memory of that for nearly a week.

"I could sleep in the dressing room," Hugo decided. He took up his valise and moved it into the adjoining space, a narrow cubby off the chamber. "Ah. This is smaller than I thought it was. All right, I could tell our host that you snore and I can't stay in the same chamber with you."

"I don't *snore.*"

"You don't. Much. But wouldn't it be wiser—that is, more comfortable to have your own space?"

"It would for you, certainly. You deserve to have a bed of your own." Bed. One word. Three letters. A perfectly ordinary item of furniture.

Yet as her lips shaped the word, the sound of it awoke parts of her body that she knew ladies ought to silence. *Bed, bed.* According to manuals of etiquette, ladies ought not to think of bed; ought not to wonder about the activities carried out there. Ladies were calm and innocent and desired to remain so.

If this was true, Georgette had ceased being a lady as soon as she climbed into a mail coach with Lord Hugo Starling.

Hugo retreated into the dressing area and picked up his valise. "I'll see to my move, then. Better to impose on your new uncle Freddie than to impose on you."

"You wouldn't impose."

"I try my best not to." He set his free hand on the mantel, as if bracing himself. "But remember that I never claimed to be perfect."

No, she had claimed that for him. And after a week in his company, experiencing the best and worst of England's coaching inns, the roughest and smoothest and muddiest and dustiest of roads, she would not take back that claim.

"Well—off you go, then," she blurted. "Good night. Not that it's night, but you must be tired. And we needn't join Sir Frederic for supper. So—I'll see you in the morning?" Impulsively, she stepped close to him and wrapped her arms about his chest.

It was meant to be a good-night hug, such as family members sometimes shared. But her belly brushed his, and his frame was solid and strong within her embrace, and suddenly it wasn't familial at all. The touch was fire, and she shivered again, then tipped her face upward.

He looked right into her eyes. They were so close now. Close enough that their noses might touch, their lashes might brush. It seemed impossible that they should not kiss. It seemed impossible that they should be apart now, having seen each other so closely.

Hugo let his valise fall heavily to the floor. His hands came about her, gentle as they slid up her back, then took hold of her shoulders.

Georgette rose to her toes, then pressed a kiss to the ridge of his cheekbone. His eyes closed like a man too close to the sun. He breathed in deeply, like a man getting air after suffocating.

Neither was a flattering comparison. But when he trailed gentle fingertips down the side of her face, pressing a kiss to her temple that was neither chaste nor lustful, something bloomed within her. It was as if her body awoke there, under the pressure of his lips, and she turned toward his touch.

He shook free and stepped back. "Good night," he said. His breathing was ragged, but no more so than her own.

"Must you be a gentleman again?"

"One of us must," he said. And he picked up his valise and the leather case of his hospital plans and left the room, closing her in alone.

Pulling in a shuddery breath, she sat on the edge of the bed. The birds woven into the tapestry flaunted themselves before her, one unaware, both trapped. She eyed the paler one, then sighed. "If you had known what was wise, little bird, you'd have flown away when you had the chance."

Chapter Nine

The following morning after breakfast, Hugo discovered what Sir Frederic had meant by *I shall put you to work*: the largest parlor of Raeburn Hall was turned into a tiny hospital for the baronet's tenants. Bedsheets covered the costly carpets peeking out at the edges of the room. A dozen wooden chairs had been brought in—from the attics, considering the state of them. A folding screen of incongruous costliness divided the room. Behind it, several tea tables clustered, holding every sort of gauze and tincture to be found in the house.

"A place to meet with patients, if you need it, and a few medicines," said Sir Frederic. He surveyed the room with a look of satisfaction. "Ah, and here come the maids with clean linens and towels. I don't know what you might use them for, but they are the sort of thing doctors always seem to want."

The effect, as a whole, was tidy and pleasing. And the patients would come to *him*, as he'd wanted in his own hospital. Maximum care, minimum waste of time and effort.

128 *Theresa Romain*

"Thank you," he said to his host. "I welcome the opportunity to practice medicine in this way."

"You probably won't be paid much. But I'll leave that to you and your patients to work out." With a clap on Hugo's shoulder, the baronet left the parlor.

Georgette walked in carrying a can of hot water, followed by a maid doing the same. "You can set that down, thanks," she told the young woman. "It must be twenty pounds if it's an ounce." Turning to Hugo, she smiled. "Hullo, Doctor. How did you sleep?"

"Perfectly well, with no snoring to wake me." In truth, he'd tossed and turned and wondered whether he'd overstepped a line—or not stepped far enough. When he finally drifted off, the endless June daylight of northern England woke him at half four.

Georgette looked fresh in white muslin, her pinned-up hair emphasizing the elegant line of her neck and shoulders. She was clean and pretty, and he could not wish for her to become otherwise. "You'd best leave now," Hugo advised. "Before the people arrive who need medical care. There might be blood and . . ." *Vomit. Cursing. Gangrene.* ". . . I don't know what sorts of other things."

"Infections? Ears full of spiders? Worst of all, tears? You're right, I'm far too fragile and ladylike to offer any help whatsoever. I'd best be going." In her free hand, she took up the handle of the other hot-water can. With effortless ease, she carried the two behind the folding screen. When she emerged without them, she thumbed her nose at him.

Hugo raised his gaze to heaven. "Fine," he said. "If you wish to help, that would be acceptable."

"Always so melodramatic," she said. "You really must try to control your enthusiastic words."

By ten o'clock, the parlor held two dozen people of all ages. Some looked ill, some might be no more than curious. Where to start?

A little boy rested his head on his mother's shoulder, dull-eyed and coughing. Pneumonia? Hugo's fingers went cold. He flexed them, quieting himself, then told the mother, "I'll see your son first."

They settled into chairs behind the folding screen. When given the chance to examine the boy more closely, Hugo realized his breathing was not labored. Thank God. He wore the ordinary childhood smells of sweat and dirt, not the sickly sweetness of an infection that had taken hold.

"This is a throat complaint," he told the boy's mother, who introduced herself as Mrs. Worrall. "It does not appear putrid. He will recover on his own, but you can improve his comfort with a tea of licorice root and peppermint. Give it to him as often as he likes."

Rather than being grateful, as Hugo expected, Mrs. Worrall put her hands on her hips. "And how am I to get licorice root, Doctor? Or peppermint? If it doesn't grow on me man's land, I can't have it. It's too dear at the apothecary's."

"Ah . . ." Hugo hadn't considered that. In his private London hospital, he intended that donations would cover the costs of care for those unable to pay. It was the right thing to do, after all. But he had not considered what to do if the physicians hadn't access to the materials they needed.

Georgette peered around the edge of the screen. "I couldn't help but hear, especially since neither of you made any effort to be quiet. Doctor, we've plenty of hot water. Is there something else I could make a tea with, for the boy to drink right now?"

Doctor, she had called him, with a little wink. Once again, he had the unsettling delight of being treated as her coconspirator.

"Yes, Mrs. Crowe," he replied without betraying a flicker of the pleasure he took in her words. "Hot water with plentiful honey in it will ease the boy's symptoms too."

For the first time, the little boy picked up his head. "Honey? I like that." His brown eyes blinked, curious.

"Then you shall have it," said Georgette.

"Doctor, we haven't ready money since we're paid in farm goods, but I'll bring you a rye loaf," said Mrs. Worrall. "I make them fine and light, better than what you ever got from a bakery."

The offer took Hugo aback, but he recognized it as a significant payment from this woman. "That sounds very nice. I look forward to a treat."

Georgette extended a hand. "Mrs. Worrall, if you and Davey will come with me to these tables? Doctor, the next patient is belligerent. I should like him to go last because of that, but he was belligerent about that, too."

"I'm surprised you didn't get on with him better, then," Hugo said.

"Oh, we got along quite well. We're already old friends." With that, she guided the woman and boy—whose names she had somehow overheard and re-membered—toward the hot-water cans and tea tables at the edge of the screen. To make a tea of honey, presumably. To send some home with Mrs. Worrall too, he hoped.

Hugo had not worked much with aides to doctors,

though he knew nuns had once commonly performed medical services. Until the Tudors had crushed Catholicism wherever it sprang forth, that is. Some women still trained informally as aides—nurses, they were called—since they could not become doctors. The academic world, in its questionable wisdom, had closed its doors to fully half the population of England.

A woman such as Georgette Frost would be capable of learning whatever she put her mind to, and likely much that she didn't. Hugo caught her notice as she finished pouring out a cupful of steaming water.

"Thank you," he said.

"I'm only helping you because you begged me," she said. "Not because I want to."

His brows lifted. "Do you mean the opposite of that?"

"Maybe." Her smile trembled, then fled, and on she went with her work.

When Hugo went back behind the examination screen, the farm laborer from yesterday was standing there. He'd removed his coat and dropped it to the floor, and was now shrugging out of his braces and tugging his shirt free of his breeches.

"So you're belligerent, are you?" Hugo wiped his hands with a clean towel.

"No, I'm Keeling," the man said. "One of the baronet's hinds."

"Never mind," said Hugo. If Georgette had truly been bothered by the man, she wouldn't have called him an old friend. "What's the trouble?"

The man lifted his shirt on one side, exposing a raw, ragged red path through the flesh over his ribs.

Hugo bent closer, studying it. It looked like a bullet wound, but not a fresh one; the skin had scabbed over.

"How did you come by this injury?" He straightened, dampening another towel in the second can of hot water.

"By a bullet," said Keeling. Which was exactly the sort of literal but unhelpful answer Hugo would have given if he didn't want to answer a question. He had to admire it.

He pressed at the wound with the towel, gently cleansing the skin of Keeling's side. Once it was wiped as clean as it could be, Hugo took another look. "It ought to have been stitched right away. I'm afraid I can't do anything to close the wound for you now."

Keeling let his shirt fall. "What kind of doctor are you?"

"Not the magical kind." Despite what he'd told Georgette once as part of a story. "It looks like you've avoided infection thus far, so you'll finish healing without complication. You'll have a scar, but it won't be obvious."

"A scar?" Keeling's sun-bleached brows lifted. "A proper one?"

"I suppose. It'll be a big one."

"Right. That's dead canny. Thank you." From the pleased look Keeling wore, Hugo guessed that "dead canny" was a statement of approval.

"Don't thank me. Thank the person who shot at you."

Keeling put his braces and coat back on, then leaned in close. "Listen." He lowered his voice. "Don't tell no one where this came from. But it's good for a man to be paid for his work, like." Grabbing Hugo's hand, he pressed something into it—then strode away.

Hugo unfolded his fist. "Shit," he muttered. Keeling had given him a bit of gold.

It wasn't a coin, but it was the amount of gold that might be in a coin if that coin had been melted down.

"Shit," he said again.

Yes, they had followed a trail of gold and gossip to Northumberland—but Hugo had never really believed the latter would lead to the former.

He rubbed a hand across his eyes, then opened them. Yes, it was gold. Gold in his hand.

He stuffed it into a pocket. Ducking from behind the screen, he called, "Geor—ah, Mrs. Crowe?"

She was at hand at once, guiding another woman with her arm around that lady's shoulders. "She wanted to see you as soon as Mr. Keeling left."

"No!" howled the woman, drawing curious looks from the dozen or so remaining people. In a more regulated tone, she added, "I want to talk to your lady, not to you."

"I'm not his—" A sharp look from Hugo cut off her sentence. "That is, I'm not a doctor."

The woman shook her head. She was about Georgette's age, buxom and auburn-haired, dressed in what seemed to be a sort of uniform among the local young women: full calf-length skirts and a colorful shirt with a scarf fastened loosely about the neck. Likely pretty at other times, her features sagged with misery now. "Please, ma'am," she said.

Hugo could have cursed again. In moments like this, when the trouble was clearly of a female nature, he would have spent any amount of his own money to send a woman through medical college. For how could one offer effective treatment if one's own sex made the patient distraught? "See what you can do to help," he told Georgette.

She hesitated, then stepped behind the screen with

the patient. Hugo stood to one side of the screen, watching the pair but unable to hear them at this distance. They bent together, a low conversation following. There was much counting on fingers, shaking of heads, counting again.

By the time Georgette left her to join Hugo, the woman was crying in a heap on the floor.

Georgette looked sober. "That's Harriett Linton. She works for Mr. Keeling and lives with him and his wife and their four children. We were discussing her, um, female cycle. She believes she's with child."

Oh, damn. "What do you think?"

"That she most likely is." Georgette looked over her shoulder at Linton, biting her lip. When she turned back to Hugo, her own eyes were full. "It's possible to have an off month, but she—well, it's far more possible that she's with child."

"Keeling's?" The bit of gold in Hugo's pocket felt heavy as lead. At Georgette's nod, he asked, "Did he force her? Or did she want to—to lie with him?"

Such subjects would, under any other circumstance, have been fraught and embarrassing. But when a woman was crying with such desperate depth of feeling, there was no time for roundaboutation.

Georgette seemed to agree, for she answered without a blush. "Neither. She didn't want to lie with him, but he said she must to keep her position. She'd been without work for a long time, and she was hungry."

Hugo shut his eyes.

This was the kind of suffering no hospital could touch: the everyday wrongs people did one another. Linton hadn't been sick, only hungry. *Only*, as though hunger didn't drive people to desperation. And Keeling had made her whore herself for bread.

His eyes sprang open, seeing the next step clearly. "We've got to get her out of that house."

"She signed a contract to work for him."

"Surely she doesn't have to *live* with him."

Georgette frowned. "Where else can she live, then, Mr. Planner?"

"Here," he said. "She should live here."

She smiled, almost. "You make awfully free with my uncle's house."

"Sir Frederic is a widower with no children." Hugo had learned that much of their host the evening before. "He has the space."

Raeburn Hall wasn't huge—at least, not to Hugo, who'd spent his youth shuttling between eight ducal estates. But it was the largest building hereabouts: three stories of trimmed stone, with some sixty rooms of all uses, or no use whatsoever. Only three guest chambers were filled at the moment: by Hugo, Georgette, and Jenks.

"She should stay here," Hugo repeated. "If your uncle Freddie wants rent, I'll pay it."

Now her smile turned the corner from *almost* to *certain.* "Why, Mr. Crowe, you will have me thinking you are a hero."

"I'm nothing of the sort. I'm just not a villain." He pressed at his temples. Maybe he ought to have brought his spectacles with him. Usually he only needed them for reading, but he was getting the devil of a headache. "I don't want to impose upon you, but—"

"I'll see Linton made comfortable," Georgette replied. "You needn't even ask."

"I know you're only helping me because I begged."

She bobbed a curtsy. "That I am. Now, whom would you like to see next?"

Four hours later, Georgette had—alongside Hugo—met everyone from a baby who wouldn't stop crying to a blacksmith with crushed toes. The baby had been hungry, so it seemed, and a measure of treacle in milk turned him happy. The blacksmith was a more difficult case, as his red-streaked toes signaled infection to Hugo's practiced eye. To Georgette's, they simply looked awful. So awful that she wanted to give him a bottle of laudanum and tell him to drink it all.

The blacksmith, a Mr. Lowe, doubtless would have welcomed Georgette's treatment. "There's a surgeon a dozen miles from here, but he'd want to take off me toes. I wouldn't let him hack me up. Ye know a medicine for me, don't you, Doctor?"

"I'm sorry, Mr. Lowe." Hugo had met every person seeking care with a calm and patience that made Georgette want to wrap her arms around him. "The only medicine for you now is a blade. It's not as simple as 'surgeons cut, physicians mend.' Sometimes a cut is needed for healing. I'd be doing wrong if I told you I could help you in any other way."

Lowe had arms like tree trunks and a hard, stubborn jaw. But at Hugo's words, he quailed and seemed to shrink. "I can't bear such a cut, Doctor."

"That's up to you." Hugo looked grave. "But it may come to your toes or your life."

The blacksmith's lip quivered—but after a taut moment, he expelled a bellows' worth of air. "Then I must, mustn't I? Let's have it done."

"Have you a wife?" Georgette asked. "Someone who

could be with you during the surgery and help you home after?"

"Aye, Mrs. Lowe is home with the bairns. Anyone here will know how to fetch her."

Hugo carried out the surgery when all the other patients had been seen. Mrs. Lowe had arrived by then, a hardy woman with a sweet, tired face and a look of great relief that her man was being treated.

Despite Georgette's bluster of the morning, she had no stomach for this sort of doctoring. She brought the supplies Hugo said he needed, then left the parlor in a tearing hurry.

Finding her way back into the breakfast parlor, she saw that a cold luncheon had been laid out. It was like magic, this silent care that servants took of their masters. Georgette's family had employed servants at the bookshop, but she had always been more likely to work alongside them than above them.

After washing her hands and face, she served herself a generous portion of food and tucked in. About half an hour later, Hugo wandered into the room. He had changed into a fresh shirt, waistcoat, and coat, yet he looked dazed and weary.

Georgette hopped to her feet and guided him— well, shoved him—to a chair. "Sit and have some lunch. If you've washed all the toes off your hands, that is."

"I have, yes." He folded his arms on the table, then rested his chin atop them. "Mr. Lowe said he couldn't bear it, and I thought I couldn't either."

"Because . . . why? Surgery is difficult?" She put some fruit and sliced mutton on a plate for him, then slid it next to his folded arms before sitting beside him. "There's wine, too, if you want it."

"Oh, I want it. No, this sort of surgery isn't difficult. I struggled because I wasn't sure I was leaving him better off." He turned his head to one side, looking at Georgette oddly askew. "How will he heal without someone checking his bandages? What will happen if the incision becomes infected? He can't travel a dozen miles each way to see a surgeon. He can't work if he cannot stand."

"Nor can he work if he dies of gangrene," Georgette said crisply. "Maybe you only gave him some chance, but on his own he'd have had no chance. Now, eat something before you swoon."

He glared at her. "Men don't swoon." But this was enough to get him to lift his head, to settle straight-backed into the chair and take up utensils.

Before he took a bite, he paused. "Sir Frederic mentioned he'd like me—us—to offer such medical services to his tenants every week as long as we're here."

And how long will that be? Georgette wanted to ask. Instead, she said, "What of the apothecary in the next village?"

"I don't know," said Hugo, as if he'd heard what she really wanted to ask. "I do wonder. What will the farm laborers do after we leave?"

"The same thing they did before." Heedless of manners, Georgette stuck an elbow onto the table and propped her chin on that hand. "They'll get along as well as they can, and most of them will be all right, and some of them will not."

"That baby." Hugo cut a triangle of mutton. "The one who cried of hunger. He needs a wet nurse, or treacle and sheep's milk. Several times a day, every day." Spearing the meat on the end of his fork, he looked at it blankly. "Building another hospital in London will do nothing to help him."

Georgette had no understanding of hospital construction. She hadn't assisted a doctor before today. She knew nothing about what Hugo had said, but she knew discouragement when she heard it.

"You helped that baby today," she said. "And if he needs help again tomorrow, you'll give it. And you'll check Lowe's bandages, and you'll fight off that lassie who wanted to show you her bosom"—this won a bark of laughter from him—"and you'll show that curious lad how to make another tincture with iodine. And whatever else might come your way."

Hugo popped the bite into his mouth. Deliberately, he chewed. "You," he said to Georgette once he'd swallowed it, "sound very certain."

"Why should I not? It's not a hypothesis. It's logic. You cannot help everyone, but you can help some people. And they'll enjoy better health than if you didn't treat them."

"You said 'hypothesis.'"

"I said a lot of things. They were all brilliant."

Hugo pushed his plate away, looking thoughtful. "You were wasted in that bookshop."

It was so difficult to know whether he meant such statements as compliments or not. "Why do you say so?"

"Because hardly anyone got to speak to you beyond pleasantries. They missed a rare delight."

Oh. *Oh.* That was a compliment, and of the sort that made a lady forget she'd decided to squelch her foolish infatuation. It was the sort that made a lady realize it was as alive as ever, and that it might even be more.

Cheeks hot, she cast about for words. "You are surely

the first person who described my speech as rare. I'm usually the one asked to keep silent. Most recently, by you."

"I shouldn't have done that." He turned toward her. He was still weary, still a little raw from the day's experiences, and his expression was unshielded. "Thank you. If you hadn't helped me, I would have begged you."

"If you hadn't begged me, I might have begged you." Her smile felt crooked and new. "I did like helping people find books they might enjoy. But I liked this even more. These people . . . your help mattered to them. And that made them matter to me, more than any book ever could."

Silent seconds ticked away. Then: "You honor me," he said quietly.

Georgette could not remember when she knew less how to respond, or when her response held more significance. "Wait a few minutes," she blurted. "I'll likely offend you in some way, and then we'll be back to the usual state of affairs. Me bumbling about after gold, you saying things like 'hypothesis' and 'hypotenuse' whenever you can."

"Hypogastrium," he said. "Hypocrisy." He drank off a glass of wine.

"That too. Golden words, every one of them."

"Right—that reminds me. I have some gold, Georgette." He related his exchange with Keeling.

"That is much less belligerent than I'd have expected him to be." She hesitated. "I picked up a clue myself, but I can't tell you exactly what it is."

For it was gossip; overheard gossip. Mrs. Norris, a tall and feline-featured woman, had said to Mrs. Hopkins as they awaited their turn to see the physician, "Did you hear, one of the Bamburgh hinds found a gold nugget in his barley field? Well, his bondager did."

"I don't believe it," had said Mrs. Hopkins. "He must've found it himself. If a bondager found anything, she'd shove it up her cunny and keep it."

That was why Georgette couldn't tell Hugo what it was. "Suffice to say," she offered, "there's rumor of more gold being found near a village called Bamburgh. Also, the wives don't like the bondagers. Though that second part is not a rumor."

"Judging from the high color in your cheeks, it came paired with entertaining remarks." Hugo pushed back his chair, stood, and offered her a hand to do the same. "Keep your counsel if you wish. Shall we walk out in the direction of Bamburgh and see whether we find any treasure?"

Chapter Ten

"This is a beach. We are standing on a beach." Georgette could hardly credit the sand beneath her boots.

"So we are," agreed Hugo. "Your powers of observation remain undimmed."

"Always so free with the compliments. How you put me to the blush." Georgette didn't mind what he said, though. She was *standing* on a *beach*.

Life in London, where even the grass was trimmed and fenced away, had not prepared her for the sight. Here the sand was rough, pitted and graveled as if the North Sea flung missiles at it. Scrubby, determined grasses clutched at it here and there. Hugo would know what they were, and whether they had vegetable acids.

But she didn't ask him; she only looked. They'd walked little more than two miles from Raeburn Hall, and the landscape had been transformed utterly. Around Sir Frederic's home, the land stretched in a gentle yawn of field and hill. Then came rocks, first poking up from the ground to interrupt the slumberous farmland—then more and more of them, looking like gray mountains had been dropped from the sky to shatter over the earth. On this part of the beach, the rocks were halfhearted among the light-colored sand, and the sky was enormous and blue and full of cottony clouds.

Before her was the North Sea, endless and, at the moment, quiet. Best of all was what was behind her. She turned to look at it again, a sigh of contentment issuing from deep within.

There was a *castle*. A real ancient castle on a rocky outcrop, such as a princess might be snatched from in the dead of night. A castle such as a king might defend against an army, or to which a dragon would lay waste before curling around the keep, fiery and selfish. The stone structure stood solid and timeless on its jewel-green outcrop, all sturdy towers and narrow turrets and walls that held in and kept out in equal measure.

She had never seen anything like this castle, yet she'd imagined such a scene so often that it seemed familiar. Like meeting someone in person with whom she'd only corresponded. *Ah, you at last. It is good to see you.*

"You want to go closer to the castle, don't you, Madam Storybook. To rap on its stone walls and swim in its moat." So sure was Hugo that he didn't even say it as a question.

But he was wrong. "No, I don't want to," she replied. "From here it looks perfect. If I go nearer, I take the chance of spoiling it. And it doesn't even *have* a moat."

He patted together his gloved hands. "Let me make certain I understand. You like it so much that you don't want anything more to do with it."

She copied his gesture. Her gloves were worn at the

fingertips. "No, Monsieur Science. Say that I like it as it is and am content to admire from where I am."

"Merely a different way of saying the same thing."

"My way is better."

"Notice that my arms are not folded. I am busy not agreeing with you."

"Don't disagree." She smiled up at him, squinting into the sun despite the shield of her bonnet's brim. "Not when you could be looking at a castle. And knowing the sea is at your back." A hesitant breeze carried the smell of salt and something unfamiliar that must be the sea itself. It was the smell of water hitting rock, of plants carried in by the tide.

"Or I could be combing the sand hereabouts for gold." He stripped off his gloves and tucked them away, then crouched, taking up a handful of the coarse sand and sifting it through his fingers. "Not that I think we will find any, but we would be remiss not to eliminate the possibility."

"That's precisely the worry that kept me awake last night. Being remiss. About elimination."

He ignored this comment, only moving on to a new spot. He was methodical in his search—of course. First this square foot, then the one to the right. She ought to help, but she liked watching the movement of his hands. They were as careful sifting sand as they had been measuring droppers of different solutions for an interested youth yesterday. They were as certain in their movements as they had been when he unrolled his hospital plans before Sir Joseph Banks.

She wanted those hands on her, cradling and stroking. But he only kept combing through sand.

He'd shown her the bit of gold from Keeling. It was pure and bright, not at all the sort of wave-lapped grit to be found on the beach. But gold such as this had been found near Bamburgh, the gossiping women had said, and there was Bamburgh Castle, large as life.

Oh, probably they should have searched the barley fields rather than the beach, but it was clear the gold had been planted along with the barley. And this was a far prettier walk than tramping through fields of just-sprouting grain.

"Do you think the blacksmith melted them?" she asked Hugo now. "The gold coins, I mean."

"And dropped them on his toes into the bargain?" Hugo held out a palmful of sand, letting the breeze catch the finest bits. "Maybe."

"It would be remiss not to eliminate the possibility."

His mouth curved. "You are a wise woman."

"So why hasn't Jenks been more aggressive? Why hasn't he made an arrest?"

"It can only be because he hasn't found sufficient proof yet. But if he had a scrap of it, the wrongdoer would be shackled from neck to ankle." He let the rest of the sand in his hand fall.

"Why are there no others around here looking for the stolen gold, do you think?" She nudged her boot into the yielding sand. "No other treasure hunters like us."

"I wondered that too. I believe it's a matter of timing."

"In what way?"

He abandoned that square of sand and moved on to the next. "As soon as the gold sovereign was spent in Strawfield, everyone interested in finding treasure flocked there. With the exception of a young woman who needed the nudge of—"

"Familial neglect and eviction?"

"You make it sound so exciting," he said drily. "But in a phrase, yes. Until there is no hope of finding the gold in Strawfield, I do not think most people will look elsewhere for it."

"As you would not have, had I not forced your hand."

"You don't always have to force my hand, Georgette, to get what you want." He held up a palmful of sand at eye level. "You could also employ more words and fewer blows with the elbow."

"A woman must use whatever weapons she has to hand. Or to elbow." She spoke lightly to disguise her confusion. What did he mean, she didn't have to force his hand? What did he think she wanted?

Not even she knew the answer to that. She had long been in the habit of trying not to want anything at all.

"No gold yet, I see," she said to interrupt her own thoughts.

"If I find anything of note, I will immediately jump to my feet and crow in triumph." He held up something small, evaluating it, then extended it toward Georgette in his palm. "*Littorina*. A periwinkle shell. Common as dust, but pretty enough. Would you like it?"

She took it between thumb and forefinger. About an inch and a half in height, it was shaped like a dollop of cream, pointed at one end and otherwise fat and twirling. Georgette took off her gloves, testing the texture of it. Small as the shell was, it wasn't fragile. Brown and gray bands ridged its outside. "So deliberate and so tiny," she said. "A little animal made this."

"Little and delicious. Have you ever eaten winkles?"

"Is that a euphemism?"

"Miss Frost, it is never a euphemism. Since you have lived in London, I presume you have not dined on winkles. They are a coastal food."

"Your hypothesis is correct." She traced the sleek inside of the shell, then put it into the pocket of her gown. "I'm glad we've been able to travel together."

"Nonsense. You would never have come with me if I hadn't caught you in a gold net." He handed her another winkle shell.

"I don't need *all* the shells you find. And the gold net, as you put it, was my idea. Perhaps we entrapped each other."

He gave her another shell.

She dropped it on his head. "For a stubborn old scholar, you're not so bad."

"I am not *old*." He took off his hat, shaking the shell and bits of sand off its crown, then laid it beside him.

"You told that Runner, Jenks, that you were thirty-two years old."

"I did, and I am. You told him you were twenty-one."

"Close enough to the truth. I will be, exactly one week from today."

He stood, pressing another periwinkle shell into her hand. "An early birthday gift, then."

She laughed, letting the shell fall to the ground.

Hugo smiled in return, but a bit sadly. "You are terribly young, you know."

"Am I? I ought to be more terrible, then, if I'm to keep company with you."

"That's hardly fair. I wasn't the one parading around London in men's clothing."

Georgette raised a brow.

Hugo cursed under his breath. "You know what I mean."

"You are far more amusing than you realize," Georgette said. "And don't worry about your age, my dear. You wear the years well."

"I *wasn't* worrying about my—"

"Turn around. Don't look."

He looked at her oddly, then obeyed with reluctance. "How abrupt you are. Now I have to know what you are doing."

"Taking off my boots and stockings, you meddling man. I want to walk on the sand. And look for gold." She suited her actions to her words. The stockings were the trickiest bit, for she had to undo her garters and roll the fragile stockings over her knee, calf, and ankle. If Hugo had watched her do that . . .

It would have been exciting, to be honest. The idea of it made a flutter wake in her belly, then slip between her legs.

When she'd tucked the stockings into the boots and set them aside, she stood. "You may look. I'm decently attired again." Her voice sounded breathless. Beneath her toes, the sand was gently rough, tickling tender skin.

He turned back toward her and glanced at her bare toes, amused. "Are you certain you don't wish to see the castle up close? Barefoot, you look like Boadicea. Ready to tread upon anything and everything."

"I ought to tread more lightly." She hissed, hopping on one foot. "Those winkle shells are sharp. And wasn't Boadicea from a different part of England?"

"She was, at that. This is practically Scottish territory, though you mustn't tell the king I said that."

"You sound as if you've been reading from Sir

Frederic's history books," Georgette teased. "How can you stand to take something from his library? I saw it this morning. The bindings are dreadful. So much tooled gilt, but the leather is cheap as can be."

"The nuances of binding escaped me. And you are correct that I went in search of a dull book last night. Without your snoring to soothe me, I couldn't sleep."

Gingerly, she set down her winkle-stabbed foot. "You chose a book over me. Ah well, I am used to it."

"That's not so," said Hugo.

The tone in which he said it, as though the words were a heartfelt confession, made her not mind at all. Was she more important than a book, then? Had he missed her company? The possibility was intriguing. Unfamiliar.

She would not press him further, lest his admission fall apart. Instead, she took a step toward him, then another, admiring the footprints held in the sand. "I needn't set a foot out of my way to go look at a grand structure. I've seen a lot of beautiful buildings since you kidnapped me in London."

"I will let the grotesque inaccuracy of that statement pass, but please note that I note it. What buildings did you like?" He made a few prints of his own at the edge of the water. His boot was large, a stomp in the sand.

If she walked closer to the water, as he did, the sand crunched wetly under her foot, and the next wash of seawater filled each toe print with a tiny pool. "I liked all of them. The Swan with Two Necks, because I've never heard a better name than that. And it was where the journey began. Then I liked the first coaching inn I ever stayed in, and Raeburn Hall—except for the library, that is." She made another footprint, then watched until the waves lapped it up. "Even Willingham

House. That was part of the journey too. It is a beautiful home."

"It might be beautiful, but it's not a home." Stomp. Stomp. Stomp.

"You don't think of it as your home?"

"I haven't since my Eton days. But then, why should it hold special feeling? It is only one of eight houses, most with estates, that my father owns across England."

Eight. Good God. "It must be lovely to be a duke."

"You keep saying things like that. I don't know if 'lovely' is the right word. Comfortable, yes. Privileged, undeniably. But lovely . . ." He nudged a boot out, then pulled his foot back before the water touched the leather. "Lovely is an hour or two with someone whose company delights you."

"That is not loveliness. That is a dream."

"Is it only that?" He looked hard at her, and she didn't know what to say.

He scuffed together a great pile of wet sand, saying, "Never mind that. What constitutes a home for you?"

She let out a caught breath. "He said 'constitutes.' My heart is thumping so hard right now." He glared at her, and she added, "I hardly know the answer to that. I don't have one."

The glare turned to curiosity. "The bookshop was, surely?"

"Oh. That. I don't think so. It was familiar enough for me to consider it a home while my parents were alive, but that was only due to habit."

"I know it wasn't ideal for you, but *that* is what sounds like a dream to me. I mean . . . it's a bookshop."

"You'd have done better growing up there than I," she said. "Doubtless you spent your youth studying diligently while I was getting into mischief and going where I should not."

"And what has changed since then?"

"I should have known you'd say that." She kicked sand at him. "I wish you wouldn't speak of me as if . . ." She cast about for words.

"Yes?"

"Give me a moment. I'm trying to think of something good."

"I do think of you as something good," he said simply. "You are an astonishing person. I didn't realize that at first."

Somehow, she kept her trembling legs beneath her. "You are terrible at giving a compliment. Or was that meant to be a compliment? I can't even tell."

"It wasn't meant to be either a compliment or its opposite. It was merely an observation."

So serious, he sounded. "In what way have I had the honor of astonishing you?"

He scuffed more sand into the pile with that beautiful, damnable focus. "You say things to people, and they are the right things. It's not something I have been able to learn despite all my study."

She walked from the wet sand out of reach of the sea, noting how dry grains clung to her feet. "And how are you to learn to say the right things if you study ancient Greek and mathematics and medicine? You'll learn a great deal, but none of it has to do with people."

"Medicine does. Or it should."

"It should. That's true. And I think today it did, don't you?"

He tapped the heel of one boot against the sand

pile, as though satisfied with it. "I think it served its purpose."

"What is the purpose of it, for you?" Purpose, purpose. Well, it was *his* word. He ought to love having it thrown back at him.

When he didn't answer, she thought she knew what he was thinking. "It's to honor your brother Matthew, isn't it? Would he have liked this? Travel, and medicine, and crushed toes and whatnot?"

He planted a boot solidly on the pile of sand, arms outstretched for balance. "Every year that separates us makes me less confident about the answer."

"Tell me about him."

"My personal history is not relevant at the moment." He stood at a careful distance.

She found a smooth, dry patch of sand and sat down, pulling her knees to her chest. "When I was thirteen years old, I kissed the boy who brought the coal. Now, your turn."

"I won't tell you something important merely because you entrusted me with an unsolicited confidence. And what sort of kiss do you mean?"

"A real one."

After the boy who brought the coal, there had been the fishmonger's son. The groom who accompanied the heir to an earldom to the bookshop. Others over time. Scraps of affection, stolen in clandestine moments—not from those with power, but from the people next to them.

In a way, they'd all been real kisses, and they had all been nothing. She took what passed for love in that moment, knowing it would not last. And so she never gave more than a kiss—though afterward, she always felt it had been too much.

"Not a real kiss," she mumbled, but he did not seem to hear.

He frowned. "I don't speak about Matthew often. People don't know what to say when I do. I hardly know what to say myself."

She pushed back her bonnet, letting it dangle down her back by its knotted strings. The fluffy clouds shielded her from the sun, and the air was mild. "Was he much like you?"

Had she asked too much of him? At first she thought he would not answer. Then he said, "I will only talk to you about him because you begged me."

"I certainly did," she agreed. "It was so undignified. A pitiful spectacle."

A faint smile touched his lips. "No, we were not at all alike. He was a mirror of me. The charming one."

"That I can well believe. Certainly if one of you was charming, it was not you."

"I have never mentioned how much I love traveling with you," he said. "It gladdens my heart to be put to so much trouble and mocked as well."

"You do love it," she said. "You'd have been so bored without me."

"I am never bored."

She began pushing together a pile of sand with her left hand.

"What are you doing?"

"Building a private hospital," she said. "My sand will receive the finest sort of care."

"It'll never stay up."

"Building a private rubble heap, then. I shall intentionally build sand castles that fall until you are overcome with horror and tell me something real."

"How you bait me." He walked to the wave-lapped

sand a few feet away and caught up a double handful of it. Then he sat beside her, plumping the great handfuls between them. "Wet sand holds its shape far better than dry. Haven't you ever built a structure in sand before?"

"I have not, in fact."

She wanted to dig her fingers into the wet sand, but Hugo hadn't relinquished it. He was shaping it, smoothing it. He made of it a perfect little dome.

"Matthew was the first person I ever knew," he said quietly. "I knew him before I was born. I never knew myself without him until he died. And when he died, I wished I had been the one to die instead, because it's easier to be the one leaving than the one left behind." He brought his palm down flat, pressing the dome into shapelessness. "There, Georgette. Is that enough of a confession for you?"

"I want to hear whatever you want to tell me." Rarely had she meant a sentence so sincerely. The feeling of it must have shone in her voice, for Hugo looked at her slantwise. It was a long, evaluating sort of look.

Then he started shaping another structure. "He had the best care money could buy, or so my father thought. But it wasn't. It was an exorbitant fee from a puffed-up physician who never put his hands directly on a patient. A stillroom maid could have done better, with tinctures and poultices. A surgeon could have, with his willingness to do more than bleed the patient and order the fire to be built up higher as he took a fee."

"You told your father all this, didn't you?"

"I told everyone this. I couldn't not say it." Abandoning the sand structure, he folded his knees in an echo of Georgette's posture. His hat still lay on the beach a few yards away, and the breeze off the sea ruffled his short hair. "My parents didn't talk about him after that. They put away all his things, and all the portraits. But they still had me, with his face, reminding them. Reminding me, every time I looked in a glass."

"Did you like that?"

"I did, and I hated it too. It's become easier to look in a glass over time. As I age, my face is less like his was when he died." He wrapped his arms around his knees, broad shoulders straining against his greatcoat. "After fourteen years without him, the loss is like the way soldiers describe their old injuries. They ache, all the time, but the ache is so constant that sometimes it can be forgotten."

"Many such men turn to opium or spirits to ease the ache."

"Yes, well, I turned to study. Medicine. Science. I attempted to learn everything. Even worse, wouldn't you say?"

She pursed her lips. "Well, I would. But you probably wouldn't like it."

His mouth tugged up at one side. "I'm getting used to the things you say."

She smiled.

"I thought . . ." He unfolded, leaning back on his elbows and stretching out his legs. "I thought if I learned enough, maybe someday I would know how to keep someone else from feeling this kind of loss."

Georgette stretched out her legs, regarding her bare toes. All ten of them, uncrushed. "That is heroic, to turn grief into good deeds."

He made a sound of disgust. "Don't be so eager to turn me into one of your bland storybook fellows."

"There is nothing at all wrong with blandness, or it would not be part of the recovery from so many ailme—ah, you're making that sound again. And well done. You almost made me forget what we were talking about."

"It doesn't matter. I don't want such an attachment again. It's too difficult when the attachment is inevitably severed."

Inevitably, he said? He might as well have cut out a piece of her heart. "No, that's true." She injected a little venom into her tone. "You should be alone all your life except for scientific books, and you should never love anyone again. That's better. More logical."

He remained perfectly calm, resting on his elbows and staring out to sea. "I wonder if you recall which of us didn't want to walk closer to the castle. Which of us thought it was best to view it from a distance; better not to go close lest one's idea of it be spoiled."

The similarity had not struck her before. "You are a fiend to bring that up."

"I thought I was a hero."

"Maybe you're both."

No, she'd never really had a home. She had never been certain of anyone's love. And she missed that love with a sharp pain to the heart: she missed what she wished her family had been, as she had missed the chance to become what they'd wanted.

She had become what she wanted instead, or so she thought. But what good was it, if she was still alone?

She dug her toes into the sand, watching them disappear. The sand was the color of her skin, which was the color of her hair. If she wore a dress of the same shade, she could vanish entirely.

But at her side, Hugo wasn't looking out to sea anymore. He was looking at her, and not as if he was trying to find where she ended and the sand began.

He looked at her as if . . . as if looking at her was the purpose of this moment.

She had been searching for a purpose, hadn't she?

She reached for his hand, trapping his stronger fingers in hers. When he sat up, looking a question at her, she took a deep breath—and quickly, before she could doubt herself, she dove over the little building of sand and pressed a kiss to his lips. It was graceless, hard and fierce and consuming, and she had never felt anything more deeply than the crush of her lips against his mouth.

That was that. She had done it. There was no going back; no pretending that she hadn't wanted this since the first time he'd offered her a shoulder and told her he wanted her to be safe.

He was warm, shockingly so. The sensation of another person's lips against her own was so heart-thuddingly sweet that she didn't realize at once that he wasn't kissing her back.

But he *wasn't* kissing her back, and he tugged his hand free of hers, and the awareness of her own foolishness bled away the heat and the pleasure.

She sank back. Pulled away. Looked down. "I shouldn't have—"

Then he pressed forward, and his hands were in her hair, weaving through the pinned-up lengths and pulling them loose. He pulled her close, closer, into his lap, and fit his mouth to hers with a determination that left her breathless and startled.

Lord Hugo Starling did nothing by half measures, and once he decided he wanted to kiss a woman, he made sure she was kissed soundly. And oh, now he was kissing her. Not just kissing her back, but kissing her with a fire that she'd not known how to light. He held her to him, her hair, her shoulders, her waist, as if he were as eager for her as she'd been for him. As if this kiss had been waiting like the castle, unknown but familiar, ready for discovery.

So she discovered him: the line of his cheekbone, the slash of his brow, seen so often but never touched. The taste of his mouth, all heat and wine, and the shoulders that seemed broad enough to bear anything. He was in her hands, and she in his, and their mouths clashed. They always clashed; they loved to clash.

When they paused, both breathing quick and ragged, Georgette gasped, "I'm only kissing you because you begged me to."

He smiled, looking deep and true into her eyes. "I don't care why, as long as you don't stop."

"I won't stop."

After a while, a light mist began to chill the air. Hugo shrugged free of his greatcoat and draped it over them both, and there on the sand they kept each other warm.

Chapter Eleven

The following morning, Hugo knocked at the door of Jenks's chamber.

"One moment," came the muffled call. When the Runner flung the door open, he was wiping at his chin with a cloth, as if he'd just finished shaving. "Mr. Crowe," he said upon spotting Hugo. "What is it?"

"I wanted to let you know, Miss Linton is currently being established in a bedchamber on the floor below. Mrs. Crowe and a maid are seeing to her comfort."

"And why did you take it on yourself to let me know?" The Runner lowered the cloth, twisting it tight in his fists.

"Pure kindness? You seem the sort of person who likes to know who's in a building with him."

"That's all? Not trying to distract me from other happenings hereabouts?"

Hugo's blink must have looked sufficiently mystified, for Jenks slung his facecloth over one arm. "Right you are, then. I'll be ready to speak to Miss Linton in a few minutes."

Hugo shot out an arm, catching Jenks before he

could shut the door between them again. "Wait. Please. Mr. Jenks—she is staying here because it is not safe for her to stay with Mr. Keeling anymore. She was imposed upon."

"I wouldn't put the matter so politely." Jenks turned in the doorway to toss his facecloth onto the bed in his chamber. Around him, Hugo saw a Spartan room, with plain wood furniture and a small glass and washstand. It suited Jenks's brusque manner, though Hugo suspected it had been intended by Sir Frederic as insult. Jenks had been packed off to a servant's room, it looked like, rather than a comfortable guest chamber.

No matter. Soon enough, they'd all be on their way, and back in London, Sir Frederic would be a genial host only in Hugo's memory.

The thought of returning to London was not as pleasant as it had been a week earlier.

"That's why I need to question her," Jenks added. "One form of lawbreaking is often connected to another. If Keeling gave her some gold for—how'd you put it? Imposing on her? Then I wonder to whom else he's given gold. And why."

The bit of gold from Keeling felt heavy in Hugo's waistcoat pocket. "I couldn't say."

"Couldn't you?" Jenks shut the chamber door behind him. "You heard about the scorched chests north of Doncaster, didn't you? The ones from the Royal Mint?"

"Yes. My—wife followed the story eagerly when she could find a newspaper."

As they began walking down the corridor, Jenks looked at him wryly. Hugo could almost hear his thoughts. *Keeping up the wife charade, are you?* "I imagine that she did. Did you hear there was a body found buried by them?"

"No, I haven't seen a newspaper since—wait, what? A body? A *human* body?"

"Discovered two days ago. Got the express an hour ago. And when an express comes on a Sunday, it's a matter of life or death."

In this case, the latter. A chill prickle raced down Hugo's spine. "That's bad news. Will there be an inquest? Have you need of me to give medical testimony?"

"No need for a doctor to testify. The body was too burned to tell more than that it had belonged to a man."

The imagination revolted from the picture thus raised. "My sympathies to the fellow, and to the fellow who found him. That had to be a terrible discovery."

"Doubtless it was."

Jenks was a master of the too-long silence. The corridor stretched endlessly before them, the escape of the main staircase far away. And in Hugo's pocket was a bit of gold from Keeling.

And near Doncaster, a man had been killed for three chests of coins.

That decided it. "Look." Hugo stopped walking, then drew forth from his pocket the bit of gold Keeling had given him. "I want you to have this. No amount of metal is worth a life."

At the sight of the gleaming bit in Hugo's palm, Jenks froze. "So I've thought from the beginning. Rare is the person who agrees with me, Mr. Crowe."

"I'm a doctor," Hugo said, knowing the reply was inadequate. *I have human feeling* would have been more to the point. "If this is a clue that will help you solve the murder or the theft, then it's yours."

"Who gave it to you?"

Despite the terse words, the man displayed no expression. Clothing, face, hair—he was determinedly nondescript, so as to fade from the memory of those he questioned. A good tool for a Runner.

Hugo weighed his response, tipping his palm so the blob of gold rolled back and forth. A petty urge to deny Jenks the information seized him. The Runner had complicated Hugo's journey north to an annoying degree, forcing him and Georgette to pose as a married couple.

Although that part had not been as difficult as it had first seemed. Truly, it wasn't bad at all. Except for the fantasies of home and hearth and bed that had begun to seize Hugo's imagination, crowding out his determination to adhere to his plan.

Georgette Frost was hell on a plan.

But. In favor of telling Jenks the truth was the burned body in Doncaster. The bullet wound in Keeling's side. Perhaps a week healed, it was too recent to date from the theft at the Royal Mint a month previous. But could it have come from a man ambushed near Doncaster, who had been killed for his rich cargo?

Then there was the weeping Miss Linton, paid in gold by a man who had raped her—or at the very least, coerced her in a desperate moment.

That settled it. Hugo held out the gold. "The hind Keeling gave it to me yesterday in payment for his medical treatment."

Jenks extended a palm. When Hugo dropped the gold into it, he squinted at it. "Must have been the devil of a treatment. Did you build him a new leg out of clockwork?"

"Hardly." Hugo wiped his hands with a handkerchief,

not wanting to remember the feeling of the gold in his palm. "I believe he was trying to buy my silence."

"Didn't work, then." Jenks looked up from the bit of gold, considering. "What's the price of your silence? It comes dear, if gold isn't enough."

Hugo tucked away his handkerchief. "Not particularly. My words are free to the right listener."

"Hmm." Jenks pocketed the gold, then walked on. When they reached the end of the corridor, the hall's great staircase before them now, Jenks halted. "You and your . . . wife . . . vanished yesterday."

"Nothing and no one can vanish. That violates the law of conservation of mass," Hugo replied. "And are you expressing a suspicion of me? I handed over gold to you, Mr. Jenks."

"Suspicion is my line of work. Just as treating people is yours."

"Fair enough," Hugo said. "Though I was intended for the clergy. Wouldn't you feel dreadful about suspecting a man of the cloth?"

"No," Jenks said. "But then, you might say the rule of law is in my blood."

"Is it? Then I hope you have a pleasant time with your suspicions," Hugo said to Jenks. "Pardon me, but that's all I need to speak with you about at the moment. I must be off."

The Runner would not move from the center of the staircase. "To where?"

"To treat the blacksmith. Mr. Lowe had all the toes on his left foot off yesterday and I want to check on his wound."

"I'll come with you." Jenks stepped aside.

Giving him the bit of gold had been the right thing to do. Hugo knew that. And yet a small part of him wished he'd tossed it to Jenks over one shoulder and walked away, whistling.

He settled for asking, "Have you any experience at caring for amputations?"

"No. But I won't be looking at feet. I'm looking for another clue." Jenks followed Hugo down the stairs, a fine wide sweep that grew more ornate with each story nearer the ground. "Lawbreakers don't respect the Lord's Day. I can't afford to either."

With the Runner trailing him like a substantial shadow, Hugo went into the parlor where he'd treated patients the previous day and collected a bag full of medical supplies. "So you're going to call on Keeling?"

"On Lowe. If the gold you gave me was once a sovereign, it must have been melted by a blacksmith. I've only circumstantial evidence thus far. I need proof to make an arrest."

"But Lowe's toes were cru—"

"Maybe he needed convincing."

"What a dark place your mind is." Hugo hesitated over an empty glass vial, then added it to the leather bag as well. The boy who'd shown such interest in medical workings the day before was, he thought, a son of Lowe's. There might be time to teach him another compound or two. "And who do you suppose convinced him so violently? Am I saving Mr. Lowe's life only for you to cart him off to the gallows?"

"That depends on what I find," said Jenks. "And whether you save his life."

"Oh, I'll save it." He glanced over the supplies remaining on the tea tables. Ah, there was the honey Georgette had used to make a tea for the little boy. Honey had healing properties on wounds. He added that to the bag as well.

"We're not making a cake, Mr. Crowe," said Jenks. "Let's be off."

"If you wish," Hugo replied. "As soon as I fetch Mrs. Crowe to join us." For somehow in the last day—or the last week, or even longer—it had become impossible for him to think of setting off somewhere new without Georgette.

It was raining as they wound through Sir Frederic's land, the sort of light rain that turned the fields soft and pliant and melted footpaths into mud. Georgette crowded close to Hugo under an umbrella, mindful of Jenks under a second umbrella a few paces behind. For his sake, she must act married; for hers, not too married, lest she dwell on the incendiary kisses of the previous day and take them to heart.

It was the sort of muddle that could drive a woman mad—or fire her imagination.

Georgette was more prone to the latter.

The smell of damp earth filled the air. At a distance, bondagers passed here and there. They all wore the same sort of garments, and it was impossible to tell one from another. What were they doing, huddled in the cold mist of a June Sunday morning? Walking to or from church? Paying calls on one another? Compared to them, Georgette was dressed impractically, her boots not stout enough and her skirts trailing in the dirt of the path. She held them up, fabric bunched in one fist, wondering what place in England she might belong.

Linton was now settled in Raeburn Hall, a process that had involved much fuss from Sir Frederic and argument from Keeling. In quick snippets as they walked, Hugo told Georgette of his conversation with Jenks. The body, the gold, the wide-cast suspicions.

"I am glad you gave the gold to Jenks," she had answered, and he looked relieved.

It had been his own, his payment for doing his work well. He ought to do what he thought right with it. And when one thought about the blood being shed for the stolen money—the treasure hunt lost its playful glint and took on a darker cast.

The darkness clung to Linton, too. Georgette had been struck by the woman's youth, and by her dreadful fatigue. She was no more than nineteen, and living on the edge of poverty. Had Georgette been, as the Duchess of Willingham might say, less fortunate in her friends, she could easily have found herself in similar straits.

Hugo had asked Georgette what her purpose was, and she'd answered that it was finding stolen sovereigns. It had not been an adequate response then; since meeting Linton, it seemed even less so.

If she claimed the Royal Mint's reward—and if she did not—she needed something more to do than exist.

They passed a number of cottages as they walked, all as similar as the garb of the bondagers. Each dwelling was stone-walled and small, with roofs of neat thatch. Flocks of sheep milled haphazardly, corralled into an order known only to the dogs that sometimes barked and herded them.

The innocent wanderings of the animals were pleasant to look on. She hadn't realized her steps had slowed until Hugo asked, "Shall we pause so you can pet a sheep? That is not a euphemism."

She welcomed the moment of lightness. "Alas, it never is." She eyed the soft ground away from the path.

"No, I don't want to pet a sheep at the moment. But you go on if you've the urge. I'll hold the umbrella."

With a laugh, he declined.

Soon enough, they reached what was clearly the blacksmith's cottage, for a forge of the same native stone stood nearby. With a steeply pitched roof and a stout brick chimney, the forge dwarfed the low-slung cottage. The smith's workshop was silent for now, but Georgette could imagine it belching coke smoke, sounding with the ring of a hammer against metal.

Once Mr. Lowe got back onto his feet. Literally.

"I'll be off," said Jenks. He peeled away, trudging across the foot-worn ground to the entrance of the forge.

Right. He was looking for clues, not paying a call of goodwill.

She followed Hugo to the cottage, the door of which was opened as soon as they drew near. Mrs. Lowe stood there, pretty and frazzled, with circles of exhaustion under her eyes. "Eee, it's champion to see you, Doctor. Missus. The mister is as bad as a bairn, blathering all the day and night."

"Is he in pain?" Hugo asked.

"Mebbe yes, but mostly he seems mor'al happy to have his toes off, like. Can't wait to be back on his feet."

She welcomed them into the cottage, a long partitioned room with a clay floor. A trestle table ran down its center. To one end of the space, a fire pumped merry heat into the room, and a pot of something savory hung over it, bubbling. Baskets of potatoes and apples were ranged around it, and onions hung from the ceiling in a rope, their leafy tops dried and plaited. A little girl and little boy banged and drummed on an empty pot with a wooden spoon, shrieking their delight. A sheepdog and thin orange tabby wound around Mrs. Lowe's legs, barking and yowling.

"If Mr. Lowe is this loud, I pity his wife," Georgette murmured to Hugo.

Mrs. Lowe directed Hugo and Georgette behind the partition, where the blacksmith lay on a bed atop a neat patchwork quilt. The couple's eldest, the curious boy who had asked so many questions of Hugo the day before, sat at the edge of the bed.

"Doctor! Nurse!" He hopped to his feet at once.

Nurse? Georgette had never thought to be called such a thing. She turned it over in her mind, liking the sound of it. "How are you?" she asked. "And how is the patient?"

"Im-patient," joked the blacksmith. He hoisted himself onto his elbows, propping himself up against the wall. "Ready to get back to work. A man's got to make a living."

"Let's have a look, then," said Hugo. Setting down his bag, he bent over the heavily bandaged foot and began to undo the dressing.

As the boy craned in closer, eager to see, Georgette crouched over the bag. She unclasped it and looked idly through the contents. Anything to look busy and not see the poor blacksmith's wound.

Although—maybe it wasn't that bad? There was no screaming, no fainting when the bandage fell to the floor. "It is healing well," Hugo said. "I believe the worst of the pain will be over within a week."

"Chopped off many toes, have you?" said Lowe.

"I haven't taken off many toes," said Hugo. "But I'm a fiend with fingers. Can't stop slicing them off."

Lowe guffawed. His son, voice on the edge of dropping, laughed in a rough crackle.

"Men," muttered Georgette. She ventured a peek at the blacksmith's foot. If she were to be a nurse—at least for today—she couldn't shy from anything. She peeked up to see Hugo's handiwork.

And . . . it looked like a foot with no toes on it. Instead of toes, a neat line of sutures traced the end of the foot.

All right. She could manage that.

Georgette stood, clasping her hands behind her back. "What does he need now?"

"Honey, please."

She blinked. "Did you call me—" That was foolish. No. It wasn't a term of endearment. He wanted the pot of honey she'd just spotted in the leather bag.

Handing it over, she watched as he dabbed it along the line of sutures. "This will help prevent infection," said Hugo.

"Only if we keep the dog away from me foot, like," Lowe said to his son. Compared to the previous day, when pain and fear had wracked him, he was hale and bluff. Such was the blessing of relief.

"You seem in good spirits," Georgette said as Hugo checked his work and covered the wound with a dressing. "How have you been occupying yourself? Spillikins? Bilbo catch? Hounding your wife to the edge of sanity?"

Lowe laughed. "Bairns' games, all of them, especially the one about the missus. Nae. I've played me smallpipes."

"Is that a euphemism?" Hugo asked. Georgette kicked him in the foot.

"It's the finest instrument in the world." The blacksmith puffed up. "Matthew, go get me pipes."

Hugo looked up sharply, his shoulders rising. "Your boy's name is Matthew?"

"It is a good name," Georgette said. "A very good one." When Hugo looked her way, she smiled at him. The tense line of his shoulders relaxed.

The youth, Matthew, returned in a moment with what looked like a leather bag stuffed full of thin wooden flutes, all dangling from a leather belt.

"Nice thing about the pipes"—Lowe slung and buckled the wide belt about his midsection—"is you can play them while you sit."

"Please don't," said Hugo.

"Please *do*, Mr. Lowe," said Georgette. "I've never heard this instrument before."

"There now, that's a canny lass you have." Lowe patted the bed, and Georgette joined the line of people sitting there. "Nothing to blow into with a smallpipes. Not like that windbag the Scottish like to play. See? You work this bellows with your right arm as you play." He demonstrated, his elbow pumping the leather bag full of air. "S'pose that's why I took to it. Bellows are me life's work, like."

Georgette pointed at the flute-looking things. "So which one of these makes the music?"

"All of them," said Lowe.

"None of them," muttered Hugo, closing the jar of honey and handing it to Matthew. "Keep that away from the dog, yes? And away from the younger children."

"I will, Doctor."

"All of them," repeated Lowe, ignoring this interruption. "See this one? This is the chanter, for playing the melody. These holes and keys let a man play anything he wishes. Then the drones give us the harmony. Tune them or shut them off as you wish."

"Shut them all off," said Hugo, rummaging in the bag of medical supplies. "That's not why we're here."

Georgette folded her arms, ignoring his groan. "That's not why *you're* here, maybe. My purpose this afternoon, as in much of life, is unspecified. Besides which, I thought you wanted to learn everything."

"It'll take my mind off me foot," said the blacksmith.

Hugo waved, a gesture of surrender, and pulled a roll of bandage from the bag. "Not too loud. I have to wrap this about the dressing, and bagpipes always send me into a froth of rage."

"*Smallpipes*," said Lowe. "Totally different, like." He hoisted the leather bag under his left arm. An octopus of pipes connected the two and was clutched in the blacksmith's left hand. The little flutes he had called drones then stuck up on their own, the chanter hanging downward to be played by both hands.

And so he began, his elbow working the bellows, fingertips dancing over keys and stops. The sound of the pipes was bright and buzzing, a light staccato piping. Quick as the ear could follow, the notes were strung together like beads in a necklace, all bright, all entirely separate.

The music curled and coiled about them in the small room, making it larger in every direction. Calling to the people in the other room, bringing Mrs. Lowe to lift the partition, her arms full of squirming toddlers, her smile bright and her fatigue lifted, for a moment.

When the tune ended with a flourish, Georgette sprang to her feet, and she and Mrs. Lowe applauded. "There, now." Lowe beamed. "Almost makes a man forget he hasn't any toes."

"Here now," said Hugo. "You still have five."

"Right, wasn't I? The smallpipes make the bagpipes

sound like an angry cat." Lowe unbuckled the wide leather belt supporting the instrument.

"Bagpipes always sound like an angry cat," said Hugo. "No comparison needed. But yes, your tune was pleasant." He tied off the end of the dressing. "If the pain gets too bad, take laudanum. Start with twenty drops every four hours. Go up to thirty if you must."

Remembering the worried mother of the day before, Georgette asked, "Can you buy laudanum from the apothecary in Bamburgh?" This was not quite asking them whether the treatment was within their means, but it would give the same answer.

"Eee, for sure." Mrs. Lowe set down the wriggling toddlers with a gentle swat on the bottom of each. "We might have part of a bottle already, like. I'll go through me stores and check." She followed the smaller children out of that part of the house.

Hugo looked gratitude at Georgette. *Right. Thanks for checking on that.* To Lowe, he added, "For the next week, walk if you can, a little every day."

Lowe handed off the pipes into Matthew's careful grasp. "Try to stop me."

"No, I won't," Hugo replied. "That's why I ordered that. And when you're sitting, keep the foot elevated"— Georgette stuffed a bolster beneath Lowe's injured foot—"and keep the bandages dry. Change them as often as need be to keep them clean."

"Because of nasty oozing?" Matthew sounded hopeful.

"No," said Hugo. "That's a problem, if something nasty oozes. It means we didn't catch the infection soon enough. My hope is that the only thing dirtying the bandage will be the walking about your father does."

"What about all that fancy sewing you did?" Lowe winked. "Pretty as a picture, like."

"The *sutures*," said Hugo, "must stay in as long as possible. Ten days, say. Two weeks would be better. A surgeon can remove them for you, if I am not at hand."

Georgette scoffed. "Who would be less at hand than a surgeon a dozen miles off?"

Hugo's look was speaking. Or rather, silencing.

Did that mean he didn't think they'd be here in two weeks? Or he didn't think *he* would. She counted off the days in her head. This was the eighth of June. In two weeks, they might still be searching for gold, might they not?

Well . . . they might not. She could no more imagine what lay two weeks in the future than she could guess at her life in two decades. For once, her imagination was failing her. She must remember: it was not safe to rely on anyone else in the world. Especially not a scholar who lived for his perfect, perfect plans.

Right. She'd have that inked on her arm, maybe, to help her remember.

"Could you show me how to remove the sutures?" Matthew asked Hugo. "In case of need?"

For the next few minutes, Hugo stitched and snipped into a wad of gauze by way of demonstration. Son and father watched carefully, the boy asking questions and the man shooting curious glances at his bandaged foot.

It was pleasant, watching a son want to help his father. A father trust his son. When people stayed together, when they cared about each other, this was how they treated each other—she supposed.

Hugo promised to return as soon as he could, to

check on the wound again. "And if you see any signs of infection," he added, "pour some spirits over the incision. The strongest spirits you have."

"Waste of spirits," said Lowe. "Are you sure?"

"If once I admit doubt, Mr. Lowe, it will not depart. I am surer than sure." Hugo looked at his bag. "Ah, you've packed it up already, Geo—madam?"

"The strange things you do call me," she murmured. "Yes, I made myself useful."

"About your payment, Doctor," Lowe began.

Hugo put up a hand. "Your son was my apprentice. That's all I could ask."

Georgette cleared her throat. "What of my help, Doctor?"

The look Hugo shot at her was veiled, but his mouth made a sensuous curve. "Yes, Nurse. I shall see to your recompense later."

Oh. Well. Yes, that was exactly what she'd hoped for.

As Hugo gave some final instructions to Lowe and his son, Georgette wandered into the front room. Mrs. Lowe was stirring her stew, and the little boy was clinging to her skirts and wailing for a bite.

"May I?" At the older woman's nod, Georgette scooped up the boy. She held him steady, one arm beneath his rear and one behind his back, then twirled with him as quickly as she could until he was laughing.

"Me next!" His sister, not much older, tugged at Georgette's skirts for a turn, and she was given the same treatment. By the time Georgette set her down, both were dizzy and giggling.

"You've a canny hand with little ones," said Mrs. Lowe.

"I lived with my cousin and her husband and four

young children for some time," said Georgette. "I helped care for them when needs must."

The reminder caught her by surprise. She'd been used to thinking of herself as extra, unneeded, once Cousin Mary and her husband bought Frost's Bookshop. Georgette was but another body to find space for, another mouth to feed. But when she played with little Eliza, just learning to talk, or soothed fractious Johnny with his never-ending eruption of milk teeth, then for that moment there was a place for her in the family.

The memory of it was warm.

"I like your cottage," she told Mrs. Lowe. "I have often dreamed of living in such a place."

The older woman's expression was thoughtful as she stirred the bubbling stew, then set aside the spoon. "A cottage is a roof and walls, like. But it isn't very nice unless there's someone nice in it, Mrs. Crowe."

The false name made Georgette glance over her shoulder, quick and doubtful.

"Aye," said the blacksmith's wife. "A good man is what I mean. Lowe looks out for us. Lost his toes, but kept everything else, and that's what matters."

Georgette hesitated, on the verge of asking how he'd met with the accident to his toes. Or how he looked out for the family. Or how Georgette might get a cottage that was more than roof and walls.

There were too many questions crowding for notice at once, and before she spoke any of them, Hugo emerged from behind the partition with his bag and the furled umbrella. Together, he and Georgette bade farewell to each member of the family in that front room, even to the suspicious cat that hid behind Mrs. Lowe when the visitors walked to the door.

As soon as the cottage door closed behind them, a figure whipped around the corner of the building. Toward Hugo? Out of reflex, Georgette's fist shot out. "No!"

The figure resolved itself into the familiar form of Jenks—now bent over, wheezing. "Right in the gut? Must you?" He sucked in a deep breath, straightening slowly.

"You startled me." She ought to apologize, but she didn't feel like it. Not after the warmth of the family circle she'd just left; not after realizing that Hugo had put a period to their stay in Northumberland.

"Forgive the wife." Hugo popped open the umbrella to shield her, though the earlier rain had dwindled to drizzle. "She has the heart of a horrid street rascal and the soul of—well, the same."

That wasn't the sort of heart she had at all. But she painted on a smile nonetheless. "I hope you're not injured, Mr. Jenks."

The Runner looked insulted. "No. I am not." He hitched his furled umbrella under one arm, adding, "Found some interesting things in the forge."

What had she thought her heart made of, for that brief instant? Now it was a stone, plummeting. "By 'interesting,' do you mean relevant to your investigation?" No, it could not be. Not that nice Mr. Lowe. Not his wife, his children, his dog, and grumpy cat.

"I do." Jenks looked at her as suspiciously as the ginger cat had. "Little drops of gold, fine as the mist in the air right now. A scatter of them. Our friend blacksmith has been working more than iron."

Hugo offered the umbrella to Georgette, taking the handle of his bag in both hands. "What will you do now?"

"Find where the gold came from."

Georgette's hands clasped the wooden handle of the umbrella tightly. Of course they wanted to find the gold. Of course they did. But . . . not yet? "If *we* find the sovereigns," she said, "we get the reward from the Royal Mint. What happens if *you* find them, Mr. Jenks?"

He looked back at the forge, then turned toward her again. "Then I've done justice."

Before she could answer, there issued a distant crack, like something heavy hitting something hard. In a wild gesture, Hugo dropped his bag and flung his arms around Georgette. She yelped, startled, and let the umbrella fall—and there came another crack.

Then was silence, so loud it echoed in her ears. The shock of it consumed her for a moment, so she did not at once notice that Hugo had slumped against her.

By the time she did notice, he was staggering upright again. The shoulder of his coat was torn, a dark stain spreading across the fabric.

She caught his hand, his elbow. Whatever she could grab hold of. "Hugo?"

"I think," he said, "that I have been shot."

Chapter Twelve

Hugo had dissected cadavers time upon time. He had performed surgeries. He had encountered the blood of wounded and dying and ill people, some of whom he could help and some he could not.

He had never realized that the smell of blood was so much stronger when it was one's own. It filled his nose and lungs, coppery and heavy.

His shoulder burned, seared by a bullet and heated by spilled blood. Leaning heavily on Georgette, he turned toward the door of the Lowes' cottage. "I need to get inside," he ground out. "With my bag. I can look at the wound there. Jenks, a hand?"

"Jenks"—Georgette spat the name out like a curse—"ran off as soon as he heard the gun fired. Likely searching for clues, but my *God*, you've been *shot*. Priorities!"

"We'll be fine. His behavior is . . . good sense." He tried to lift his right arm, to rap at the door, but he couldn't move it. The attempt made his shoulder scream. "He can . . . triangulate. Two shots—did they come from different angles?"

Georgette slid an arm around his waist, then hammered at the door with her free hand. "If anyone else had said that, I'd think he was out of his head," she said crisply. "But since it's you, I'd say you're not as bad off as I thought."

"I'm fine."

"One more lie like that and your hair will catch fire. It happens all the time in storybooks. You really ought to read them."

"You made that up." Speaking each word was like carving a shape from stone.

"Anything to distract you while I . . . aha. Mrs. Lowe, might we impose on you again?" The blacksmith's wife had finally opened the door, her progress evidently slowed by a child clutching each of her legs. When she saw Hugo, her eyes went wide, and she stood back at once to allow Georgette to usher him back into the house.

Bleary and chilled despite his burning shoulder, Hugo faded from the present moment. He was dimly aware of quick speech, the cry of a toddler, a great sweep of crockery—and then he was pressed and shoved and heaved, gently but firmly, until he was laid out on the long trestle table with a cloth beneath him.

"I've got the doctor's bag," called Matthew. The wrong Matthew. It was good to think on the name, though.

"Best take off the coat so I can see the wound." Hugo spoke the words from far away.

"How do you sound so calm?" Georgette tugged at his coat on the uninjured side, easing the fabric over his hand and down his arm.

Because it happened to someone else. Someone who had left a blacksmith's cottage satisfied with a job well done, dissatisfied with the lonely cold he stepped into afterward. "Would it improve the situation if I frothed and raved?"

"It would be much less disconcerting than this eerie sort of composure."

"Maybe I'll scream in distress while you remove my coat." More hands were helping now, lifting Hugo at the side to help him free of the garment.

"Maybe I will scream too," she said. "To share the burden of panic with you. By the bye, you have the most terrible luck with coats."

"I do, when you are around." Though he was lowered prone again gently, the jar to his injury made him grit his teeth. It had the effect of snapping him into the present moment, concentrating the shock of the bullet wound to his shoulder. No, not quite the shoulder itself. The trapezius muscle. If the bullet had ripped muscle instead of injuring bone and tendon, he was a lucky fellow. Luckier still that it had missed the subclavian vessels; if it had not, he could have easily bled to death by now. "I think the wound is not dire. Georgette and Matthew, this shall be a test for you."

Mr. Lowe stumped from the rear room and came to stand beside the table. "What's all this?" He peered up and down the length of the table, his expression turning from surprise to worry. "What happened to Mr. Crowe?"

"Good, you are getting in a piece of walking," Hugo said. "A little every day."

Georgette bent to speak in his ear. "Now I know you'll be all right, Doctor. You can't help but see to the patient's care, even now." There was a tremble in her voice.

"Is that—was Mr. Crowe *shot*? Who did this?" the blacksmith asked.

"We didn't see." Georgette brushed her hand against Hugo's knuckles. "But—he protected me. After the first shot, he protected me."

"That's what a man does for his woman," said Mr. Lowe.

"I would have done it for anyone," Hugo protested.

"Would you? See if I thank you again, then," Georgette sniffed, but the caress of her fingers over his hand was gentle as ever.

From the corner of his eye, Hugo saw Mrs. Lowe hand off the younger children to Matthew. She came to press against her husband's side. "Good God. I never thought they'd . . ." She covered her mouth, muffling the words. "Doctor, you're innocent. You've nothing to do with the affairs about here."

How mysterious. Not that he had attention for *mysterious* at the moment. "It appears I do now."

"Hugo," said Georgette. "I have cut your shirt a little, and the waistcoat, so the wound is exposed. It looks as if the bullet went into the muscle above your shoulder bones—"

"The trapezius." Ha. He knew it.

"—and stuck there."

And *stuck* there? Damnation. "Then we shall have to dig it out."

"Dig it out? Um. What if we don't?" Georgette sounded tentative.

He looked steadily up at the ceiling of the small house. It was a nice ceiling, pitched high and solidly beamed. "I will die slowly of lead poisoning."

A chorus of gasps followed.

Hugo tried to smile. "Only joking. I don't know. I might be all right. But I'd rather not have a bullet in me, so the wound can close. And if the bullet carried any cloth with it, that could cause infection."

Georgette replied first. "You've convinced me. What do you need?"

"A looking glass, if one is available."

"There's the one I shave by." Mr. Lowe limped to fetch it.

"Are you going to take a bullet out of your own shoulder?" Georgette bent over him, her features sharp with strain.

"Trapezius." His jaw clenched. "I can do it. I don't want to ask you for help."

The words slipped out easily, too familiar after hearing them time and time again from Georgette. How many times had she said she didn't need him? Didn't want him to help her? She had wounded him long before a bullet lodged itself in his body.

"Oh." Her cheeks went the sudden pink of one who had been slapped. "What do you mean by that? Are you—is this pride, or do you distrust me?"

It was pride, but not entirely of the *I don't need you if you don't need me* sort. He simply didn't want her to see him bleeding.

And he *did* want her help, even though she never wanted anything of him. He wanted her to care whether he recovered or whether he bled out on the blacksmith's table.

He wanted a damned lot more than that. But all he could do was shake his head.

The vivid color in her cheeks began to subside. She pulled in a deep breath, then blew it out slowly. "Strong spirits. We'll need that."

"For the wound?" asked Mrs. Lowe.

"And for me." Again, Georgette brushed Hugo's hand gently. "Guide me through this. I will do it for you."

Her gaze was steady, unblinking. Her eyes were like a glass in which a man might see reflected whatever he wished. *I care for you,* a man might see. *I will be brave for you, to give you solace. I want to spare you pain.*

He turned his head as far to the right as he could, catching sight of the bloodstained edge of his shirt and the torn muscle. It hurt more when he looked at it.

"Fine, then," he said. "Get the medical bag, and I'll show you what is needed."

Lowe returned with a hand-sized glass, and his wife brought a bottle of something spiritous. Georgette held it up, giving it a little shake—then she took a quick belt from the bottle, shuddering at the liquor's strength. "That ought to cauterize a wound on its own."

"No cauterizing. Cleaning to prevent infection." Hugo gritted his teeth, then said, "At the count of three, pour. One. Two."

She splashed the wounded muscle with the alcohol.

Fire ripped him, a shock of burning pain that raced all over his body. His scalp prickled, his legs spasmed, his hands clenched into fists. For several seconds, he could only struggle for breath—then he growled: "Good God! I said wait until *three*!"

"Would it improve the effect if I had?" She stood over him, bottle tipped at what Hugo could only view as a threatening angle.

"This is no time for you to throw my words back at me." He eyed the bottle. "Again. But gently."

"Right. Gently. I'll remove the bullet gently, shall I? As if such a thing is possible." She disappeared from above him, the sound of her footsteps crossing the main room. "Mrs. Lowe, might I have that laudanum?"

"I don't need it," called Hugo. "Come back. Let's finish this."

When Georgette returned, she held a little bottle fashioned of brown glass. "Are your patients this terrible to you? Drink it or have it dashed in your face. Thirty drops, isn't that what you suggested to Mr. Lowe?"

"Aye, it is," said the blacksmith. "I'll—I'll be off in the corner. Or the other room. I'll—right, then."

His limping footsteps faded away. Mrs. Lowe mumbled something about watching the children, and she, too, fled.

And it was just Hugo and Georgette and the bullet. And the laudanum.

So be it.

"Hold up the glass where I can see the entrance of the bullet," he ordered. "Thank you. Yes, it's much as I thought. This ought to be straightforward. You'll need access to both the front and back of the muscle, in case the bullet has fragmented."

She hoisted his shoulder, easing her own beneath him. "You're not as heavy as I expected."

"I was heavier before I lost some blood."

"So saucy. It is also possible that I'm very strong." She wedged something beneath him—his wadded coat, he realized, now used as a bolster. Then she took up the bottle again and counted out drops of laudanum into a large spoon. ". . . twenty-nine, thirty."

"I don't need it."

"Do take it, Hugo. Please. I don't want to hurt you."

He was powerless, always, against a *please*. Swallowing the drug, he mumbled, "You will. You already have."

The laudanum was bitter on his tongue, so bitter it covered the taste of his words. Maybe she thought he meant the prodding at his raw wound. He hoped she did not; he hoped she understood how much more he intended.

As the laudanum began to pull him away from the present, thickening his speech, he gave her scrambled instructions. "Remove the bullet with that—no, the next instrument. Yes. That one. . . . No sutures on the skin. It needs to heal from the inside out. . . . Clean the wound with boiled salt water and cover it. And then . . ."

And then . . . though it was hardly midday, he sank into twilight.

Chapter Thirteen

Removing a bullet from a man's shoulder—beg pardon, *trapezius*—was, Georgette decided, not much different from carrying laundry and books beyond the point of exhaustion. One kept in mind what one had to do, and one did it without thinking or feeling. Because if one thought about it, or allowed oneself to feel, then it would all be too much.

But when the bit of surgery was done, and the lead ball wrapped in gauze and the wound cleaned and covered, she felt emotion aplenty. Mostly relief: that the bullet had not fragmented; that she had got out the shreds of cloth it carried into his flesh. That Hugo's slumberous breathing was strong and steady, and that she had not injured him further.

The Lowes came back into the main part of the house then, and Georgette apologized for the disruption to their day. She was cleaning the used medical instruments with more of the boiled salt water when Jenks came into the cottage with a slam of the door and a stomp of booted feet.

"Couldn't find any sign of the assailant," he said,

"beyond some footprints at the other side of the forge. The ground didn't even hold the shape well. Too muddy. This everlasting mist is the worst."

Right, right. Jenks had been trying to find the person who had fired the gun at them. And before that, he'd been looking for gold in the blacksmith's workshop. And he had found something? Some evidence?

Right now, she did not care, for Hugo was asleep and bleeding.

"You, Mr. Lowe." The Runner leveled a piercing glare at the blacksmith. "I see you're moving about. Been on your feet long?"

"He's been in the house." Mrs. Lowe had returned to her pot of stew over the fire. She stirred at furious speed, not looking around. "Only just got up when the doctor and his missus came back in, like."

"I asked your husband." Jenks folded his arms.

If Hugo had made the same gesture, it would mean he was about to change his mind. Georgette ventured a touch to his right forearm. How long before he would be able to fold his arms? To throw? To embrace?

"I didn't do anything to the doctor!" The burly blacksmith pressed against the wall of his small house, as if trying to vanish.

"Then who would?" Jenks pressed. "Who would want to hurt the doctor?"

Or me—or you, Jenks. The bullet could as easily have struck the Runner, or Georgette herself. Was it a warning? A threat?

Hugo's eyes were closed in sleep, deeply shadowed. He seemed larger, laid out the length of the table. It was strange that a little ball of lead could have caused a strong man to bleed so, or that thirty tiny drops of liquid could have knocked him on his arse.

He had trusted Georgette to help him. He'd placed himself, literally, in her hands. Thank heaven she had proved worthy of his trust.

This time. She could not forget the shade of his voice when he'd said she'd hurt him, or that he didn't want her help. He might not have trusted her if the need were less immediate. She was not, after all, able to teach him anything he did not know.

Replacing the final medical supplies in the leather bag, she snapped it shut.

"I would never hurt the doctor," Lowe was saying. "He saved me life."

This was not an answer to Jenks's question, but it must have been satisfactory enough for now, for he turned his attention to the prone Hugo. Quickly, Georgette described what had passed. "The bullet is out now, but he can't live on this table until he's fully healed. Somehow, we've got to get him back to Raeburn Hall."

"There's no 'somehow' to it. I will walk."

This from Hugo, of course. His eyes remained shut, but he sounded perfectly alert. At his voice, Georgette's heart gave a startled kick. Curse the man; bless the man.

"I don't think that's wise," she replied. "Especially because you're meant to be asleep."

"I don't do things merely because I'm meant to. I do them if I believe there's good reason to." His eyes opened; then his lips curved. No one had ever looked so peaceful and so bullheaded at the same time.

She was not quite able to prevent her own lips from returning his slight smile. "I've no doubt of that. But as a personal favor to me, let us have one of Sir Frederic's carriages sent over for you."

Jenks sighed. "Mr. Lowe, I will return to speak with you another time. When you haven't the distraction of a man being chopped up on your table."

Georgette stuck out her chin. "I did not *chop up*—"

"Pax, please." Hugo swung his feet to the side of the table, then gingerly rolled upright. "No one chopped me up. I cannot stay on the table forever. I am awake and can walk back to the Hall. Everyone is correct, including me."

Without his coat on, his shirt and waistcoat clung to the lines of his chest. The sliced fabric over the right shoulder hung loose, showing the bandaging packed over his bullet wound. He looked like a pirate who had gone through battle.

The sight was, to say the least, appealing.

"I'll have more questions for you, Mr. Lowe," Jenks repeated. He eyed the man's wounded foot, and when he spoke again, his tone was less harsh. "When you're up to it. I believe we could help each other."

"Aye, then," Lowe agreed cautiously.

"In the meantime, I'll speak with Mr. Keeling," Jenks said. "Which is his cottage?"

"You'll pass it on the way back to Raeburn Hall." Brow puckered, Lowe gave the Runner directions. "But surely—he wouldn't—do you suspect him of doing . . ."

The remainder of the question was crushed beneath the weight of Jenks's stony stare. For a second time, farewells were exchanged. Hugo slipped his uninjured left arm into his ruined coat, and off they set.

The Keeling cottage was a slog along a muddy path. Low and thatch-roofed, it was nearly the same size and construction as the Lowes' house. Yet everything looked a little different. Maybe it was the scragginess of the smoke from the chimney, or the rust on the edges of the tools leaning against the side of the building. The house itself looked wary.

Georgette kept to Hugo's side in case she should be needed for support. They both hung back as Jenks knocked at the door. When it opened, a worn and sour-looking woman confronted the Runner. He questioned her briefly.

"Me man's with Sir Frederic, much good will it do him." Mrs. Keeling stood in the doorway, one shoulder hitched against the frame. "He's trying to get that bondager back from the Hall, but I won't have her here again for love nor money." With that, she shut the door in his face.

Jenks did seem to have that effect on people.

He rapped at the door again, then tested the handle. Mrs. Keeling wouldn't answer, and she had evidently latched or braced the door from the inside.

Eventually, then, on they went.

In later days, the process of getting a wounded, woozy, and stubborn Hugo back to Raeburn Hall was not one on which Georgette would prefer to dwell. He continued to refuse help, insisting that his feet were fine and could carry where he needed to go.

So they made progress along the path, slow and then slower. Jenks walked ahead on his own. Georgette held an umbrella over herself and Hugo to block drizzle, so she knew the trickles at his temples were the perspiration of effort. He was pale, and his breath came short and labored.

Yet he would not let her help him again, save for holding the umbrella. Which hardly counted as help, for he carried the bag of medical supplies in his left hand.

"Your stubbornness will be the death of me," she grumbled.

"That is medically impossible," he said. "I know my health well enough. This walk won't be the death of me, so it certainly won't be the death of you."

By the time they arrived at Raeburn Hall, they were all cold. Georgette's knuckles were a frozen vise from clutching the handle of the umbrella, and likely Hugo's were the same from carrying the medical bag.

After handing over these possessions to the capable butler Hawes, they found Sir Frederic in the study. With a generous fire built up, the small room was warm and soporific and pleasantly dim, scented of tobacco and coal. Their host was dozing, his head lolling against the upholstered back of the grand chair behind the polished desk. His hands were folded across his padded waistline, the picture of comfort.

Until Jenks called his name.

"What's that?" Sir Frederic jerked upright, his graying hair mussed and wild where it had pressed against the back of the chair. "Resting my eyes, that's all. What—Jenks? Mr. Crowe, what has happened to your coat?"

Hugo's jaw clenched. "I regard the damage to my coat but little." Once Georgette was seated, he eased himself into another chair with a groan that betrayed his fatigue.

"As you ought," Georgette retorted, "considering that a part of you was damaged as well. Surely that is far more significant."

"What's this?" Sir Frederic's brows lifted. "You've been hurt?"

Jenks held up a hand, seating himself on the edge of the baronet's desk with feet braced on the floor. "Hold a moment. Before we start reading out each other's diaries and wailing with sympathy, I need to speak to Mr. Keeling. We were told he was here."

The baronet's scowl at Jenks turned bewildered. "But he's not anymore. He left"—he looked at the clock on the mantel—"nearly fifteen minutes ago. Enough time for the warmth of the fire to drug me into a doze. Strong as laudanum, ha!"

"I doubt that," Hugo said mildly.

"Let me see . . ." Sir Frederic shuffled about some of the papers on his desk. It was huge, ornate, beautifully varnished to a mirror-deep gloss. Georgette could hardly look at it, for it threw her own reflection back horribly distorted.

The bookshelves were old and lovely, though, full of books in a scatter of different colors and heights. Unlike those in the library, it looked as if these had been collected over time from different sources, chosen according to interest and actually read.

"Ha, there it is." Sir Frederic laid hands on a sheet of foolscap and flourished it at Jenks. "Keeling has been plaguing the life out of me today, trying to get his bondager to move back into his house. Wrote me a note about it and everything."

Mouth a flat line, Jenks took the paper from him and skimmed it. Georgette craned her neck to try to read it—and as if noticing, Jenks held it up higher and closer to his chest.

Hmph.

"This says," the Runner commented at last, "that you owe him recompense. For what?"

"Why, for housing Miss Linton. What else could he

mean? I warned him before, he needs to be patient. Wait for the harvest and not try to reap his oats earlier." Sir Frederic paused, blinking. "I say, that's a clever one." With this inscrutable observation, he pulled forth a small pocketbook and scribbled a few lines in it.

When he looked up from his writing, he was all solicitude. "Now, what happened to Mr. Crowe? And his coat? His coat looks dreadful."

Hugo looked at Georgette. It was a speaking look, one she easily interpreted as *I lived it. I haven't the slightest urge to tell it. Especially if we're all to talk about my coat again.*

A fair point. "Just this," Georgette began, and she told Sir Frederic everything that had passed.

Almost everything. When she mentioned that Jenks had searched for clues while Hugo was treating Mr. Lowe's foot, the Runner kicked her in the ankle from his perch at the edge of the desk. This was both unnecessary *and* ungentlemanly. She hadn't planned to mention the scatter of fine gold droplets Jenks had noticed in the foundry. That seemed like a knowledge he and Hugo and Georgette had earned for themselves. With bullets and blood, no less.

"Good heavens," interjected Sir Frederic every few sentences. "You don't say! . . . Oh my . . . my, my, my . . . You did? . . . Oh, dear . . ."

When Georgette had acquainted him with all the particulars, everyone in the room exhaled at once. Only now did it seem their walk was truly over, her hands warm and her gown drying at the hem.

"My, my, my," said the baronet again. "What a dreadful morning for you. Simply dreadful." He looked about the study. "I haven't a decanter in here. Ridiculous oversight. I haven't yet had time to make this room my own, not entirely. But the wine cellar is up to London standards."

He rang for a servant—and when the butler appeared, Sir Frederic beamed. "Hawes, pick out something sprightly for us to drink. A Madeira, let us say?" He looked to the others expectantly.

"Indeed. Mrs. Crowe ought to have something fortifying," Hugo spoke up. "She has been through an ordeal."

"*I* have?" Oh, the stubbornness of him. "I'm not the one with a hole in my shoulder."

"Trapezius."

"Right. Right. I'll drink something fortifying if you'll drink double."

"I can't agree to that," Hugo said. "It would be excessive to drink so much wine after consuming laudanum. Besides which, it's not my sprightly beverage to promise away."

"*Minha casa é sua casa.*" The baronet's round face wore a genial smile. "Picked up a bit of Portuguese over the years. Yes, Hawes, a Madeira," he decided. "I had a pipe of it shipped from Portugal to my home in London last year, and it soon became a favorite. Had to bring it along when I inherited the baronetcy. The wine cellar here was *nothing* when I arrived."

Hawes soon returned with a crystal decanter on a silver tray polished to a diamond brightness. Wealth, wealth, wealth. The butler laid the service on the desk before the baronet and set a quartet of glasses down, then bowed from the study. Sir Frederic poured out, handing each person a glass of liquid the color of burnt sugar.

Georgette breathed it deeply, scenting spice and sweetness and the bite of alcohol. It smelled, of a sudden, like the most delicious and necessary drink imaginable. She tipped her head back and gulped it down.

"My dear!" Sir Frederic looked pained as she reached forward to set down her glass on the desk. "Take care. That wine is older than you!"

Not to mention, it was fortified with strong spirits that made her wheeze. The Madeira was sweet and coffee-bitter, with a warming bite as she swallowed it. "Sorry about that. I'm not at ease. This morning was not what I expected."

"You did well." This grunt came, surprisingly, from Jenks. He was holding his own glass dubiously. After he spoke, he set it down untouched.

Then he turned a dark glare on Hugo and Georgette. "You were both fortunate. But this is no longer a matter for amateur involvement."

They all peered at him curiously—then Sir Frederic spoke first. "What sort of matter are you discussing?"

"The gold. The bullet. Two bullets, to be accurate." Jenks's words were clipped. "Possibly the injury to the blacksmith's toes. Mr. and Mrs. Crowe, you two will stay in Raeburn Hall for safety until my investigation is concluded."

If Jenks had directed this order toward Georgette alone, she would have protested until her tongue went numb—or more numb than it already was from the gulped-down Madeira. But because he included Hugo, and because Hugo had bled on her hands today and drifted into unconsciousness, she would agree with anything Jenks asked.

Again, she was glad Hugo had given Jenks the bit of gold from Keeling. How had she once thought it beautiful? Finding gold that came coupled with gunshots was too great a risk for the possible reward.

Still. Even if she wouldn't take a dangerous chance, she couldn't stop wondering about the truth. Keeling gave out little pieces of gold. Lowe had been melting gold. Which of them provided it to the other? Or did they both get the gold from someone else? Were any sovereigns left, or had they all been melted into unrecognizable bits of metal?

As questions twirled and spun through her mind, Sir Frederic set down his own glass and leaned forward, resting his hands on his desk. "What," he asked, "did Mr. Lowe say about this morning's events?" His gaze flicked expectantly from one to the other.

Hugo sipped at his Madeira, looking every inch the gentleman despite his damaged clothing and bandaged shoulder. "Etiquette forbids asking probing questions of a man while bleeding onto his table."

"Well, I don't believe it does," Georgette replied. "But I didn't happen to think of asking Mr. Lowe his thoughts while Mr. Crowe was, as he said of himself, bleeding all over the table."

"Yes, of course." The baronet sank back into his chair, drumming his fingers on the desk. "But you *are* recovering, Mr. Crowe? You appear to be."

"I appear to be, yes." Hugo took one more sip of Madeira, then lined up his glass on the desk beside Georgette's and Jenks's.

His was not the certain reply for which Georgette could have hoped. "Aren't you able to heal? Didn't I clean the wound aright?"

"Oh yes," said Hugo. "You did perfectly. I only mean that not everything has been as it seemed today. But what has been true, and who has been honest, I cannot say."

Sir Frederic looked taken aback for a moment— then he laughed. "You sound like Jenks. Suspicious of everything, the old fusspot." Jenks made a resentful noise.

"Here, finish your Madeira," added the baronet. "Have another if you like. Two more, since your lady suggested it. And I'll order a nice beefsteak for dinner. Got to strengthen your blood."

They all parted, though not without more questions in Georgette's mind. As easily as planning a menu, a bullet wound was thus dismissed by Sir Frederic. Hugo, too, seemed all too willing to forget that a lead ball had passed through his shoulder—pardon, *trapezius*. And Jenks? He was no more or less single-minded than ever. For them all, this was much like any other Sunday, albeit with a few unusual events to be taken in stride.

But something in Georgette had been changed when Hugo cast himself in the path of a bullet, guarding her. Protecting her heart.

No; silly Georgette, to think so. No, he had only made her heart all the more vulnerable.

Chapter Fourteen

The next day, Hugo did not ask Georgette to check and clean his wound. In fact, she suspected that he never *would* ask. The barb he had tossed—not asking for help, not wanting her help—had found home.

But since she knew it needed to be done, and since he had got the wound by throwing himself in the path of a bullet to protect her, *and* since she couldn't bear the idea of him going through further pain alone, she decided she would see to the matter whether he asked her or not.

First, she had to find some strong spirits—and strong spirits were to be found with her host. Sir Frederic was in his study, wearing a perplexed expression as he paged through a cloth-bound volume.

She rapped at the frame of the door. "Beg pardon, Sir Frederic."

He looked up, and a smile flicked on as soon as he saw her. "Ah, good day to you! Do call me Uncle Freddie, please." With a confidential wink, he stage-whispered, "In case that dreadful Jenks is about."

That dreadful Jenks, Georgette knew, was *not*

about—though where he was, she was not sure. He was
gone back to the Lowes' cottage, maybe, or speaking
with Linton, or tracking Keeling.

Not so long ago, Georgette could not have imagined anyone whose enthusiasm for locating the stolen
gold sovereigns surpassed her own. Now she could not
fathom what carried Jenks into the grim rain and
through thankless conversations time after time, when
the only reward he foresaw was that of knowing justice
had been done. Justice was all well and good, but it
wouldn't keep him warm or provide him with pleasant
company.

But maybe he felt strongly enough about justice
that it took the place of the personal and the comfortable. Perhaps that was what it was like to have a
purpose.

"I confess, Uncle Freddie," Georgette said, "I am
here to beg you for spirits. I need to check and clean
Hu—my husband's wounded shoulder." The lie about
their marriage was more difficult to speak each time,
for it had to cover too much truth.

Sir Frederic set down the volume atop a stack of
others on his desk. "No idea what to do with these
books," he mused. "I suppose it's time I ship them off.
Well, that's not why you're here. Let me see—spirits.
Spirits, spirits." He eyed the decanter of Madeira.
The level of liquid within it was much lower than it
had been the previous afternoon.

"Not that," he decided. "Brandy would be more
medicinal, surely. But all the brandy I have is excellent." His brow puckered with distress. "It seems a pity
to pour it out."

"I'm not going to waste it. But I do understand,

you don't want a fine vintage used for anything but drinking before the fire. Have you nothing terrible?"

His eyes widened. "I would *never* keep anything terrible in my cellars." He looked doubtfully at the decanter. At the stack of books before him. At the fireplace, the window, then the decanter again. "No, no. What am I saying? The wound must be cleaned. You and Mr. Crowe must visit the wine cellar and select whatever you think best. Hawes can give you the key."

What a different sort of life, to have so many fine things that one was unable to use them. Yet Sir Frederic was not unwilling to help; he had been more than generous since Georgette and Hugo had arrived unannounced and unexpected at his door.

So she thanked him, promising to use the smallest possible amount of spirits, and retrieved the key to the wine cellar from the efficient Hawes. Then she fetched Hugo. He was reading in the library, his gold spectacles perched at the end of his nose. He was coatless, but his shoulder was pressed by a waistcoat and shirt.

"You oughtn't to have anything pressing on your injured trapezius," Georgette said by way of greeting. "It must be painful."

He looked up from his book, then rose to his feet. "Good day to you. You said trapezius. Well done."

"I'm not here to have my pronunciation praised. I'm here to drag you off to the wine cellar and splash something dreadful onto your bullet wound." She brandished the key at him, a huge, old, toothy piece with an ornate head.

He closed the book and set it aside with a look of distaste. "I cannot muster the proper enthusiasm for that subject. A pity."

"Do you mean the subject of having your wound

---

cleaned? Or are you reading about vegetable acids again?"

"The latter." He removed his spectacles gingerly with his right hand, nursing the shoulder, then rubbed at the bridge of his nose with his left. "Poor vegetable acids. I am sure we cannot live without them, yet I do not foresee a time when I will need to know of them in detail."

"You won't, unless you become a botanist. And though I wouldn't place that out of the realm of possibility, right now it's more important to place brandy on your shoulder."

Hugo folded up his spectacles and tucked them into his waistcoat pocket. "You are enjoying this, aren't you? Throwing caustic liquids at me?"

"Yes, I am. Because it's helping you."

When he blinked at her as if surprised, a sudden shyness made her add, "And because it's good for your medical career. You'll make a much less high-handed doctor if you know what it's like to be a patient."

"I probably ought to be offended by your use of the phrase 'high-handed,' but I grant the logic of the argument. Lead on to the wine cellar, then, and we shall see if our host stocks anything suitable for irrigating a bullet wound."

They made their way to the cellar door, which Georgette unlocked using the great key from Hawes. Rather than leave it in the lock, she pulled it free and stuffed it into the pocket of her gown. "I don't relish being locked in," she told Hugo. "I suppose I'm growing as suspicious as Jenks."

"I'm hardly going to chide you for displaying caution. Would you like me to descend first with a lantern?"

She would in fact like that, and once he had one lit

he preceded her into the wine cellar. Stone steps, narrow and unprotected by a railing, led into the earth. Georgette picked her way down carefully, left hand trailing against the wall.

Inside the cellar, the lantern flung forth a candle-brightness, and light wells cunningly set into the walls let in dim, filtered daylight. The room held a pleasant, dry coolness, bounded by stone walls and a ceiling curved like sloping shoulders. Stone ribs supported the ceiling, and the floor was flagged in the same buff stone from which the walls were constructed.

She had never seen a space like this room, which appeared snatched from a castle and stuffed incongruously under Sir Frederic's modern home. Along one side, barrels and casks were lined up. They stood on end, hooped in thick bands of iron, their contents branded on the lids. Their wood was pleasant-colored in the gentle daylight, everything from clean new ambers to deep gray browns of great age. At the other side, shelves formed a wooden grid along one wall, long as the room and divided into squares by vertical posts. Each was some degree full of glass bottles. Some were stacked horizontally, their bottoms turned out. Some were as fat at the bottom as an onion. These stood upright, listing slightly as if drunk on their own contents.

Some bottles were brown, some green, some dulled with age. Some were labeled by hand; others had press-printed labels. Some bottles were identified with letters scratched into the glass; some were unlabeled, but wooden plaques nailed to the shelves below identified the contents. It was a greater variety of spirits, more elaborately catalogued, than Georgette had ever imagined.

This, then, was Sir Frederic's true library. Not the room with the gaudy-bound books; not even the study.

One could learn a great deal about a person by examining his library. Sir Frederic's wine cellar told Georgette that he had traveled a little, bought a lot. That he liked to indulge himself so often that indulgence had become a habit. But many collectors were the same way. Book collectors, such as those who came to Frost's in search of rare volumes, would spend any amount to acquire what they wanted.

Perhaps that, too, was what it was like to have a purpose. She had wondered about that more and more since embarking on her journey with Hugo.

After the journey, she'd no idea what would come. But for now, her purpose was cleaning his wound. Finding stolen gold. Preparing to leave.

No time like the present, was there? Especially since she was with Hugo. Who wasn't wearing a coat, and who looked delicious, and who loved nothing more than preparing for anything he could think of.

"While we are in this cellar," Georgette said, "we could look for the stolen gold. Keeling comes to Raeburn Hall as he pleases. Doesn't this cellar look like the perfect place to hide something? How often do you think someone looks into every corner of this room?"

"Not often at all." Hugo trailed his fingers along one shelf, looking over the bottles resting there. "But Jenks has searched the whole house. And no one can enter the wine cellar without a key."

"Ah, yes. As Lord Science, you must consider every possibility and potential difficulty," she said. "But Bone-box, the horrid urchin, knows that someone who could steal four trunks of sovereigns from a Royal Mint would not stick at the theft of a wine cellar key."

"Meaning, if Jenks only searched once, he ought to do it again?"

"Or we ought to," said Georgette. "If someone is going to find the gold, it might as well be us. I lost my taste for it when you were shot, but—"

"Now that I'm recovering nicely, you've got a lust for treasure again?"

He blinked, evidently taken aback by his own words. Word? One word—*lust*, dropping unexpectedly into the room. It landed perfectly, like the first snowflake falling to nestle amidst the winter grass. The prelude to more, much more.

Or was she hearing only what she wished to? Looking for signs of her own desire in him? No one had ever accused her of lacking imagination. She fumbled for words. The right words. Words that would not reveal the tumble of emotion awakened by the sound of his voice, the movement of his hands.

"What looks good?" she asked, faltering.

"All of it, really." Hugo's brows were doing a sort of gymnastic affair, lifting farther and yet farther as he scanned the cellar shelves. "For drinking, that is. For pouring on a wound? I can't blame our host for being reluctant. He has thousands of pounds' worth of spirits down here."

"Fine. We'll get some lye."

"Not the same thing." He pulled forth a bottle of amber-colored glass. "Here's a malted whisky. That ought to hurt like the devil."

"That's how you know it's effective. I'll draw some off and we'll have this done."

Hugo handed her the bottle. "I will have to take off my shirt."

"Yes, that's true." She worked at the bottle. The cork was not pushed in completely, as though the bottle had been previously opened and enjoyed.

"I don't have to take it off all the way," Hugo added.

"I will not be offended if you do." She deserved an award for achieving that level of understatement.

When Georgette looked up from the cork, he was working at the buttons of his waistcoat. A grimace tightened his features.

"Let me, let me." She set the opened whisky bottle atop one of the barrels, then crossed the flagged floor to stand before him.

"Got it." Hugo slipped the last button free. Once he shrugged out of the waistcoat, grimacing again, he laid it aside atop another barrel. "I can't forget, I've got my spectacles in the pocket."

"I promise not to step on your waistcoat."

The fine linen of his shirt was enticingly thin, hinting at the outline of his torso. Could she see the dark hair on his chest? Would he need her to help him remove his shirt?

"See anything you like?" Hugo asked.

She reddened. "That is the most obnoxious question possible, so I cannot possibly answer 'yes.' Besides which, you are completely trespassing against the professional environment in which I'm conducting—"

"That's a lot of words to say 'Hugo, you caught me staring.'"

She could have clouted him, mainly because he was correct. He was also smiling—a quick, tentative flash of humor that vanished too quickly.

"All right, so you caught me staring. Should I apologize or tip you a saucy wink?"

"Let us say I was not offended."

He copied her words, the wicked man. It was not a strong statement of besottedness, alas. But it was better than no statement at all.

Next to be removed was the neckcloth. Hugo coaxed at the knot with the fingers of his left hand, wincing as he raised the right to assist.

"Let me help," Georgette said. "And don't say anything stubborn like, 'no, I don't need your help,' because you do."

"How often I have wanted to say the same thing to you. But you always become enraged when I so much as hint at the matter."

"Such hyperbole. You sound as if you're full of spirits already." Though she managed to keep her voice steady, a tremble began to resonate through her body. She was *undressing Hugo*. Her hands shook, her lips felt dry.

Desire was most distressing—but pleasantly so.

With his neckcloth off and laid atop the waistcoat, she was able to unfasten his shirt at the neck. She could see the dark hairs of his chest now, not merely imagine them. She wanted to touch them, to learn their texture. To feel the warmth of his skin and his steadily beating heart.

"You are shivering," he said.

"I am cold," she excused, drawing nearer. He smelled good, like spice and soap.

"So you always say."

Well, what else was she to say? It was the only response that preserved her dignity. She couldn't always be flinging herself into his arms, hoping he responded.

Up and off came the shirt. Yes, she saw something she liked. She saw Hugo, half bare, his chest and abdomen planes of muscle and bone. On his right side, the ridge of muscle from shoulder to neck—the trapezius, she would remember as long as she lived—was covered with a bandage tied off beneath his arm.

She liked the sight of him, yes, but the bandage made unease swim through her. "I hate that you were wounded."

"Georgette, I'm fine. Or I will be eventually."

She was no nurse; she could not keep her eyes dry at this evidence of his injury. "I wish it had not happened."

"I do not. If someone shot at us again, I would take the bullet for you. Every time."

She swallowed, but could not speak.

"I'm fine," he repeated, "because you are not injured. Now. Let's get the medical part over with, shall we?"

With hesitant movements, she undid the bandage. The wound was both better and worse than she had expected. She remembered it dimly from the day before, the dread that came coupled with Hugo's unconsciousness. What had happened to the bullet she had dug out? It must still be in the bag of medical supplies. *Ugh.*

Absent the blood and fear of the previous day, the wound appeared tidy. The *worse* bit was that it was there at all.

Hugo tilted his head, trying to glimpse it. "Can't see it. I should have brought a glass. But the bandage doesn't look bad. Within a week I might have full use of my arm again without pain."

"Does everything take a week to heal? Toes? Gun-shot wounds?"

"This one will, I think. The shot came from a small gun like a pistol, and from far away. If it had been closer, or the gun larger, the bullet would have passed through me. It could easily have broken some of my bones or hit a major blood vessel." Again, he craned his neck to one side. "If one must be shot, this is the way to do it."

Georgette retrieved the bottle of whisky. "If you keep talking about this, I shall cry, and then I'll be humiliated."

"Why?"

"Because I want to be as strong as you are," she blurted.

He looked at her with deep eyes. "Dear one, dear one." His voice was quiet as he gathered her into his arms. "There are so many ways to be strong. Honesty is one of them. Courage. Threats." He stroked her back. "Boldness. Intuition and determination. We'd never have got here without you."

"Since you were shot, I cannot think that a good thing."

"Then I must convince you otherwise."

He was very warm, and his arms about her were strong, and his hand on her back was gentle. And was he *aroused*? They were body to body, her hips pressing to him, and against her abdomen she felt the growing swell in his breeches.

He cursed, releasing her and stepping back. "Sorry."

"No. Wait." He had said honesty was a way to be strong? Well, then. "I want to know something. When you kissed me, while we were at the beach—did you want to, or were you just being kind after I had kissed you first?"

As long as Georgette did not ask, she could hope for the former. She had never meant to let herself tumble for a scholar, but Hugo had a way of being . . . *more.* More than she had expected, and leading her to be more than she had thought she could be. A friend; a nurse; a traveler. A woman desired?

As long as she didn't ask, she didn't know. It was better to know.

"I have told you and told you," Hugo said, "that I am not especially kind."

His jaw was set, his booted feet planted firmly on the floor. He looked like a man braced against a strong wind—or a man whose body and mind were at war.

"Pour the whisky on me," he grumbled. "It'll knock some sense into my head."

"Why sense?" she asked.

His expression was stormy. "Because even though you said you didn't want my help, you've had it during this journey. And I don't want to take advantage of the situation. Especially since I swore I'd see you safely to your brother."

She had to laugh. "So you think I'm hungering for you out of gratitude? Because you hired that coachman in Doncaster and paid his fare?"

"Well . . . gratitude doesn't hurt." The tense line of his shoulders relaxed a little. "Except that in this case, it might. And I don't want it to. You to. To be hurt."

"Lord. Hugo. Starling. If you are not especially kind—though I think you are—I am not particularly grateful. I've done what I wanted." She took a deep breath of the cool, wine-scented air. "And I want to do more."

"God help me." His left hand clenched into a fist. "I can't stay with you, you know. I have to go back to London. I have a hospital to build."

"Your stubbornness will be the death of us both," she said. "I'm not asking you to stay in North-umberland. I don't know how long I'll stay myself. I'm not thinking about a month from today, or even what happens when we leave this cellar."

"A rare gift, not to be tormented by so many plans."

"Perhaps it is." She stretched out a hand, as she'd wished to, and laid it on his chest. His heartbeat thundered under her fingertips; his skin was warm. Drawing her fingertips down his chest, his abdomen, she teased at the dark hairs that trailed toward his breeches in an intriguing line.

He jerked away, then took up the bottle of whisky and splashed it on his own wound with a hiss. Then he slammed the bottle down onto the barrel again. "There. That's done. Now I'm all yours."

If only. If she thought a month ahead, she would wish it to be the past week, again and again. "Like-wise," she said. Stepping close to him, she put her tongue to his collarbone. At the right, it was whisky-scented and hot to the taste. She trailed light kisses, the tip of her tongue, from one side of his collarbone to the other. He groaned, clutching at her shoulders.

"I've an idea." He twirled her about, then pushed her backward to bump against the wall of shelves. He caught up her hands. "Hold tight."

Mystified, she grasped the vertical post holding up a set of shelves.

He cursed again, and it sounded like praise. "May I . . ." His hand reached forward. She nodded, wanting nothing more than to have his touch. Liking that he wanted to touch her.

At first, his hands were determined but gentle as they traced her curves. He wanted to touch her, and he wanted her to like it. When had she ever been touched in this way? Had anyone else ever been so sweet? Not the boys she had kissed, who wanted what they could get of her. Often, when a woman was touched, it was rough, as though she were an object to be shoved out of one's path—or it was tentative, as if she were fragile, hardly human.

Hugo touched her now with a reverence that seemed leashed wildness. Wide-splayed fingers, stiff with the effort of restraint, cradled her outthrust breasts. Pleasure was a spike, driving her toward him weak-kneed. His troubled right arm, low at his side, found the curve of her hip and pulled her closer. Again, he was stiff against her. Clutching the vertical bar, she rubbed against him wherever she could. Her hip into his palm. Her thighs wide, her core pliant and damp. She twisted against him, craving more and more of his touch, until the shelves behind her rattled.

Rattled again. Rattled so alarmingly that she released the bar, turning.

"We'd best move, or I am going to break this . . ." She peered at the handwritten label below the shelf. "Brandy from 1795. Good God, it is older than me. I am sure Sir Frederic paid a fortune for it."

"Come sit, then, upon the famous Madeira." He took her hand, swung her in a neat semicircle toward the line of great barrels against the opposite wall, and helped her hop onto one of the largest. The barrel was old, with a lid of new wood atop it. It was as high as her waist, like all of them, but wider around than it was tall. Half a ton of fine wine, and she was sitting atop it, drunk without tasting a drop.

"This is entirely improper," Hugo said. "I acknowledge that. I have to acknowledge that."

"I acknowledge it too, but I don't care." She leaned back against the stone wall. "What has propriety done for us?"

"A good question. Thank you for asking it." He crouched before her. "Shall we explore what impropriety has done for us? Will you lift your skirt?"

Biting her lip, she pulled the pale blue fabric up to the tops of her boots.

"More."

Her shins, so he could see her stockings.

"More."

The skirt rose to her knees.

His hands covered her knees, tracing their bones and bends. He lowered his head, whispering against her stocking. "*More.*"

A throb of desire arced through her. Her sex clenched, damp. With trembling fingers, she rucked up her skirts more, until the garters of her stockings were revealed.

Hugo inhaled, sharp and shuddery. With his left hand, he followed the line of her garter. His fingers walked the ribbons, slipped beneath to touch the skin of her thigh.

"More," she said.

Slowly, he lifted his head. "You will be the death of us both." A smile, feral and enticing, crossed his features. "The little death."

And he spoke no more, for his mouth was on her thighs, on the curls of hair between. She gasped at the shock of it, gentle as the brush of a feather, intense as a storm. Her thighs tensed, knees falling apart—wide, then wider, as his lips and tongue found her most intimate places.

Together, they quested for her pleasure, her hands in his hair, his mouth pulling and licking at her sex. He was unmaking her, shaking her apart, and when she thought he had drawn her as far as she could be drawn, he pulled her to a higher, tighter pitch of pleasure. She was gasping his name, grasping his hair, heedless of everything in the world except the feel of his tongue. Then paused for a second, just enough to slide his left hand between her legs—and one strong finger slid into her at the same time he licked her heart of pleasure.

She fell apart at once, quaking under his touch, loving his touch, sighing his name.

When he rested his head on her thigh, breathing hard through his own desire, she opened her passion-drugged eyes to look at what they'd made of themselves.

Lord Hugo Starling, half bare and scented of whisky, had touched her as no one had touched her before.

Lord Hugo Starling, his muscle raw from being pierced by a bullet, had protected her from being shot.

Lord Hugo Starling, his words fighting her with each mile of travel, had never hesitated to bear her company.

She had not experienced so much of love that she would shy away from it, even in these small forms. Small enough, maybe, that to him they seemed only right, or sweet, or pleasant for an afternoon.

She had experienced enough of love to know that it was following her on quiet feet, ready to pounce. To capture her for him, and never to let her go.

Oh, she had been wrong: this afternoon, these illicit kisses and touches amidst a fortune in wine, would not be enough. The pleasure of a moment only made her want more.

Foolish fairy-tale reader that she was, she feared she would be satisfied with nothing less than ever, ever after.

Chapter Fifteen

Georgette never did search the wine cellar for gold sovereigns that day. And the following day, Hawes refused her the key, claiming that the oldest ports had become too agitated in the presence of an unfamiliar visitor. As if the bottles were people!

Although the way she'd twisted against the shelves, she'd probably stirred up more than a bit of sediment.

Jenks stood firm in his resolve to keep Georgette and Hugo within doors, so in the days that followed, she searched for gold sovereigns in the public rooms of Raeburn Hall. It was a fruitless search, undertaken with more determination than hope of success. Sometimes Hugo searched with her; sometimes he saw to patients who burst through the doors of the Hall in pain or with an illness.

In whatever way they spent the day, they seemed always to be under the watchful eyes of servants, or of Jenks, or even of Sir Frederic. It was enough to make Georgette wish she had never returned the wine cellar key to Hawes. With the excuse of Hugo's snoring— or was it Georgette's?—they kept to their separate chambers for a propriety no one much cared for anymore. At Hugo's side during the day but hardly able to touch him, she wondered what she had done to deserve such torment.

Well, no, she didn't wonder. She could think of more than a few examples.

Georgette peered in when patients came to consult Hugo, but he rarely needed her help. Even so, she always chatted with Matthew Lowe when he came from his parents' house to report on his father's healing. Since Hugo—whose own wound was healing nicely— was barred by Jenks from calling on the blacksmith, and the blacksmith could not walk to him, Matthew traipsed between the foundry and the Hall each day to provide the latest news on his father's health.

On the afternoon of a sunny, beautiful Friday that would have been much better spent outdoors, Matthew ventured as usual into the grand parlor of the Hall. "Pa and me, we both wonder if mebbies the sewing . . . um, the *sutures*"—the youth corrected himself—"could come out now."

"It's the thirteenth?" Hugo counted on his fingers. "No, I only put them in six days ago. Best not to take them out yet. Could he manage his way here tomorrow? I told Sir Frederic I'd spend the afternoon seeing patients, as I did last Saturday. I could check his sutures then."

"Can't you come see him, like?" Matthew twisted his cap in his hands, mouth screwed up in thought.

"If you'd like to have words with Jenks about that, please do," Hugo said. "I have tried to convince him his safety measures are excessive, but he won't be swayed."

Georgette raised her eyes to heaven. "How true that

is. Jenks said he couldn't have anyone interfering with his investigation, and he swore he would shoot Mr. Crowe again if either of us ventured out of the Hall."

"No," said Hugo in response to the boy's silent confusion. "It does not make any sense. But there you have it."

"I'll see how Pa does, then," Matthew said doubtfully. "I'll try to get him here t'morrow. Mebbies we could work out some crutches."

"If you can't, then come yourself to tell me how he goes on," Hugo said.

Matthew agreed, ready to depart. "Wait!" Georgette said. She had to do something so she didn't feel utterly useless. "Take some more honey with you. Here, I'll ring for it right now."

"Canny idea, that." Matthew settled his cap at a precise angle. "What the dogs didn't eat, the babbies did. Haven't put any on the sutures for a day or two."

With a jar of honey in hand, he bowed his way out.

Hugo seated himself in one of the wing chairs by the fire. "Please sit, Georgette, so I'm not being rude."

"Oh, anything to avoid rudeness." She dropped into the twin of his chair, facing him. "Enjoy the seat while you have it. These will be moved out tomorrow, replaced with those horrid hard chairs from the attics."

He stretched out his legs. "So it is planned."

"You love plans."

A thin smile bent his lips. "I do, yes. But what good does it do these people to make me a part of one here? Is it not better they should see the apothecary in Bamburgh, since he'll always be there?"

The thought of departing was troubling him? She guessed so, from the crease in his brow. Good; let him worry over the idea. Let him consider making a home somewhere besides London. Somewhere he wouldn't have to be alone with only his hospital plans for company.

"What an illogical question," she said.

"Is it really illogical?" Hugo looked so taken aback that she wanted to climb into his lap.

But there was a footman messing about at the sideboard across the parlor, and she had to behave. For the moment. "Of course it's illogical. Better they should see the apothecary than no one at all. While they can see you, though, better they should see you."

"How clearly you put the matter."

"Did I? Good. I am translating 'stop dithering' into your preferred vocabulary."

He ignored this. "If being shot wasn't so annoying, I would brave Jenks's wrath and visit Lowe. Waiting about for patients to come to me feels like wasting time."

She bit down hard on the words that wanted to spring forth. *Isn't that exactly what your hospital is intended to do? Bring the patients to you, to save the physician's time?*

Save it for what, was the question. As Hugo had nothing to do at present but read about vegetable acids and refuse nobly to steal the wine cellar key, she guessed he felt time to be ticking away fruitlessly. Certainly he reached for his nonexistent watch often enough, as if checking on the progress of his life.

"Whether you go to them or they come to you, you help people." Envy flashed through her, almost battering through her polite smile. He always knew what to do. There was always something he could do to be useful.

In short, he had a purpose. She was beginning to detest the word.

"I do," he granted. "But when I leave, no one else will care for these people as I have. And I don't mean that no one will care as much, or as well. I mean that other medical men will literally offer different care."

"Not to imply that you are arrogant—but is that not all right?"

"Probably it is arrogant." He looked troubled. "But most physicians would have bled Mr. Lowe to remove the infection from his blood. That is exactly the treatment that led to my brother's death."

Georgette stretched out her feet, knocking the toe of one slipper against Hugo's boot in sympathy. "Mr. Lowe is doing well. Maybe there are times a patient needs to be bled, but in this case he was fortunate you were here."

He knocked her slippered foot with his larger one. "Surely there are times it is right to bleed a patient, or it wouldn't be such a common practice. Yet I cannot think of any at the moment. If one's body does the healing—which it does, far more than any medicine I could offer—then the blood needs to carry the healing about."

Georgette held up a hand. "Wait. Healing isn't a *substance*. And you're starting to plan again, aren't you? You have that sort of distant, distracted look, and it's not because you've left off your spectacles."

He folded his arms.

"Aha. Yes. You *are* planning something."

He rolled his coat-clad shoulders, testing the movement of the wounded muscle. "I don't know what causes healing. And my plan, so to speak, is small: I need to talk to the apothecary. The nearest surgeon is too far away. The apothecary will be the best source of care for these people once we're gone."

He said *we're*, but it wasn't a together-sounding sort of word. It spoke of a time when they would be gone from here, and he would have his hospital to build.

Don't go, she wanted to beg. But such had always been his plan, organized as if there were boxes to tick. The travel, the gold, the return, the hospital. Adding in "the apothecary" was a subclause to the gold. So, she supposed, was she.

It was more difficult to be honest about what she wanted outside of the hidden bounds of the wine cellar. Truth had seemed smaller there, easier to admit.

She stood up, knowing manners would make him creak upright as well. "Good luck to you. I admit, I'd prefer you not to be shot again, so perhaps you could ask Jenks to have the apothecary sent here."

He stood to match her, face set in grave lines. "It seems silly, maybe, to care so much. But for a younger son of a duke, for whom so much of life is plotted out and inessential, any chance to"—he halted, fumbling for the right word—"to *matter* must be seized."

"Poor sons of dukes," Georgette murmured. "They have the most difficult lot in life."

"It has been some days since I was provoked into cursing in your presence. Please do not goad me into ending my proper streak."

"What has propriety ever done for us?" She could *feel* the curious gaze of the footman on them, so she settled for drawing a finger along his jawline.

He caught her hand up in his—and before releasing it, he pressed it to his lips. "I have a plan for you as well, Miss Impudence. Do not think I have forgotten that tomorrow is your birthday. You told me the date of it when we visited the beach."

"Oh . . ." she replied with stunning inadequacy.

"Beg pardon, but right now I'm going to see about having the apothecary summoned," Hugo said. "Until later?"

"Uh—" she replied.

"Right," he said. "Glad we're in agreement."

When he left the room, she sank into the embrace of the wing chair. Let the servants look and wonder; they couldn't see through her proper facade to the turbulence of her dreams.

So easily, Hugo's plans set her to dreaming: not of a treasure in gold, but of kisses. Of looks that made her tremble and flush; of nearness that made her ache with want. She could almost forget that she and Hugo were in Northumberland only because of rumor and stolen treasure, not because their lives were truly connected.

But if they were . . . it would be like home.

She'd dreamed of a cottage once, all hers, planted about with flowers and herbs and vegetables. Something that would allow her to be fine on her own, not reliant on help that might never come.

Now her dream was changing, the little stone cottage stretching to three stories and some sixty rooms. The soft Kentish landscape wiped into starkness and space and rain-soaked fields, with a castle in the dim distance to keep guard over the border with Scotland.

And she wasn't alone in this dream, for Hugo was with her. He wanted to be with her, just as . . . as she wanted to be with him.

She must have dozed, for a hammering at the door

of Raeburn Hall jolted her upright. Heavy lids blinking, she looked about. The cold grate—the slant of the afternoon light—oh, right. She was in the parlor. About an hour must have passed. Surely that wasn't enough time for the apothecary to arrive? Would an apothecary knock with such urgency?

She stretched, rolled her shoulders, and shook off the clinging threads of drowsiness. Then she strode to the entrance hall to see what the fuss was about.

Already, a crowd had gathered there. Everyone from Hawes, who managed to look not at all curious, to Linton, who managed nothing of the sort. Oddly, there was no one present whom Georgette did not recognize from the household.

And then she saw Jenks, leaning against the door. Folding a paper and stuffing it into his coat pocket. Looking inscrutable as ever, but with a flick of urgency to his movements.

"What is it?" Georgette was the first to ask the question everyone wanted answered. "Another express?"

Jenks blinked, as if only now noticing the number of people about. "My apologies for the disruption. Yes, another express."

"Are you going to tell us what is in it, Mr. Jenks, or should I pick your pocket later?" Georgette asked.

"I wouldn't recommend you do that, Mrs. Crowe," said the Runner. "I suppose I can tell you all. The news will be in papers soon enough. This express comes from my colleague in the village of Strawfield, in Derbyshire. Three of the six stolen trunks of gold have been recovered, and one of the four thieves arrested."

"Bless my soul!" Sir Frederic had emerged from his study, blinking owlishly at the hubbub. "Half the gold, one of the thieves. That is progress, is it not? That is true progress."

"The thieves," Jenks added with asperity, "call themselves 'the John Smiths.' The man arrested swears he cannot identify any of the others."

"One thief caught, though," Sir Frederic said heartily. "That is good! Surely the most important thing is recovering the gold. Let the other criminals go where they will. If they haven't the gold, what harm have they done?"

"A great deal, sir," said the Runner. "The so-called John Smith who was arrested has killed a woman in Strawfield. Four guards at the Royal Mint, too, were killed. And the unfortunate whose body was found burned near Doncaster is likely another victim of the thieves."

The hubbub turned to a hush. Even Sir Frederic's bluff cheer vanished.

"People get so excited about the gold," said Jenks, "that they forget about the blood spilled. But I have not, and I won't."

Six lives for six trunks of gold—good Lord. It was not a worthy trade. There were other human losses that might be related, too. Like Lowe's injured foot. Keeling's harassment and rape of Linton, for which he recompensed her with a bit of shining metal.

"Now that the Derbyshire investigation is concluded, should we expect the nation's treasure hunters to move north, Mr. Jenks?" This was the contribution of Hawes, whose question was posed in a silky accent without a trace of anxiety. "Shall I prepare more rooms, Sir Frederic?"

"No need for that, surely." Jenks was the first to

answer. "If anyone comes hunting for treasure here, he'll be disappointed."

"Because there's nothing here! I have been telling you so." Sir Frederic clucked, his round face the picture of wounded pride. "Well, you are to be leaving soon, then. Yes?"

"I didn't say any of that, Sir Frederic." Jenks's impassive stare met the baronet's, then held it until Sir Frederic blinked, shuffling his feet. "And no, I'm not leaving yet."

In his tone was a mild chastisement to their host, but Georgette felt it directed toward herself as well. She and Hugo had met no one else looking here for the stolen sovereigns. This meant that she alone, of all the gold-mad seekers in England, had pursued the stolen sovereigns so relentlessly north. She alone had stalked this Bow Street Runner, using his intelligence to sneak her way along the correct path.

She was ashamed. She had thought only of the glitter of the coins, of what they could do to change her life. She had forgotten all those people whose lives had already been changed, and those whose lives had been ended.

"I will help you, Mr. Jenks," she said. "However I can."

Chapter Sixteen

Why were these men so stubborn? Jenks, as Hugo once had, refused her help. "Keep yourself safe," he said. "That will be help enough. And don't do anything foolish that will force me to shoot you or Mr. Crowe."

Hugo, like Jenks, was busy for the rest of the afternoon. While Jenks did God knew what in response to the news contained in the express, Hugo did, in fact, meet with the apothecary. The two men parted happy on both sides—one having learned more about rural medicine, the other having got to pick the brain of a physician who also happened to be a duke's son.

In short, everything seemed to be in process without her. Which meant that Georgette awoke the morning of her twenty-first birthday with nothing to do but formulate a scheme.

She had forgone so many pleasures for years, working in the bookshop for her parents. Working for Cousin Mary and her husband. Doing whatever was needed. Love had been confined to the occasional kiss with an almost-stranger at the servants' entrance to the building. It had taken place in seconds, only to be soon regretted.

At least, that was how life had been before she clambered reluctantly into Lord Hugo Starling's carriage. Now she knew what love was, and a moment was no longer enough—even as she feared it. So easily, she could let her hungry heart love him. But she must not, for to love someone was to need him, and she had no illusions that he needed anything of her. Every touch, every kiss between them, she had begun.

She would begin something new, now. Something for them both, but also just for her, to hold to in the moments after their journey was ended. Once the gold was found or lost forever. There would still be a reward.

It was her birthday, and she wasn't going to forgo any pleasures today.

Hugo collared her in the corridor as she exited the breakfast parlor. "Good morning, Madam Birthday. You look lovely."

She curtsied. She had contrived an out-of-the-ordinary gown today, and she liked feeling the skirts swirl about her legs. To a white muslin dress, sweetly embroidered and beaded at the bodice, she and Linton had stitched an overskirt of sheer golden silk. The fabric had begun life as a shawl, but it was far more useful for making one pretty than keeping one warm. "Thank you for the kind wishes, Lord Non-Birthday. Fine feathers make fine birds—but if you want to tell me the bird is fine too, I won't mind."

"The bird makes the feathers fine." He took his spectacles from his waistcoat pocket, then put them back.

"Are you fidgeting?"

"Not at all." He hesitated. "Maybe. I told you yesterday I had a plan in mind. But I do not know whether you will like it."

"I don't either. I haven't enough evidence to go on until you tell me what it is."

He smiled faintly. "I have had an influence on your vocabulary, I see. I do not know whether that is a good thing."

She leaned against the brightly papered wall of the corridor, tucking her hands neatly behind her back. "Of course it's a good thing. I'm teasing you, and you could use teasing. What is the gift?"

"It's . . . no, it's no good. I'll take you to the apothecary in Bamburgh, and you can pick out sweets or powders or whatever you like."

His level of hesitation was intriguing. "Every time you demur, I become more certain I am going to like the gift. As long as it's not a bullet through your other trapezius, which Jenks would contribute if we left the house."

He leaned against the wall beside her, nudging her hip with his. "Well. I thought I would give you a day. The whole day, in which I'd do as you wished."

"Like a servant?" She wrinkled her nose. "But servants are paid to take orders."

"Not like that, no. Like . . . a friend. Or something. Because I know you like to be with people who care about you."

The "or something" was intriguing as well. And the rest of the offer was too sweet, shaking her as if she'd breakfasted on chocolate and wine rather than toast and tea.

"Who would not wish to be with people who care about one?" She spoke lightly to cover the embarrassing depth of emotion evoked by his simple words.

It was a normal wish, surely. For Georgette it had always been her fondest one. Doubtless there were people for whom love was a bedrock, hardly noticed in its steady permanence. But when one grew up with parents as busy as they were distant, love was a shifting sand. What allowed a structure to be built one day might be the same thing that toppled it the next. She was never certain of anything, except that she must work as hard as ever she could. To become indispensable in small ways, which were better than no ways at all.

What could she work at now, though? The offer of a day of Hugo's time left her uncertain of how best to use it.

He would do as she wished, he said. "But," she realized, "you cannot give me the whole day. You are promised to see patients in the parlor beginning at one o'clock."

He let his head fall against the wall with a thud. "You are right. How could I forget?"

"How could you have arranged two things for the same time? Tut, tut. Your admirable plans have outgrown themselves."

"What about tomorrow instead? If that would do, I could—"

"Stop." She placed her fingertips on his lips, gently. "It is a wonderful gift, and I want it today. We shall just have to make excellent use of the morning."

"Do you have something in mind?"

"In fact, I do." She traced the shape of his lips with careful fingertips. "If you will truly do as I wish, then I want you to love me."

Yes, Hugo thought at once. And then: What had he got himself into?

Catching her fingers up in his own, he pulled them from his lips. "What do you mean by love?"

"I don't know." She looked troubled. "What does it mean to you?"

Why could she not ask him about vegetable acids, or about the composition of the bullet that had pierced his shoulder the previous week? Something easy to answer. Something definite.

"It means . . ." He twined his fingers with hers. "Oh, a million little things. And before you ask, no, that is not a precise number. That's only an estimate."

She swung his hand with hers, bumping it lightly against the rail of the wall. "Hmm. Give me a few examples from that million."

He pondered this. In his early life, love had been inextricable from the double soul he shared with his twin. So long and so well had they known each other, it was as if they shared a life, and whatever happened to one was known and felt by the other.

But Matthew was gone. Had been gone for a long time, and so was that idea of love. Love now was smaller, more everyday. It had to be, or the pierce of it, the loss of it, could not be borne.

"Love is . . . laughter after a joke that isn't all that funny," he said. "Asking how a day was, and listening earnestly to the answer. Splitting the last tart instead of eating it all oneself."

Somehow he was managing full sentences, when she had asked him to *love her*, and her hair smelled sweetly of some sort of flowery soap. He could remember what it had looked like unpinned, down about her shoulders. Though she'd been wearing scrubby boys' clothing at the time, she had been beautiful. She could not help it. She was joy, and intrigue, and mystery. She was brave in ways he had never thought of being brave.

"It is," he added, "putting down a book for one's companion when one only wants to read."

"That is love indeed." She sounded grave.

"You are teasing me? After I thought up such excellent examples?"

"Not at all. I like them very much. I have seen more of such examples shown to others than I have known myself; that is all."

He wanted to punch the whole indifferent world. Instead, he said, "Well, what can I do for you? Shall I pick up a book and put it down when you speak? Shall we find a single tart to split? But since it is your birthday, I will likely give you the whole thing."

"No, that's not what I want." She dragged in a deep breath, then blurted, "I want you to make love to me."

Yes, he thought again—then sense collared him. "What? I—no, I can't do that."

"Because you are . . ." The minx. She flicked her gaze down to his breeches. "Incapable? Oh, dear. How unfortunate."

"*Not* for any anatomical reason. But because I'm here to protect you."

"From what?"

He looked about, catching sight of a maid at the end of the corridor. She was out of earshot, but this was *not* the sort of conversation one had before servants. Tugging at Georgette's hand, he pulled her into the nearest chamber and knocked the door shut behind them.

It could serve equally well as a parlor or a storage room, so full was it with furniture. A wardrobe stood against one wall; a trio of wing chairs were arrayed before the cold fireplace. A small pianoforte was stacked with sheet music, and ornaments cluttered the mantel. It was all free of dust, which meant the servants had likely finished in here for the day.

This would do. This would do very well.

"What do you think you must protect me from?" Georgette shook free of his grasp, then walked to the wardrobe.

Her question ought to have been easier to answer. "From . . . from . . . danger," he fumbled. Sentences were more difficult to form when *make love to me* echoed in his ears like the silence after a gong was struck.

"I'm not in danger right now." She pulled open the wardrobe doors, one after the other, and peered inside. "Oh, how cunning. Look, the right is all drawers and shelves. The left could fit all my gowns and leave room for me besides."

Suiting her actions to her words, she stepped inside the cavernous piece of furniture. "Without any gowns in here, I think there's room for two. Won't you join me?"

"Your wish today is my command." He crossed to stand before the wardrobe, then eyed it with skepticism. "I understand wanting to avoid the servants, but why must we go into a small enclosed space?"

She pressed against the far wall of the wardrobe, crouching. "So you can't get away from me."

"I've no desire to."

"Good, but not good enough." She swallowed. "What do you desire?"

"Many things."

Her eyes were clear as the morning sky. "Please be more specific."

He stretched out his arms, bracing each hand against the partition in which she stood. His wounded muscle hardly twinged now. "Do you want a hypothesis? A hypotenuse? A hypocaust?"

"No. I want . . . a purpose. A plan. Now that you've caught me in the wardrobe—"

"Is that how it went?"

"—surely you've a plan for me."

She looked so desirable, all flushed with hope and a beckoning smile. Not a siren at all; just Georgette, joyful and clever. When she turned the full force of her enthusiasm on him, a delightful sort of quiver raced down his spine.

He tried to fight it. "It smells horribly of camphor in there. You cannot think I could seduce you under such circumstances."

"It's not a seduction if I ask for it. And you can consider the camphor a challenge. Can you bring me to pleasure without the help of a barrel of Madeira?"

If she put it *that* way . . .

He clambered into the wardrobe.

It was even more awkward than he'd expected it to be. His shoulder banged the back of the piece; his boots trampled the hem of her gown. The wardrobe was not quite as tall as Georgette; it required a slight duck of her head and made Hugo crouch. Or bend— but if he bent, his face was almost in her bosom.

Very well, he'd bend. And he'd swing one of the doors shut around them too. "I'm only doing this because you begged me," he said. "Though if you'll give me a moment, I shall beg you."

"For what?" She sounded breathless. In such tight quarters, in the near dark of the wardrobe, every word echoed, every movement of hers pressed against him.

Lord Hugo Starling, youngest surviving son of the Duke of Willingham, always made the intelligent choice. The logical choice. The choice with the long view in mind.

"To touch you," he said. "A bit. Or a lot, but—not irrevocably. I don't—mustn't—"

"You hesitate now?" She found his hand in the darkness. "As if a few minutes in a wardrobe would mark the difference between propriety and ruination?"

"That depends on how those minutes are spent." He had ideas. He had nothing but ideas.

The first of them was lifting their linked hands to her breast.

She moaned, pressing into his touch. Her hand slid up his arm to his shoulder. "We have passed days and nights together. If we were compromised, it happened long ago."

But she had not been, because he had seen to that. He'd spent wakeful nights on the floor, or locked into a chamber down the corridor from hers. He'd seen her safely to bed, and safely to rise.

Now, though, she'd been compromised beyond a doubt. He had seen to that, too.

"*Compromise*," she added, "is only a word for rules made by others."

Strictly speaking, she was right. "So is *law*." His fingertips made slow circles about her nipple, drawing it to a tight peak within the bodice of her gown. "So are other ideas with which we live, like *propriety*. And *manners*."

"None of which is relevant right now. Oh—oh, I like that. What you're doing with your fingers—do that forever."

He was hard, stone-hard, and getting harder with each caress. "If I weren't watching out for you, I'd do so much more than this."

"I never asked you to watch out for me." Her legs opened to a wider angle, knee bumping the door of the wardrobe. She slid up the line of his thigh, riding it.

Oh God, he could feel the warmth of her. He wanted to be in that sweet heat, plunging deep. "I know, I know." He thumped his head against the low ceiling of the wardrobe. "I'm doing it because it matters to me. I want you to be all right."

"And why would groping me only a little be the thing that keeps me all right?" Her hips rolled, pressing her more firmly against him.

So many clothes, so little space, and the scent of camphor was making him dizzy.

"Damn your unassailable arguments," he said, and ignoring the protest of his injured shoulder, took her in his arms. Booting open the door to the wardrobe, he half dove, half toppled, landing on the carpeted floor of the little room. Georgette fell atop him in a tangle of limbs, laughing.

But when he caught her lips with his, she stopped laughing at once—and she returned the kiss with delightful enthusiasm. It deepened, sweetened, flamed hotter, and then her hands were in his clothes and his hands were in her bodice, and she was stroking his belly as he rolled and pinched one of her nipples.

He hadn't planned for this. He had planned a hospital, he had planned to leave, he had planned—oh *God*, she was undoing the fall of his breeches and taking his cock in her hands.

With her gold-and-white skirts rucked up, she straddled his thighs. A bridge to temptation. She held his shaft, and he had to grit his teeth not to pump his hips. "What are you doing?" he groaned.

"How will you love me?" she asked.

"With my hands." He gasped as she stroked him, long and hard. "With my mouth. But not with my cock. I can't—we can't."

Her cheeks flooded with pink. "I never thought to hear you say that word."

"You thought about me saying *cock*?"

"I have thought about many things"—she worked his length in her fist, taking cues from his every twitch and quiver—"that you would never suspect."

"I'm getting the idea now."

"And why can't I have everything?"

"It would"—he shuddered from scalp to toe—"it would take away your choices. You could never choose another to be your first."

The movement of her hand paused. "And?"

He cast about for threads of sense. "If you fell pregnant, we'd have to wed. You'd have to tailor your life to suit mine." An image flashed through his mind: Georgette, surrounded by papers and plans, joyless. "I wouldn't force those choices on you, or take from you any others."

"I see. Very noble." With a slow slide, she began stroking him again. "Very logical."

"Ugh." Nobility and logic were stubborn bastards. And he was only human, and if she kept touching him like that, with her sex visible and lovely when he did no more than lift a drape of her skirts . . . oh, it would be the sweetest disaster imaginable. Right now they wanted the same thing, but only in this moment. Eventually the future would become the present and split them from each other.

"What will you give me instead, then?" she asked, and he had an idea.

"You'll like this," he said. "I think." He shifted to sit

upright, and they faced each other—sitting on a carpet
in a near-forgotten room of a near-forgotten Northumberland manor house, their clothes awry, both
desperate with arousal.

"We can do this together," he suggested. "I'll touch
you, you touch me."

Her eyes fell closed. "Yes. Yes."

Their bodies moved closer together, close enough
for hands to roam. For him to pluck at her hard nipples, to stroke her neck and the soft skin of her inner
thighs. To wait until she was rolling her hips, making
little moans of anticipation, before he caressed the
folds of her sex. He sank one finger deep, then pulled
free and buried two in her. She was wet and tight and
wonderful, wriggling and coaxing, her touches on his
shaft growing ragged and fractured until, riding his
hand with a cry of passion, she climaxed.

He had waited only for that, and he spilled with a
force he had not experienced in years, jetting hard
and hot over her fist. The shock of it seemed to go on
forever, to end far too soon.

Georgette flopped down beside him. Spent and
panting, he drew a handkerchief from a waistcoat
pocket and wiped her hand clean, then tucked the
soiled cloth away.

"That was wonderful," she said. "I loved it. Both of
it. Them. The—thing you did . . ."

"Likewise." He was too fuddled to say more. He'd
meant to honor her birthday, but he had received this
unimaginable gift. An interlude of passion and sweetness, respect and mischief.

He never wanted to leave this room. Which was just

as well, because he couldn't move. He felt as pliant as if he'd melted into the carpet.

After an interlude of recovery, during which sense returned in a slow wash, he shoved himself to a seated position and righted his clothing. Stretching and drowsing, Georgette did the same to her bodice and skirts.

How much time did they have? He pulled out his watch—oh, no he didn't. Damn. He still had not got it through his head that his watch was gone. Well, there was a clock on the mantel, and if it had been wound aright, they had several hours before patients would arrive at Raeburn Hall for treatment.

"Come sit with me," he said. Shoving his way between the too-large wing chairs, he settled into one and held out his arms in unmistakable invitation.

She accepted it. "Thank you," she said.

That was all she said, and he could pretend it referred to anything. Everything. *Thank you for being awkward with strangers so I could dress as a boy and harangue them. Thank you for stopping the carriage so I could pet a sheep. Thank you for planning a wonderful hospital.*

Thank you for holding me.

"You are welcome," she said, nestling against his uninjured shoulder—and he realized he had spoken his last sentence aloud. "Does this hurt?"

Yes. It hurt. But not because of the bullet wound.

As she settled deeply into his arms, he felt a great weight on his chest. It was the pain of a heart being squeezed, the heaviness of knowing she had had to live so long without being treasured.

Today, he hoped he had made her feel treasured.

But what about all the days after? Who would be there for her then?

She would say, he knew, that she didn't need anyone. But what she needed and what he wanted her to have were increasingly disparate.

"Let me take out your pins," he said. "So you can be more comfortable."

She lifted her head, obliging. Pin by pin, he loosened her hair. Only one side, the side that she wanted to rest upon him, then he set the pins aside and held her again.

He cradled her like that, looking into the empty grate at nothing in particular. Just sitting, being with her, minute after minute. Time ticked by, and there was nowhere else he wanted to be, and no one else he wanted to be with—and then a light snore told him she had fallen asleep.

He smiled. "I told you you snored," he whispered.

She snored again. It was a sweet little sound, not one that would ever wake him from slumber. It was quiet, a sound of peace and comfort.

"I wish you had been adored every day of your life," he said.

"Mm?" Without opening her eyes, she made a questioning sound.

"Nothing, nothing. Go ahead and rest." With the arm that embraced her, he pulled free the rest of her hairpins, letting her hair down in long waves. They spread over her shoulders and back like a cloak, not like an intimacy revealed.

"You have me," he whispered. "For now."

She didn't hear him, dozing as she was, but he shouldn't have added "for now." He had always planned for theirs to be a temporary alliance; it seemed he needed reminding of that fact. Soon enough, he would be back in London, and she'd be with her brother, and they would all plan themselves a tidy little life.

Logic. Forethought. He must remember these. For when he was guided by anything else, the result was pain that lasted a lifetime.

Chapter Seventeen

The mind of Lord Hugo Starling tended to be a cluttered place. His thoughts were scattered between what was now and what was next, budgets and books, hospital plans and memories he would prefer to avoid, people to visit and letters to write.

Writing these things down eased the chaos within. Order without made him feel more at peace.

But in the wardrobe with Georgette, in the wine cellar with Georgette, on the beach with Georgette, he had written nothing, yet he had been at peace. He had been *then*, wholly then, and he had enjoyed the moment as he dwelled within it.

He had held her, and it had been a gift.

The realization came that afternoon, as he scanned the patients gathering in the makeshift waiting-space of Sir Frederic's largest parlor. He felt as though he could diagnose any ailment, cure any ill.

It was a feeling unbolstered by fact or evidence. But it was a nice feeling all the same.

And he hadn't done so badly by these people. There was the boy who'd come in the previous week with a throat complaint. He was sitting in his mother's lap, wiggling and chattering to Georgette as he—ate honey from a jar with a spoon? *Georgette.* There was nothing she would not do for these people. He only hoped the bees of Northumberland were up to the task she set for them.

Keeling was here, which meant he wasn't with Linton, which was to the good. And there was Mr. Lowe, working his laborious way across the rich parlor carpet on makeshift crutches. His booted foot held his weight; the heavy bandage on the other was dirty and dusty—but not, as far as Hugo could see, stained with signs of infection. Good, good. He had been walking about, then, not always using the crutches.

When Hugo left here, as he must, these people would be all right without him. He'd met the apothecary the day before. A young man named Simpkins, he had brought an ingenious traveling case full of tinctures and tonics and compounds and unguents in stoppered vials. Hugo had taken note of their arrangement, with thanks; Simpkins had requested recommendations on a few medicinal volumes, with the same.

Best of all, Simpkins did not feel called upon to bleed those who purchased items from his shop. If people kept all their blood, they had a far better chance of healing.

Or so Hugo thought. But he was generally right about what he thought.

He had cleaned his hands and was emerging from behind the folding screen, deciding whom to see first, when he spotted Jenks. Jenks, moving among the chairs, making some brief inquiry of each person followed by a penciled note in a pocketbook.

Hugo crossed the room to his side. "Mr. Jenks, what are you doing?"

"Checking who's been here in the last week. Need to put you on the list, don't I?" The Runner wrote another note, then turned toward the doorway. "Here we go, then."

Servants were filing into the room: housemaids, kitchen maids, scullery maids, footmen. Grooms and stable hands, with straw in the mud of their boots. Gardeners, their hands dirty from their work. The cook, the butler, the housekeeper. Linton entered too. As each filed in, mystified—and the maids more than a little horrified at the state of the carpets—the room grew closer. Crowded. The farmworkers already present shifted their chairs or vacated them entirely, pressing against the far wall of the room.

Last of all, Sir Frederic entered. His bulk filled the remaining space nearest the doorway. "What's all this, then, Mr. Jenks? Are we to put on a show for you?"

"You summoned the entire household?" At Jenks's nod, Hugo's bewilderment grew. "Did some contagion pass through? Does everyone require treatment? I've no supplies for inoculation, but I could—"

"It's not a medical matter, Doctor." Jenks tucked away his pocketbook and pencil, then clapped his hands. "Your attention, please. Your attention, everyone."

Hardly did he lift his voice, but silence rippled through the room, stilling every tongue. Every eye turned to the Runner, curious or wary.

Hugo took a step back. Whatever Jenks had planned, it surely didn't involve him. He didn't need to be in the man's pocket. In fact, he could check over the medical supplies and make sure the servants had laid everything out as he—

"Don't think to slip away, Mr. Crowe," Jenks said.

Hugo halted, startled. "I beg your pardon?"

Jenks turned his attention back to the room as a whole. "I've gathered you all here because you were in this house sometime over the past ten days. That is when I last searched the house and found it free from criminal evidence. This morning, I found a cache of the sovereigns that were stolen from the Royal Mint in May."

The pause that succeeded these words was heavy. The news was so sudden that Hugo could hardly take it in. After all this travel, all these weeks, the coins were just . . . found?

"All of them?" asked Sir Frederic, at the same time Georgette said, "Where?"

"Not all of them. A small number." Jenks frowned. "They were placed upon my bed. Clearly, a taunt. And most likely it came from someone here in this room."

With narrowed eyes, he scanned the gathered throng. The room was beginning to grow too warm. "There might be a person or two I've missed. Someone who came to be looked at by the doctor last week, but who didn't return. If you know of any such person, name him now."

Keeling spoke up at once. "Me wife isn't here this afternoon. She's been here mebbies three times in the past week."

What a prince, throwing his wife's name out for suspicion. Jenks seemed to feel the same way. "I've spoken to Mrs. Keeling recently and am satisfied of her innocence."

"That's more than I can say, like," the hind grumbled.

"Sir Frederic," said Jenks. "Which of these people have you invited, and who entered unknown to you?"

The baronet looked about the room helplessly. "Why, every one of them was welcome. Today. Last Saturday. The first Friday of the month, when I see all callers." He drew up his stocky form, puffing his chest. "The only person here I did *not* invite was *you*."

"Hmm." The Runner seemed unperturbed. "You weren't expecting other visitors, were you? A niece, say, and her . . . husband?"

Oh. Shit.

Hugo's gaze flew to Georgette. Amidst the crowd, tucked between a footman and a housemaid, she looked as calm as Jenks. She even shot Hugo a wink.

The woman loved melodrama. But she was right in her calm: they hadn't done anything wrong. Much. Besides lying to a Runner about who they were.

Sir Frederic was speaking again. "Merely because I don't confide all my plans in you, Mr. Jenks, doesn't mean they don't exist. I don't want to tell you everything, because I don't know you."

"Nor do you know your other guests. Or your tenants, with whom you've met only a few times since attaining the title." Jenks was as calm as ever.

Sir Frederic took this in, his puffed-up chest sinking like a balloon. "Can it be?" His whisper carried through the silent room. "My own niece? My nephew by marriage?"

What? "Come now, Sir Frederic," Hugo said. "We're perfectly innocent." He snatched at a vague memory. "You must know that. Mr. Keeling gave gold to his bondager before we ever arrived."

The baronet went the color of a custard. "You accuse me of conspiracy? With my own hind?"

"They gave me the gold," shouted Keeling. "When I was away south looking for work, before the planting begin here. I came across them in a pub and they gave me the gold and told me they'd kill me if I told!"

"If any of that were true," Georgette said, "then you have done something most unwise by telling. But since none of it *is* true, you've only made an ass of yourself."

But no, he had done more than that. In the silent room, whispers dropped and rippled out. Wondering whispers. No-smoke-without-fire whispers.

Hugo spoke above them. "I never had the misfortune of meeting Mr. Keeling until I entered this house. And I never had a piece of gold likely to have come from a stolen sovereign until he gave me one."

"Likely to have come from?" Jenks turned to Hugo. "You don't know, though."

"No, I don't know. But the circumstantial evidence—you found it yourself. The gold had been melted down."

This would be a *wonderful* time for Mr. Lowe to speak up. Hugo caught his eye, but the blacksmith only shook his head. Furiously. Frantically.

"Mr. Lowe," Hugo pressed.

"I never knew where anything came from," he cried. "It just appeared, like. Gold coins, and I were to melt them down. There was a note. But I didn't do it, because I knew they were stolen, and a man in a hood came into the foundry and crushed my foot with me own hammer."

A man in a hood.

"Before you arrived here, Doctor." Jenks considered. "But not before Mr. Keeling did."

"I had to melt it," Lowe added, leaning heavily on his crutch. "Drop it into cold water so it made blobs no one would recognize. Then I'd get to keep me other foot, and me hands, and even some of the gold. But what's a man to do with gold hereabouts?"

"A man can do anything with gold," said Sir Frederic.

"Not here. The shops in Bamburgh won't take it, nor I can't eat it or feed me family with it. And I can't make meself a new set of toes with it."

"I *am* sorry about the toes," Hugo said. "They are—"

"You saved me life, Doctor, and I don't mean to fault you. But I wish I'd never seen that gold."

"I could wish it had never been minted," Jenks said. "But then none of us would have the undeniable pleasure of being here today." His voice held a touch of triumph. "A few of you must stay. Mr. Crowe. Mrs. Crowe. Mr. Keeling. Everyone else is free to leave for the moment."

"Wait," said Hugo, even as the other people stirred and shoved and immediately made for the door. "Mr. Jenks. The lady and I are innocent. What sort of evidence do you need in order to believe us?"

"For a start, I'd need to know who you really are."

No. Impossible. If he told the truth, then Georgette would be ruined. He had done too much to ensure her safety to compromise it now.

"If you're married to the lady," said Jenks, "then you're culpable for any crimes either of you may have committed. If you're not, then I could take her up for licentious behavior."

"No," Hugo blurted. "No."

Jenks regarded him narrowly. "Or," he added, "she could leave. Just leave, as if she were never here. And you could start telling me what you know."

She could be free. Georgette could just . . . go. Go away from this inquisition, and the amputations and the honey and the empty library and full wine cellar. She could be done with this whole coil.

The idea should have made him soar. But so much had altered that he was too muddled to know how to feel.

"May I speak to the lady in private?" Hugo asked.

Jenks lifted his chin, catching the eye of some of the servants before they filed out. He made a complicated set of motions with his hands, which they seemed to comprehend. When he turned back to Hugo, he said, "Very well. You'll be locked in this room. I'll see Mr. Keeling shut away somewhere secure, then I'll return. And I'll need answers from you then."

The door lock was turned with a dreadful grinding that seemed very loud.

"Alone at last." Georgette tried for lightness. The chairs set up in neat rows had been scrambled, some overturned. She busied herself dragging them back into order. Not that it mattered, did it? Hugo would not be seeing patients that day.

"Georgette." He stood at a careful distance. "You must blame everything on me. Take some money and leave. Throw yourself on Jenks's mercy and tell him who you are, and that I spirited you away with the promise of bringing you to your brother."

She let a chair fall with a muffled thump. "That is both correct and entirely inaccurate. *No.* Hugo, I'm not going to compound a lie and leave you in the lurch."

"Georgette. I'm fine." He gave a twist to his gold signet ring. "I'm the son of a duke, remember? Everything is lovely for people like me. But if you stay, you'll be ruined."

The bit about dukes' sons was true; she'd told him

often enough. But his plan didn't sit right with her. "Ruined for what? Not for such purpose as I have. Not for my dream of a cottage in the country."

He sighed. For the first time, she thought he looked much older than she. "You think life is like a story and you want to live inside one. But this is reality."

"I assure you, I am not unaware of that."

"If you want your cottage, you must help to save yourself. If you don't want your choices to be seized from you, this is the one you must make."

"But how can I get the cottage without the gold?"

"There's no gold, Georgette. There never was." He was standing before the fireplace, and he turned to cuff the mantel, hard. "This is not the sort of treasure that does anyone good. Jenks will chase it in dribs and drabs until July, and then it'll be done."

She could not have been more surprised if he had slapped her. "I knew you never wanted to come along, but I didn't realize you never thought there was hope."

"There can always be hope." His fingertips ground at the stone of the mantel, as if trying to crush it. "But there has to be a plan, too. And the original plan is rubbish, Georgette. Let it go now that it's rubbish. You can't be Mrs. Crowe anymore. You need to go back to being yourself."

"Even so. That doesn't mean I have to leave."

He didn't say anything; his jaw worked on unspoken words.

And she realized: "It *does* mean that, doesn't it? You want me to leave, because I was never part of your plan. Your perfect hospital in London to honor your brother. If I am compromised, you'll be stuck with me, and you can't pursue your own aims."

He had never made any bones about his determination. He had never promised he would stay with her.

He'd taken care to keep his distance; he'd done no more with her than what she'd asked. *I'm only doing this because you begged me.* Ha. She'd been the first to make that joke, but the joke was on her.

"This is not a tragic ethical dilemma." Hugo turned to face her, one hand on the mantel. "It's not. Not even close. You should leave and protect yourself. It's the right thing to do."

She could almost laugh. "At last, you're granting that I could protect myself. When I never asked you to protect me at all."

But he'd felt the obligation all the same, she knew. And at some point between the time she took his hand and the time she loosed her bodice for him, he thought he'd failed in it. Otherwise he wouldn't be looking at her like this, with such a plea in those deep blue eyes. She loved them, but she could hardly look at them. There was too much and too little feeling in them at once.

Carefully, deliberately, she set one of the hard wooden chairs upright and sat in it. "Your idea of what is right," she said slowly, "has been determined by someone who died years ago."

He turned on his heel, away from her. Smacking into the folding screen, he cursed, steadying it with an outstretched hand. When it settled into place again, he knocked the end panel flat into its neighbor. There was the table, so carefully laid out with medical instruments.

"You mean my brother Matthew." His tone was clipped. With sharp gestures, he began tucking the instruments away into the long leather case in which they were stored. "But everyone's decisions are guided by someone who has died. My father, for example. He's the duke because his father was, and before that an uncle, because the direct line broke. And you—what would your life be now if your parents had lived?"

She wanted to pace, but she did not want to draw close to him. So instead, she sat, all in knots. "I promise you that I am not guided by what my parents would want me to do."

"No, rather the opposite. You think of them, and you react. You live in stories. Who pins a future on the promise of a reward from the Royal Mint?" With more force than necessary, he snipped a pair of scissors closed and shoved them into the case.

"You did the same," Georgette pointed out.

"No. I pinned mine on the hospital plans. The reward was not the end in itself. It was the means to make the hospital happen."

"And the hospital? Is it not for Matthew?"

His hands went still. He looked at them as though he'd never seen them before. "It is. It was. But it's for—many things."

"And all our travel? Our time together?" She searched within, finding a kernel of bravery. "Was it all in service of your plan?" *What have I come to mean to you?*

Her words seemed to snap him out of a reverie. With quick and practiced gestures, he finished replacing the instruments. "It wouldn't have happened without the plan, but that doesn't mean it was only because of the plan. I did what I wanted to do."

"Yes, as did I." She laced her fingers together in her lap. "And a bit more, too."

He fumbled the latch of the case. "You cannot mean that I disrespected you?" He looked toward her, stricken. "I would never want—"

"No, no. That's not what I meant. You have never disrespected me."

No, she meant that she had fallen for him: deeply, irrevocably, hopefully as a girl in a *conte de fée*. And foolishly, too, for she knew she and he were not the same. He was a scholar, with training in innumerable fields. She was self-educated, best at carrying things where they needed to go. Where she was Cinderella, he was vegetable acids. Where she was adventure, he was a plan.

Though for a while, she'd lived along the edge of his plan and liked the backbone it gave her days. And she had thought that he liked the chance to leap outside its bounds, maybe. To stop and pet a sheep, or to make a castle in the sand.

No, it was not a maybe. He *had* liked it. But not enough. That, more than Cinderella or Rapunzel or any old tale told and retold by the French and Germans, was the story of Georgette's life: *you are not enough.*

She tried again, desperately. "You took a bullet to protect me. Doesn't that mean anything?"

This time he succeeded at latching the case. "It means I am not a villain, Georgette. That's all I've ever been able to say."

"I'm better with words than you are," she said, "and that's not how I'd describe you at all."

He said nothing. Maybe there was nothing more to say.

"Well." She slapped her thighs, then rose to her feet. "I ought to be going, ought I not? You have been most clear about that. You are right, I need a purpose. And I won't find it here."

He dropped the case to the table, then strode toward her. "Georgette . . ."

The key tangled with the lock of the parlor, the noise drawing her notice.

"Jenks," she said. It was too soon; they had agreed on nothing. "What will you tell him?"

But it wasn't Jenks who the servants guarding the door admitted to the room. It was a tall dark-haired man with sightless blue eyes and a stout wooden cane in one hand. He slammed it to the floor, then tilted his head, listening.

"Georgette," he said. "You are in here, the servants told me. And Hugo, yes? Hullo to you both."

Oh, damn. Damn the man.

Years too late to be of any good, and with the most unwelcome timing ever, her elder brother, Benedict, had made an appearance.

Chapter Eighteen

"Your timing is terrible," Georgette told her brother as soon as the shock of introduction and the obligatory greetings were completed. "Lord Hugo and I were just having a towering argument."

"And I missed it? What a pity. That *is* terrible timing."

"No," said Hugo. "You didn't miss it entirely. But I believe we shall have to leave it unresolved."

He had packed up his medical case. The chairs were in a neat line. The parlor door was no longer locked, and somewhere Keeling was informally imprisoned.

So many questions remained unanswered, but for Georgette, this was the end of the journey. Hugo's plan had always been to see her to her brother, and there was nothing more important than the plan. *Leave*, he had told her. For a moment he'd forgotten that she could not safely travel alone. But now it was a moot point. Benedict had saved the day.

Sometimes she hated Benedict.

"How did you find me?" she asked. "And why now?"

"I was determined to find you by your birthday, to make sure you were all right."

Georgette groaned.

"If you are making a horrid face, you know I cannot see it," Benedict replied. "The effect is wasted on me. And I found you after much clever investigation and labor."

"Did you really?" Hugo was seated in one of the little chairs from the attic, his large frame incongruous upon it.

"Ah—much labor, at the very least." Seated, Benedict held his cane lightly across his lap. "I began by visiting the Duchess of Willingham. Is she here, by the bye?"

"Of course not," said Hugo. "Why should you think such a thing?"

"Because my sister is with you, and you wrote me that she was a guest of your mother's."

Hugo bristled. "And so she was, when I wrote you."

Georgette placed a hand on Benedict's elbow. "Leave that," she said. "I suppose you followed us north, the blond woman and the bespectacled man with the ridiculous long leather case."

"I beg your—"

"Not far off," Benedict said smoothly. "And as to the why, it wasn't entirely because of your birthday. I've much news."

"Oh God." Georgette flopped back against the hard rungs of her chair. "There's a woman in it. You've met someone."

"I have, and I hope I haven't bollixed my chances too badly. I've much more to do before I can declare myself to the lady. But no, the real news is this: I was there in Derbyshire when three chests of stolen gold were found. And I've come to give you money, Georgette."

Jenks poked his head through the doorway. "All finished here? Mrs. Crowe, you're free to leave. With your brother, if you wish."

Mrs. Crowe, mouthed Benedict with an exaggerated play of his features. Fortunate for him he could not see Georgette's response.

Jenks stepped into the room. "There's nothing more for you to do here, Miss—Madam. If you go now, you needn't be mixed up in the story of the theft at all. And there will," he added grimly, "be a story."

"But Hugo . . ." She looked at him.

He gave his signet ring a twist; he gave her a wry smile. "Will be fine," he replied. "You're free, Georgette."

Such a beautiful sentence, under ordinary circumstances. But nothing about Hugo Starling was ordinary to Georgette.

"I will be packed in time to catch the evening stage," she said.

"And I will go with you," said Benedict.

It was done, then. She'd known from the beginning, she shouldn't count on a scholar for love. If she gave him her heart, she'd get a hospital plan in return. For an embrace, an experiment; for a kiss, a treatise on vegetable acids.

She'd wanted so badly to be loved that she'd fancied herself in love with him, despite her better judgment.

So she was telling herself now. But the pain in her heart as she stood was more than a fancy.

"I thought I could love you," she said in a voice pitched for his ears alone.

"Why?"

He always asked why. He had to ask.

"Because I was a fool who ignored the empirical evidence before me. My hypothesis was incorrect."

"I am sorry for it."

It wasn't as though he hadn't warned her. His heart was for people as a group, not for one person who could draw close to him. It was a good heart. It just wasn't hers.

Hoisted with her own petard.

Sometimes she hated Shakespeare, too.

With Linton's help, Georgette was soon packed. In fact, Linton was soon packed too.

"I never wanted to be a bondager," she explained as she placed the last of her possessions into a valise. "I only wanted honest work. I could find that in London, don't you think, Mrs. Crowe?"

"Georgette, please. Or Miss Frost, if you must." Enough lies.

"Yes, Miss Frost." The woman looked hesitant. But they were almost of an age, were they not? They had simply lived their lives in different worlds. "Well, when we get to London, I thought I might do what you did here at Raeburn Hall."

Seduce a duke's son? "Er—which thing?"

"Help a doctor. I'm strong, and I'm never ill."

This made sense. "I'll pay your way," Georgette promised. "Since my brother is flush with cash and throwing it about." Not that she meant to take a cent from him. She still had her own savings, thanks to Hugo's generosity on the way north.

Not that she was thinking about Hugo at the

moment, either. "And the baby? How will you care for the baby, Miss Linton?"

"Linton will do, miss. Or Harriet if you like." On her lips trembled a hesitant smile. "If I'm known as a widow, and I could find a good job, then I could take care of the baby respectably."

"You should be a widow," Georgette said, heartfelt. If she'd had a pistol in her hand right then, she wouldn't have answered for Keeling's life.

The stage was not due to arrive in Bamburgh for hours, but Georgette fled Raeburn Hall rather than waiting to walk with Harriet and Benedict.

The days were long this far north, and the sky held its blue tightly. It would still be daylight when they left Sir Frederic's lands for good. It seemed the day would never end.

Well. A lady's twenty-first birthday ought to be momentous, ought it not?

The air was cool and fresh, salt-scented as she wound closer to the beach along a familiar path. But she had not come to see the sand this time. She did not build with it; she did not look at the impressions her feet left behind.

She had come to see the castle.

It was stark and bright in the determined light of late afternoon. The stone of its outcrop burst gray and jagged from the lush green of grass and the sifting sands.

She stripped off her gloves and dropped them, then picked her way over the rugged earth until she reached smooth lawn, then the curtain wall of the castle.

This close to it, she could see the wear on the ancient building. The stone battlements that seemed freshly cut from a distance were worn by time—and possibly a Scotsman's weapons. The turrets that had looked as smooth as Rapunzel's tower were ordinary rock, rough at the seams.

This close to it, she could see the color of the walls, too. The castle wasn't all brown and gray, as she'd thought from a distance. It was those colors, yes, but it was also cream and rose and russet. It was golden, and some stones winked with tiny bits of shiny mineral. It was less perfect and more vivid than she had thought.

And it was beautiful.

After she had looked her fill, she retrieved her gloves and walked away. There was no need to look back.

She made her way to the coaching inn in Bamburgh, arriving in plenty of time to buy tickets for the stage. Linton was waiting there already, a valise in each hand.

Two lives packed within a pair of leather bags. It was good to be able to depart so easily, was it not? If one wasn't going to stay, it might as well be easy to leave.

She laid out the money for tickets: threepence ha'penny the mile. She counted out silver coins, reserving some for meals and lodging. Then she turned about, tickets in hand.

"Benedict!" He had arrived while she was occupied with the tickets. "Where is your trunk?"

"They're holding it for me inside the inn," her brother replied. "Will you walk with me before the coach comes?"

"I suppose," she granted reluctantly. They stepped onto the pavement, walking a smooth line before the tidy row of shops and homes that bordered the principal street. Benedict moved easily, guiding himself with thumps of his hickory cane. His strides were longer than Georgette's.

"You've changed," she said. "You don't seem bothered by your blindness." When she'd last seen him, the loss of his sight was new. He had never been morose or bitter, but for a while he had been—to excuse the expression—at sea.

"I used always to be leaving," he explained. "But now I have somewhere to go."

"Where is that?"

"Edinburgh, if the lady will have me. Though I've much business to conclude first. I won't be a barnacle on her hull."

"Please tell me that is not a euphemism."

He laughed. "Call it a figure of speech."

"You said you had money, though. You found half the stolen sovereigns."

"Ah." He halted, folding his hands neatly on the head of his cane. "I am afraid I was deceptive there. I do have money for you. And I was present when the stolen sovereigns were found. But the events are not connected."

"I don't understand." She, too, halted, shaded by the awning over the entrance to a milliner's shop. "How are the events not connected?"

"I went to Derbyshire thinking I had to have that gold to fund the life I wanted. But in the end, it was the easiest thing in the world to say someone else had found the trunks."

"Why?" Oh, lovely. She was taking after Hugo now.

"What I thought I wanted changed. And how I thought I could get that life changed too."

"That is vague and unhelpful." She looked about for something to kick.

He smiled. "Brother's prerogative. In short, my pride was less important, and allowing a space for someone else in my life was more so."

"How sentimental."

"You know me, always reading those old fairy stories. Oh, wait—no, that was you." With a flourish, he held out an arm. "Shall we walk on, Mrs. Crowe?"

"Please, don't call me that. It was an idea of Hugo's." Or maybe it had been hers? She couldn't remember now which of them had first offered a false name. Always a bird. She should have flown away when she had the chance, just as she'd told the little bird in Sir Frederic's tapestry. "It wasn't wise. But then, nothing to do with Lord Hugo Starling is wise."

"I rather thought the opposite," Benedict said, falling into idle stride beside Georgette. With one hand, he held her elbow; the other used his cane to bring the world to echoing life around him. "But then, you have spent more time with him lately than I."

She didn't want to talk about Hugo. "I already bought my ticket for the stage. And Linton's—that is, Harriet's, too. I don't need any money from you. Especially since you didn't claim the Royal Reward." Her brow knit. "Wait. Where did you get money, then?"

"From the sale of our parents' bookshop. I thought to use it for something else, but—it was a gamble that didn't meet with success." He smiled. It was a smile much like her own. "Or not with the sort of success I expected. So, the money from the sale is intact. And half of it's yours."

"I don't need you to give me guilt money, Benedict. I've never needed help from you before, and I don't now."

"What is this arrogance? No one can get by without

help. Hugo helped you all the way here, with his time and his money. I'm helping you now."

Brothers. "If you want me to push you in front of a carriage, you're going about it the right way."

He laughed. "My reflexes are excellent. And when you say you won't accept help, what you're doing is denying every good thing someone else does for you."

She had not thought of it that way, that denying an offer of help could be a form of selfishness. Or that even worse was accepting help while insisting it was not wanted.

Again and again, Hugo had tolerated that. Whatever it took to reach her destination, he helped her get it. How could she not have seen the sacrifice piled on sacrifice?

Or was it a sacrifice, if it was what he wanted too? He had also wanted the gold for his hospital. For his perfect perfect hospital. And when she tried to help him in return, he told her to go away. For her own sake, he said. For her own good.

This was the heart of it: to Georgette, help meant *I love you*, and she didn't want it unless she knew it was real. To Hugo, though, it was a simple kindness. He'd made no gestures of devotion; he had only reciprocated. She took his hand; she kissed him first. She pulled him into the wardrobe.

I love you. Do you love me in return?

He didn't. He was sorry for her, that was all. She had deluded herself, and that crushed her heart. But a heart was only one part of a body. And the rest of hers was fine.

She should know by now that she could not rely on anyone else to give her what she wished for. A pity that one could not create love on one's own. But one could create a home, and somehow she would.

Somehow. She would. Somehow.

"Let me not call it help." Benedict broke into her thoughts. "Let me call it justice. What I wish to give you is not guilt money, and it is not aid. It is no more than what you deserve."

She narrowed her eyes.

"You're making some sort of strange face at me," he said. "I can tell, because your fingers have gone all tight and clutchy on my arm. What is it?"

"How is it justice?"

"Ah!" He swung his cane in a jaunty swoop before striking it again on the pavement. "Because you are no less a child of our parents than I am. It is not fair that their every possession should have come to me, as a male and the eldest."

"But that—" She frowned.

"That makes sense, doesn't it? It made sense to me."

It did make sense, when he put the matter like that. How like their parents, to be careless of her even in death. "They didn't want me. Mother and Father, I mean. I always knew it, and I tried to be as little bother as possible. But they didn't want me."

"They didn't," Benedict agreed.

She stumbled. Halted. The words were a gut punch, one for which she thought she'd been prepared for years. But some blows, there was no way to prepare for.

Benedict reached out a hand, closing it on the cap of her shoulder. "I put that badly. I am sorry for that. They didn't want me, either, Georgette. They didn't want children at all, for children were a distraction from their own pursuits. There's nothing wrong with either of us."

"And with them?"

"I don't know." He looked up at the sky he could not see. "They did the best they could."

Georgette squared her shoulders. She patted Benedict's hand where it rested. "No. I don't think they did."

The elder Frosts would never have been warm and sentimental, but they could have made their children as welcome as customers. They could have valued them as members of the family as much as they valued help in the shop.

Benedict squeezed her shoulder, taking comfort, then let his hand fall to his side. "That's true. I've always thought of them from a child's point of view. But thinking back as an adult, it's clear that they weren't very good parents, were they?"

"Ah, well. You got away."

His smile was crooked. "I had to. You can't imagine what it was like growing up among all those words and being unable to read them. At least, not as well as they thought I ought. If I tried harder, they were sure, the letters would stop swimming about and switching places before my eyes. If I really wanted to, I would appreciate the books as they did. But I couldn't. By the time you were three years old, you read better than I, and I was twelve."

She had been so young then, she hardly remembered a time her brother had lived at home. She missed him as one missed an idea, no more real to her than the longed-for cottage or a castle from a storybook.

Yet she'd seen a castle. And now, here was her brother.

"Still, I should have stayed," he said. "I shouldn't have left you alone."

"I did all right. You'd have been less happy if you'd never gone to sea, and I would not have been more so."

She didn't know if this was true, but he looked relieved.

Probably it was true. There were as many ways to be all right as there were people in the world.

She was all right when she remembered her parents. They had given her shelter and food and clothing; they had seen to her every bodily need.

It had not been enough for a child as hungry for affection as she'd been. But she was a grown woman now, and she knew she would not starve from lack of love.

"We turned out fine, didn't we?" she decided. "Neither of us wanted to stay in the bookshop, but why should we? Our parents devoted their lives to an occupation they loved. We ought to do the same."

Benedict offered his arm again, and they turned back in the direction from which they'd come. "I intend to."

"As a sailor? I know you are miraculous, but the Royal Navy will surely not allow it."

"No. As a traveler, sometimes. And a writer."

"A writer," she mused.

"Do you doubt? I'm extremely witty. And I've a turn for an anecdote. Though most of them are not appropriate for sisters."

"Nonsense. Inappropriate anecdotes are the best sort."

"I cannot argue with that."

She hesitated. "Benedict, I'm afraid. I'm afraid if you give me money from the bookshop, I won't see you again. Will you make sure that doesn't happen?"

He hauled her tightly against his side, pinning her in

a quick hug. "You know I will. I'll visit you wherever you are. And once I'm settled, I hope you'll visit me, too."

"Don't crush my bonnet! It's my only one." She struggled away, smiling. "And yes, I will visit you."

"What will you do now? I could travel south to London with you, or I could pursue my other errands. Shaking free of my various commissions, turning myself into a civilian."

"For your lady, to whom you do not want to be a barnacle? Go, do what you need to. Miss Linton and I will be fine traveling south."

"As a rumpled, vulgar boy?"

She coughed. "I didn't think you'd have heard about that."

"Hugo's letter was informative. Here, you ought to have it in case you need to bribe your way into Willingham's good graces." He patted his pockets, drawing out a paper. "Is this it?"

"That it is." She recognized the tidy, slashing handwriting at once. "Thank you. And no, I will not travel as a boy. I'll be Miss Frost, a respectable woman of moderate means. I don't want to follow someone else's dream anymore. I don't want to fit myself into the corners of someone else's life."

"Fair enough," said Benedict. "That's why I went to sea. London is big enough, surely, for you to find a corner of your own if you wish."

"I think so. I have learned that I like helping people. When I do, I matter to them—but better yet, they matter to me." The coaching inn was drawing close; soon their walk would come to an end. "I'll find a purpose somehow. I want one, you see. Having money isn't enough to carry me through the rest of my life; there's got to be a reason to get up each day.

I have a whole week to think of one before I arrive in London."

"If Hugo could hear you, he would wilt at the notion of so little planning."

"Let him wilt."

"Please tell me that is not a euphemism."

She choked. The first laugh she'd had since toppling from a wardrobe with Hugo that morning. Ages ago. "I wish we knew each other better, Benedict."

As they halted before the coaching inn, he pulled her into another rough hug. "We will see that we do. How can I find you once you reach London?"

She thought about it. "Write to me care of the Duchess of Willingham. After all, I am her guest. Hasn't everyone said so?"

Chapter Nineteen

Locked in the parlor again.

Damn. Double damn. Exponential damn.

He'd thought to do so much good in this room, and now—there was too much furniture, and he was alone, and Georgette was gone, and nothing was any good.

Which was no excuse to stew. Stewing turned one's thoughts into mush. At the table set up for medical supplies, he unclasped the long leather case that had become his most dependable companion and extracted his hospital plans.

He unrolled them flat on the table, bending over to peer at them closely. He didn't have his spectacles on, but he knew how every line looked. He knew every change he had made too. Flipping the pages over, he looked at the list of dated notations. Here a window, there a wall.

He hadn't made any changes since arriving in Northumberland. Was that because everything was perfect?

No. Nothing was ever perfect. Getting as close as could be, though—that had mattered to him. Just now, the heart had gone out of him. These precious plans were but ink and pencil on paper, rolled and unrolled so often that the paper had become soft as cloth.

With one fingertip, he traced the line of the roof. If it were ever built, it would be a fine roof. He squinted, wondering if his hand would look like Matthew's. If he imagined fiercely enough; if he squinted until light was no more than a pinprick.

That was no good either. Matthew remained stubbornly gone, and Hugo's hand was his own. It would never look again like his hand at eighteen, when he had become a twinless twin.

The hospital was to honor Matthew, yes. Georgette had been right about that. And maybe Hugo, for his part, had been wrong. If the hospital was intended only to honor the dead, what sort of a purpose was that?

It was meant to benefit the living, of course. But perhaps old Sir Joseph Banks had a point: the best way to care for people was the way they wanted to be cared for. Hugo had seen Lowe in his home, and the blacksmith was thriving. How well would his recovery have gone away from his family? Away from a son to put honey on the sutures, and a dog to try to lick it off?

Well, the dog's contribution probably hadn't helped. But for the rest of it . . .

Hugo had cocked up, and royally. He had planned for everything except the unexpected—and Georgette Frost had been nothing but unexpected since he came across her in boys' clothing, waiting for a coach to take her away.

Some part of him had never wanted her to go away. But logic was stronger. Forethought. Doing what was wise. Time and again, he'd done what was wise. He had sent her away, and sent away his friend, too. To be wise. So they could do what they wanted to do, without him.

God*damn* it.

The stubborn lock creaked and crunched, and the parlor door swung open. "Mr. Crowe," came Jenks's voice.

Hugo emerged from behind the half-folded screen, leaving his hospital plans where they lay. "Mr. Jenks. Would you like to see me jailed?"

"I'd like to see your ring." The Runner held out a hand.

Hugo frowned. "If you must." Tugging the signet free, he crossed the room to Jenks and dropped it in Jenks's palm.

"Old gold." Jenks held it up, holding it close to his eye. "I never forget a detail, Mr. Crowe. Or should that be Starling?"

"Ah." Now that Jenks had spoken the word, it was a relief. "You know who I am."

"Doctors don't wear signets, my lord. Not unless they're something else, too. I took the liberty of searching your chamber this morning—"

"*What?*"

"—and checked the plates in your books. Lord Hugo Starling." Jenks made a little bow. "Pleased to make your acquaintance."

"You don't sound terribly cut up about the fact that I lied about who I was."

"You didn't lie about the fact you were a doctor, which was the most important thing to the people hereabouts." Jenks returned Hugo's ring. "And today, you *did* keep lying about who you were to save that woman you were with. Which was the most important thing to me."

"You searched her room too." It was not a question.

"Of course." Jenks stood aside. "You're free to go too, Lord Hugo. I can't hold the son of a duke."

That was sudden. And unexpected. Hugo had done the *worst* job preparing for the unexpected. "I don't want you to let me go because of who my father is. I want you to let me go because I'm innocent of anything to do with the theft from the Royal Mint."

"What does the latter matter as long as you've got the former?" Jenks spoke blandly as ever.

"It matters, Mr. Jenks."

The Runner regarded him narrowly—and after a moment, his manner softened. "So it does. And I've come to believe it, proof aside."

"You have?" Hugo looked at the signet, then tucked it into his waistcoat pocket where his watch ought to have been. "Then why did you lock me in here if you knew who I was?"

"I needed others to think I thought you were guilty."

"And why do you believe I am innocent? Not that I am trying to persuade you otherwise."

By way of answer, Jenks walked across the room to the folding screen. "Pretty," he said. "Must have cost a mint. Don't you think? It's rich, even for a baronet."

"Ah . . . yes?"

Jenks regarded the expensive panels. "Do you know the names of the guards who were killed at the Royal Mint?"

"Ah . . . no."

"No one ever wonders about them. But they gave their lives for that gold, and it has their blood on it." One by one, he collapsed the panels. "Their names were Harris. Sweeting. Davidson." He gave the screen a push, sending it crashing to the floor. He looked up, eyes cold and hard. "And Jenks."

"Jenks," Hugo repeated, understanding dawning. "Your brother?"

A slight nod. "My brother. That gave me the justification to take an assignment I would have wanted all the same."

"I am very sorry for your loss," Hugo said.

Another slight nod. An expression—though of what, Hugo could not be sure—flickered over the Runner's impassive features, then was gone.

"How strange," Hugo said, "that we Londoners should end in Northumberland, and both of us because of a lost brother."

Jenks tilted his head.

"I had a twin, you see," Hugo blurted. "Everything I've done since he died—really, everything I've done since he was born—has been affected by that."

Words uncorked like the old bottle of whisky that had helped him heal, he told the Runner everything. Matthew's death. Hugo's medical career. The hospital plans he carried with him everywhere. His attempts to get it funded. The falling-out with the duke.

"I thought I could help people in a way I couldn't help Matthew," Hugo finished. "That's the purpose of the hospital."

"But is the point building the hospital, or helping people?"

"It's . . . both." The answer was tentative. "It's using the hospital to help people in a way no other building or treatment or medical professional is able to."

Hugo realized something then. "You trust in my innocence, you say, but here is proof. Look—here, on the back of this page. I date all my changes to the plans. Here, on the date of the theft from the Royal Mint, is a set of changes I made after dining with the president of the Royal College." He gave a short laugh. "I annoyed him dreadfully, and he did the same to me. So when I returned home, I made alterations that were the opposite of everything he'd recommended."

"Hmm." Jenks skimmed the line of changes. "You've hardly left anything unaltered."

An apt description as any of the journey northward, which Hugo had begun in utter certainty. He'd been so sure he knew every step, the next one, the one beyond. Nothing had gone as he'd thought it would.

It had been easy for him to say he and his father didn't speak anymore. He was still the son of Willingham, with a ducal carriage whenever he wished it and a quarterly allowance generous enough to meet his every need and want.

What more could I sacrifice than I already have? he had asked his father. He had lost a twin, yes. But there were many other types of closeness; more than he had ever dreamed before he began dreaming rather than merely planning.

Georgette had helped him see that. He had found her dreams the happiest sort of contagion.

She had helped him savor passion. Revel in romance. Experience . . . love?

He had, after all, stopped reading when she wanted him to. He had crossed the country for her. He had taken a bullet for her.

It wasn't love as he had ever felt it before. This was a sturdy feeling, built brick by brick from fondness and laughter and annoyance and lust and mischief and admiration.

Sometimes in chemical equations, the sum of the whole was greater than the parts. He did not know why, or how. But it was possible in nature, and so it was possible in Hugo. He had not added up the sum of what he felt for Georgette, but it was surely greater than all the little parts of which it was made.

Because it was love, he knew now. He loved her, and he had told her to leave.

And for the second time in his life, he had lost half of his heart.

"What are you going to do now?" Hugo asked. "Has your investigation come to an end?"

"Nearly. Yes." Jenks eyed the folding screen with distaste, then picked it up and leaned it against the wall. "I told another untruth. No one left gold in my room."

"I don't understand."

"Three thieves, Lord Hugo. Three thieves not yet caught. Or two, if the poor devil who got himself burned near Doncaster was one of them."

"You are turning them against one another," Hugo realized. "If a thief is here, he'll wonder which of his comrades has taken such a rash step."

"Just giving them a little nudge," admitted Jenks. "They'll do the rest themselves. And soon, I'll find a piece of the puzzle that hasn't fit anywhere else. Something that's not as it ought to be, or something out of place. Like a board that's a different color, showing where something's been pried up. Or—"

"A wine barrel," blurted Hugo.

The wine cellar. The old bottles, the old barrels, the new ones. The largest of the barrels was the one of

Madeira, atop which he had thoroughly debauched Georgette.

"The barrel of Madeira," he said aloud. "It is old, but the lid is new. It bears investigating, Mr. Jenks."

"The Madeira." Jenks looked struck. "I searched every corner of that wine cellar—but barrels don't have corners. Never thought of the gold being hidden inside one of them." He eyed Hugo dubiously. "If the gold is there, you'll get the reward. If you want it. If you want your name in this business."

"Now that . . . she . . . is gone, it's all right." Hugo considered. "I could use a bit of the good sort of notoriety."

"The one who finds the gold will get that, make no mistake." Jenks turned toward the door. "No time like the present for a search, wouldn't you say?"

"Wait." Hugo called him back. "Mr. Jenks. When you take the money back to London, will it help? Will it help with the loss of your brother?"

"Damned if I know," said Jenks.

"Damned regardless," said Hugo. Or so it seemed. Doing nothing was no way to help with grief. Yet doing something was never enough.

But when Faust had tamed the heavens and the earth, he found that his soul was his own after all. Maybe someday, somehow, there was peace to be found.

Maybe it could come, despite all his hesitation, in the form of another person.

"I will see the criminal brought to justice," said Jenks. "Justice can't help my brother now, but it can help Mrs. Keeling. Miss Linton. All the bondagers and hinds hereabouts."

"So you mean to arrest Mr. Keeling?"

"Aye." Jenks copied the local dialect. "And," he added, "Sir Frederic Chapple."

It all unraveled quickly after that.

As Hugo and Jenks soon found, thousands of gold coins were in the barrel of Madeira. And who had put them there? Who had had access to the barrel, from London ever-northward?

At some point, the gold had been in Derbyshire. At some point, half of it had been removed and stowed in the barrel.

"Anyone could have stolen the key to the wine cellar." Sir Frederic's left hand was cuffed to a chair in the grand parlor. It had taken some wrestling to achieve this. "I am innocent, Mr. Jenks! I would never tamper with such a fine Madeira."

"Mr. Keeling might," Jenks said. "And I notice you're not willing to adulterate wine, but you don't say anything about being unwilling to steal gold."

Sir Frederic turned an unhealthy curdled color.

He made a most unlikely criminal, this well-fed and comfortable man. But Keeling, held in a separate chamber, could not cast blame enough upon Sir Frederic. "He planned it all. He knew me from a boy. I was only following his orders."

"I'm not a bad man," Sir Frederic insisted. "The theft—it wasn't for me. I did it for my tenants. The doctoring, the money—I want them to have good lives."

"And none of the money went toward these fine furnishings?" asked Jenks. "Or the barrel of Madeira in which the coins were stashed? The wrong thing for a fine reason is still wrong."

"No one was meant to die," said the baronet. "It

wasn't so very wrong. If no one was hurt. I say . . ." With some effort of his cuffed hand, he pulled forth a small pocketbook and pencil from his coat. He scrawled a little note, then stuffed the book and pencil back in his pocket.

And pulled out a pistol.

He aimed it at his own temple, hand quivering. "It wasn't supposed to go like this."

"See here," said Hugo. "I'm a good doctor, but I can't piece brains back together."

"Tell me," Jenks said. "Tell me how it was supposed to go, Sir Frederic."

With quavering hand holding the gun, Sir Frederic told him.

He had begun planning the theft as soon as he inherited the baronetcy several months before. He couldn't bear to live in Northumberland and run a baronetcy without money; he, used to all the comforts of life.

For years, he had sponsored a ragged school—education for children of the streets. It was good, he thought, to see them educated. He wound up with dozens upon dozens of grateful youths growing into respectable trades, positions in great houses, advantageous marriages.

He also wound up with a few criminals in his pocket.

After their years in London, these men had scattered. But Sir Frederic knew how to find them, and he collected them. Two from London, one from Derbyshire, one from Northumberland. They did not know one another; they only knew him. They called one another John Smith. And they all accepted his plan: steal money by following his instructions, and they would share it out together.

But it didn't go as it was supposed to go.

The first problem was that the guards were shot, not evaded.

The second problem was that the John Smiths stole a new sort of coin that hadn't yet been released to the public.

The third was they couldn't keep from flashing the gold about. Smith One had given a coin to his lover in Strawfield, then later—accidentally, he swore—killed her. He was arrested.

Smith Two had given a bracelet of reworked gold to his amour, a maid near Doncaster.

He had been killed by Smith Three—Keeling—who had given gold to Linton.

"I expected the thieves to distrust each other." Sir Frederic closed pouchy eyes, the pistol quivering in his hand. "I counted on it. But I didn't expect them to betray me. And they all did. They all betrayed me for love."

The story was as pitiful as it was dreadful. But it was not yet complete, Hugo realized. "What about Smith Four? You said he was a Londoner. Is he still at large?"

"I've said enough." The baronet pressed the pistol more tightly against his temple, drawing in a deep breath.

"You're from London, Sir Frederic," Jenks said blandly. "Maybe you're Smith Four. Someone used a pistol like that to shoot Lord Hugo, here. Oh—you didn't know he was a lord? Yes. Son of the Duke of Willingham."

"Careful, Jenks." Hugo wasn't unwilling to put Sir Frederic to the verbal rack, but he didn't want the man pushed too far. His finger was on the trigger, and if he pulled it, that would be an end to the truth.

"I've enough to arrest you, Sir Frederic," said Jenks. "Whether you shot Lord Hugo or not."

"But I'm the High Sheriff," whimpered the baronet. "I lead law enforcement in this county."

The Runner smiled—almost. "And I've a warrant from King's Bench. There's always someone above you, Sir Frederic, unless you're the king. And even then, you can be declared mad and your son set to rule in your place. Never think you're too strong to fall."

Hugo recognized that sentiment. Unspoken, it was the motivation for his father's preoccupation with what was proper. A duke could lead society by pushing its boundaries, or by dwelling on every manner and rule. Matthew's death had made Willingham pursue the latter. Even a duke's son could die.

"Put the gun down, Sir Frederic," Hugo said. "Don't let the gold take another life."

"But I am ruined."

"Ruination is what you make of it," said Jenks. "I'd say my brother was ruined when someone murdered him, but that's only my view."

A quote came to Hugo's mind. *"Modo liceat vivere, est spes."*

Jenks frowned. "You know we don't speak Greek. Be reasonable, my lord."

"It's Latin," said Hugo. "Publius Terentius Afer. Terence. 'Provided they are allowed to live, there is hope.'"

"Hope," said Sir Frederic. "Do you think—is there hope for me?" The idea seemed to buoy him. With a shaking hand, he lowered the pistol.

Jenks seized it at once.

"I've sent word to the closest constable," he told Hugo. "He'll muster a force to keep the prisoners secure. These criminals will all be bound over for the assizes."

"What will happen?" Hugo asked.

"Keeling will swing, I've no doubt. Sir Frederic will be jailed until his case can be investigated further. He didn't actually steal the money or kill anyone . . . unless he was the fourth John Smith. He might end up in Newgate yet."

"And Mr. Lowe?" Hugo held his breath.

Jenks was silent for a long while. "He lost his toes," decided the Runner. "He was threatened and injured. I believe he served as accomplice only under duress."

Hugo was satisfied with that. "And Mrs. Keeling? How will she be taken care of?"

"Mrs. Keeling never stops talking," said Sir Frederic. "If you once ask her what she wants, she will never stop complaining until the end of time."

"Then that's what we should do," Hugo said. "We should ask her what she wants. If she wants to stay on the land, some of Sir Frederic's fine things could be sold to give her an annuity."

The baronet moaned.

"And you, Mr. Jenks? What now?"

"For now, I'm taking charge of the gold. I will see it returned." He looked sharply at Hugo. "What about you—Mr. Crowe?"

What about him?

His hospital plans were laid out on the table at the end of the great parlor. Hugo crossed to it, then took them up. Studied them, the long list of alterations. They were good. Very good. If such a hospital were ever built, it would be the world's wonder.

But he'd had blinders on for too long, to think that the only way to make up for the loss of Matthew was with a grand gesture. A new building that would never allow another life to be lost.

No matter high or thick its walls, no hospital could keep illness away. It could not wall off decline and death.

But that was all right, for it wasn't the building that would make the difference. It was the people within it. The physicians and surgeons and nurses, and the supplies they had, and the way they were trained. And one could do as much good—maybe more—with a series of small gestures as with a large one.

Such as showing a Northumberland youth how to dress a wound and put in sutures. Such as, one day, paying for his tuition to attend medical college, with the understanding that he would serve an area of England that had no doctor.

Hugo couldn't protect his brother Matthew. He hadn't been able to protect himself, as the torn muscle of his shoulder reminded him. But when it mattered, he had protected Georgette without thought or hesitation. When the critical moment came, his own body had known what to do. Not with logic or forethought; with heart. He had shielded her with himself.

Once upon a time, he'd been certain of always making the sensible choice, the wise choice. He'd thought of himself as too sensible for love.

But his heart knew how to be wise too.

She thought she could have loved him, she'd said. Perhaps he could convince her to give loving him another try.

If not, he'd let her know how loved she was. She deserved to know. She deserved love, with no caveats, no limitations.

"You're returning to London with the gold?" he asked Jenks.

"Once I send the required expresses and get replies, yes. The Mint needs to be informed. They might even send a guard to accompany me."

"I'll go with you too," Hugo said.

He had scientifically minded men to meet with. He had Georgette to find. And find her he would.

If he needed to, by God, he would hire a Bow Street Runner. It wasn't as though he didn't know one.

Chapter Twenty

July 1817

With her thumb, Georgette could cover the face of the king.

She flipped the gold sovereign, marveling at its lightness. An advance on her first pay from the marchioness, so she could have her gowns tailored to appear "less academic."

The Marchioness of Stoneleigh—Tess, to her family—was a kind and fluttery employer. Upon arriving in London, Georgette had imposed upon the Duchess of Willingham with extreme politeness. She showed Hugo's letter to the duchess and asked not for house-room, but for Her Grace's knowledge of some genteel employment.

The marchioness, having tea at the moment with her mother-in-law, had perked up. "Can you governess? Have you ever been a governess?"

Georgette answered carefully. "I know French and grammar and mathematics. I'm not much of an artist, though. But I love caring for children."

By the end of the day, Georgette had been installed in the nursery of the Stoneleigh town house.

The marchioness was overwhelmed as could only be a woman with little to occupy herself. What was she to do, besides grow an heir? And so everything that came her way, from correspondence to appointments, seemed an intrusion that took her aback.

Georgette did not envy her idleness, though she wouldn't have minded the marquess and marchioness's riches.

The three little children—Hugo's nephew and nieces—plus one more on the way, reminded Georgette of living with Cousin Mary and her husband and children. In the two weeks since she'd arrived in London, she had called on her relations once, finding the shop lively and the family's chambers as crowded and chaotic as ever. A day maid was helping, and Georgette's former chamber had been given over as a second nursery. It was a good change. Cousin Mary had given her a cracking hug and said how glad she was to see Georgette had landed well.

"I worried about you so," she said. "Even though I knew you were with a duchess."

"A marchioness, now," Georgette added, skipping rather a lot of the events in between her departure and the present moment.

"Just between us," whispered Mary, "the new maid isn't working out. She's lazy as can be. I do miss you."

"Would you like to hire a respectable widow?" Georgette offered. "She's the farthest thing from lazy. She's young and strong and kind, and she's expecting a child. She needs work, and she will work hard." After traveling with Harriet Linton for a week of difficulties borne with patience and good cheer, there was no recommendation Georgette would not give her.

Georgette gave Mary the direction of the boarding-house where Linton was staying. "Call on her soon, won't you?"

Mary would. Mary did.

So they were both settled. The oldest Stoneleigh child was five, young still for having a governess. Georgette remembered herself at that age, turned loose in the bookshop to educate herself. Never encouraged to play.

So she taught the little lord and ladies to count in French and began working with them on sums. But she also fit together puzzles with them, listened to their silly poems, and laughed more than she'd ever thought she could.

Their favorite game was when Georgette plumped down with them onto the nursery floor and said, "Ask me as many questions as you wish." She heard about everything from childish fears (where does lightning come from?) to curiosities (what does a whale eat)? Sometimes they all went to the home's library together to find an answer, if the marchioness wasn't at home to callers at the time. Georgette knew better than to violate the determined manners of high society by trooping children through the house.

Besides which, she didn't want to embarrass Tess and the marquess. They had welcomed her. There was space for her here, within this family.

And it was new, uncluttered by old memories and heart-sorrows.

Well. Mostly. The marquess looked a little too much like his younger brother Hugo for heart-sorrow to be entirely absent from her days. And when the children asked her a question to which she didn't know the answer, she couldn't help but think of him. A man who wanted to learn everything was exactly the sort of person such moments called for.

But she was doing what she had always known she must: build a life in which she didn't rely on anyone else.

It wasn't what she wanted. But she'd been fine in the past, and she was fine now. Better than fine. These people . . . they mattered to her. Her fondness for them made the sun more cheerful as she woke each morning and dressed for the day ahead.

And today, she had a half day off. Time to shop for a new gown with her gold sovereigns, which were nothing more scandalous now than any other coin of the realm.

The scramble after the Royal Mint's reward was over, and the gold sovereigns were to be found all over England.

Lord Hugo Starling's name had been in the society papers. Even before he returned to London, he was a hero—right alongside Callum Jenks, the Bow Street Runner, who couldn't be bothered with any of the attention and was soon dropped from all mentions of the case.

Hugo had wanted notoriety, and he had got it. She was glad for him. She tried not to think of him, though.

She was not successful.

When she turned around, ready to leave the nook that served as her chamber in the nursery, she believed for a moment her thoughts had conjured him in the doorway. But—he was really there? She shrieked to see him there, large as life, blocking her passage from the room.

"Hu—Hugo?" Her heart thumped wildly. "You startled me. What are you *doing* here?"

"I live in London. I'm only sorry it took me so long to get back. Jenks had to wait for the guards to arrive from the Mint, you see, and I had promised to travel with him. And Lowe's sutures—"

"Never mind." She took up her reticule. "If such reports are all you have to give, then you have my congratulations. I am about to leave, though. Please let me pass."

"Are you due time off?" His dark brows lifted. "Can you walk out with me?"

She couldn't tell him no, even though the last words she'd said to him had been a declaration of love—to which he'd said only *I'm sorry*. "Once the maid arrives to take my place, yes."

The nursery was four floors from the pavement, tucked under the eaves of the brick town house. A slant-ceilinged and cozy space, it was newly papered and floored in new and clean-scrubbed pine. A small carpet in a geometric pattern covered the center of the room.

"Your father had this newly refitted," Georgette explained. "The roof leaked, and the home needed some other repairs. It's nice now, isn't it?"

Hugo searched the lines of the room with his eyes. "You don't feel ashamed to accept my family's help?"

"I'm working for my bread. I could never be ashamed of that." She smiled at the three small children playing at the other end of the room. They hadn't yet noticed their visitor. "You see, I had a purpose all along. I like looking for things, and I like helping people. Especially if I find the things, and especially if the people I help say 'thank you.' Lottie—" She raised her voice. "Here is your handkerchief."

"Miss Frost!" The little girl leaped to her feet, then ran across the room and tackled Georgette's legs.

"Or if they do that." Georgette smiled. "That is even better than words."

"Do I get a hug too?" asked Hugo.

"Uncle Hugo!" Lottie flung herself at Hugo.

"I meant from your governess," he said. "But this is nice too."

A maid scratched at the door frame. "Miss Frost?"

"Elizabeth, thank you. The children are in your care. I'm ready to walk out, and I'll be back by six o'clock."

"But Miss Frost. Lord Hugo." The maid bobbed a curtsy. "His Grace the Duke of Willingham has called here, and he wants to see you both."

"What an honor," Hugo said. "I find myself overcome."

Georgette hushed him. "We'll be right down. Thank you."

As they descended the stairs, Georgette asked Hugo, "To what *do* we owe the honor? Why would your father call for you here?"

"I expect because I've been jawing on about you since I arrived in London. And Loftus and Tess have been jawing on about you since you took up employment here. *Do* you have a halo and wings? I have heard you are an angel."

"Damned with faint praise," she said. "And here I thought I was getting on well with them."

"Ha." Outside the door of the house's formal parlor, Hugo paused. "Whatever the duke has to say, I'm on your side."

"Why, what do you think I did?"

Almost before the question had left her lips, though, he had opened the door.

Georgette had never met the duke, but she would have recognized him at once from the society papers. When he stood, in his bearing was the confidence of generations of nobility—and in the stubborn line of his jaw was a strong resemblance to Hugo.

"Your Grace." She curtsied.

Introductions were completed all around, and then the duke grunted, "I wanted to meet Miss Frost. And you, Hugo—I wanted to give you something."

He shuffled forward, wincing.

"Is the gout bad?" Hugo asked.

"Not so bad as it was. The lemon juice is helping, I think."

Lemon juice! Georgette speared Hugo with a glance.

But then the duke stretched out his hand, and in it was a watch—and she forgot all about teasing Hugo when she saw his expression. He wore a naked sort of look, as if he had so much feeling it could not be hidden.

"Matthew's watch," he said at last. "You kept it."

"I did," said the duke. "I needed it. But you needed it too. You should have it now."

Hugo hesitated—then closed his father's hand about the watch. "No. Keep it, Father. I'll remember him always. I don't need the watch for that."

The duke left his hand outstretched, uncertain, then drew it back and replaced the watch in his pocket. "Be considerate," he said. "Don't make a spectacle. Be mindful of appearances." He shook his leonine head. "Such advice doesn't always make sense, does it?"

"I'm not sure what you're getting at," Hugo said.

"I'm . . . proud of you. For what you did in Northumberland. And I think your idea about quarantining ill tenants . . . it was all right. That is—if you'd advise the medical men nearest each of my estates, that would be all right too."

Georgette had never seen Hugo's brows lift so high. "Will your medical men listen to me?"

"They will if I tell them to."

Hugo muttered something that sounded like, *always a blunt instrument.* "I would prefer to be listened to because they are interested in my ideas and find merit in my methods. But I suppose as long as I am listened to, it doesn't matter why."

The duke cracked a thin smile. "It's good to be a duke's son."

Georgette laughed. "I have often told him so."

"Well. That's all I came to say," said the duke. "Hugo, you're sure about the watch?"

"Quite sure. Thank you."

"All right, then." And that was the end of the conversation. Inclining his head in a silent farewell, the duke made his careful way out of the parlor.

"Do you want to walk out now, Georgette?" asked Hugo. "There are a lot of things I need to tell you. Or maybe you should sit and have some tea."

"How mysterious you are." She sank onto the nearest settee. "Here I am, sitting. No need for tea. What have you to tell me?"

Many things, as it turned out, ranging from coins hidden in the barrel of Madeira to the nature of Sir Frederic's treachery.

"I should have known he was no good," she replied.

"His books' bindings certainly weren't. And so you have claimed the second part of the royal reward?"

"In a manner of speaking. That is, it's mine, but I won't keep it." He was pacing, an excited sort of agitation she had never seen him display. "I realized a single hospital in London is not enough. What I want to do is teach—or make it possible for others to learn—the combination of surgical and medical care that will allow a doctor to meet a patient's every need. Not only in London, but across England. Education for boys like Matthew Lowe, who could attend medical college and return home to practice."

"It sounds brilliant. But—wait. Wait. Your hospital? You are giving up on your precious, precious hospital?"

"Oh, I'm not giving up on it." He paused in his pacing, shooting a sly smile at her. "I will donate the plans to either the Royal Society or the Royal College of Physicians. I haven't decided which. It depends on which institution will allocate more money for it."

"You are pitting them against each other," Georgette realized. "Nicely done. I hope the hospital is built someday."

"Whether it is or not, I shall use my station as the son of a duke—"

"Finally, he admits his privilege."

"—to do what has not been done before to help people. With the reward money, I will endow scholarships to cover tuition at every medical college in the country. And I can use my own income to see that the families of youths who travel to medical school are not left impoverished by their absence. Because the point isn't to have a hospital. It's to help people regain and keep their health. That's the best way to honor Matthew. Not with a building."

How earnest he was. There was none of the bull-headed attention to detail that had marked his obsession with the hospital plans. He seemed . . . free.

"It all sounds brilliant," she repeated. "Another in your line of wise choices."

"Only wait. Here comes the wisest ever." He dropped to one knee, pulling the signet from his finger. "You told me from the first moment of our trip that you found me acceptable."

Her heart began to thump hard, as if waking after a long sleep. "I said I found your *idea* acceptable. Is that ring for me?"

"Yes. Right." He held it out to her, checking his balance as he leaned forward. "Will you have it?"

She took up the ring, considering. "The last thing I said about you was that I loved you. Then you apologized."

"And I apologize again, this time for the apology. What a dreadful thing it was to say. I wanted to protect you from everything, and I had not planned for love."

"You do rather a lot of planning." She held up the ring. "Am I meant to be evaluating this, to see whether it's made of melted sovereigns?"

He cursed. "No. Sorry. You're meant to be deciding whether you want that on your finger. I should have said so at once."

She slid the ring onto her finger. "It doesn't fit."

He lurched to his feet, then flung himself onto the settee beside her. "Then I'll get a different one, if you want it. What I'm really asking is whether you'll marry me. Because I love you, with all your honesty and humor. Your confidence and your wish to find the best in people."

She wanted to say something, but all her thoughts had scattered like dandelion seed.

Then he took her hand, too-loose ring and all. "I love the way you reached out to me, the way you shared your feelings with me, the way you learn everyone's names and notice book bindings and persuade people to play the smallpipes and—"

"Now you're just babbling whatever comes to mind." A smile was tugging at her lips.

"Whatever comes to mind is something I love about you."

"My toes."

"Certainly. Though I'd love you if you had only five, or none at all."

"My ability to disguise myself as a boy?"

"Let us place that within the category of 'creativity and resourcefulness.' And yes."

She stared at him in wonder. "You are categorizing the things you love about me. You mean it, don't you?"

"Of course I mean it. I'm not saying this to be *kind*."

She snorted.

"I was guided by love before I realized what it was," he said. "All those trips to Frost's Bookshop, when I wanted to make sure you were all right—it was because I cared about you, Georgette. I wanted you to *be* all right. I didn't know what that meant for you, or what it might look like to me, but that was what I wanted."

She looked at the ring, fashioned of old gold. A band of history. "Am I proper enough to be your wife? I don't mean for you, but for your family. I don't want to be the cause of a breach."

He pressed a kiss to her hand. "Nonsense. I've told

you before, if my mother doesn't like you, it won't be because of your gown. And my father is only beginning to like me, so I think we shall do well together. Tess cannot say enough good about you, you angel, which means Loftus also cannot. Beware, Miss Frost, or you shall find yourself tonnish."

She hesitated—then laughed, a bubble of sheer joy at his words, his feelings, his body beside hers.

"Will you marry me, then?" he asked. "Do you think you could love me?"

"I know I could, Hugo. I know I do. I tend to be wholehearted and enthusiastic. Perhaps you noticed?"

"I noticed, yes. But to make sure I have all the empirical evidence I require, I'd welcome a demonstration."

She obliged. It was a spirited demonstration involving lips and hands. It would have involved more, but the parlor door was open, and there was no sense in causing a scandal. For now.

"Do you love me only because I begged you to?"

"Are you marrying me because I begged you to?"

At once, they both laughed. "I asked you to marry me," Hugo said, "because I want nothing more. I probably ought to have told you this sooner, but I have a cottage. It's in Edinburgh, not far from where your brother's lady lives."

"I know," she said. "Benedict wrote to me after he and Charlotte were wed, and he mentioned it."

"If my father is sincere—and I think he is, because he does not make suggestions only to be kind—then I will need to visit his estates as time permits. I'll want to travel about, teaching at medical colleges if needed too. And if you would like to work with nurses and befriend the apothecaries, that would be . . ."

"Acceptable?" she asked.

"Much more than that. So. Travel—but home must be somewhere. Do you want to go to Edinburgh? Where do you want to go?"

She smiled. "That's the same question you asked me at the beginning of our adventure. At that time, I wanted to go away on my own."

"And now?"

"Now I am determined that we shall travel together. But not quite yet. I cannot leave the marchioness until she finds another governess."

"You truly are an angel." He sighed. "Very well, I'll be patient. But only for a short while. And then, to the cottage?"

"To the cottage," she agreed.

To a home, together.

If you've enjoyed *Passion Favors the Bold*, you won't
want to miss the first of Theresa Romain's
Royal Rewards novels, available now!

In the game of seduction, everyone wins. . . .

FORTUNE FAVORS THE WICKED

Indecently Lucky

As a lieutenant in the Royal Navy, Benedict Frost had
the respect of every man on board—and the
adoration of the women in every port. When injury
ends his naval career, the silver-tongued libertine can
hardly stomach the boredom. Not after everything—
and everyone—he's experienced. Good thing a new
adventure has just fallen into his lap. . . .

When courtesan Charlotte Perry learns the Royal
Mint is offering a reward for finding a cache of stolen
gold coins, she seizes the chance to build a new life
for herself. As the treasure hunt begins, she realizes
her tenacity is matched only by Benedict's—and that
sometimes adversaries can make the best allies.
But when the search for treasure becomes a discovery
of pleasure, they'll be forced to decide if they can
sacrifice the lives they've always dreamed of
for a love they've never known. . . .

Praise for the novels of Theresa Romain

"One of the best books I have ever read, bar none . . .
Romain's exquisite prose and extraordinary
storytelling skills take us on a splendid
and unforgettable journey."
—*Fresh Fiction* on *Season for Desire*

"Theresa Romain writes with a
delightfully romantic flair."
—*USA Today* bestselling author
Julianne MacLean on *Season for Surrender*

Books by Bestselling Author
Fern Michaels

___The Jury	0-8217-7878-1	$6.99US/$9.99CAN
___Sweet Revenge	0-8217-7879-X	$6.99US/$9.99CAN
___Lethal Justice	0-8217-7880-3	$6.99US/$9.99CAN
___Free Fall	0-8217-7881-1	$6.99US/$9.99CAN
___Fool Me Once	0-8217-8071-9	$7.99US/$10.99CAN
___Vegas Rich	0-8217-8112-X	$7.99US/$10.99CAN
___Hide and Seek	1-4201-0184-6	$6.99US/$9.99CAN
___Hokus Pokus	1-4201-0185-4	$6.99US/$9.99CAN
___Fast Track	1-4201-0186-2	$6.99US/$9.99CAN
___Collateral Damage	1-4201-0187-0	$6.99US/$9.99CAN
___Final Justice	1-4201-0188-9	$6.99US/$9.99CAN
___Up Close and Personal	0-8217-7956-7	$7.99US/$9.99CAN
___Under the Radar	1-4201-0683-X	$6.99US/$9.99CAN
___Razor Sharp	1-4201-0684-8	$7.99US/$10.99CAN
___Yesterday	1-4201-1494-8	$5.99US/$6.99CAN
___Vanishing Act	1-4201-0685-6	$7.99US/$10.99CAN
___Sara's Song	1-4201-1493-X	$5.99US/$6.99CAN
___Deadly Deals	1-4201-0686-4	$7.99US/$10.99CAN
___Game Over	1-4201-0687-2	$7.99US/$10.99CAN
___Sins of Omission	1-4201-1153-1	$7.99US/$10.99CAN
___Sins of the Flesh	1-4201-1154-X	$7.99US/$10.99CAN
___Cross Roads	1-4201-1192-2	$7.99US/$10.99CAN

Available Wherever Books Are Sold!
Check out our website at www.kensingtonbooks.com

More by Bestselling Author
Hannah Howell

__Highland Angel	978-1-4201-0864-4	$6.99US/$8.99CAN
__If He's Sinful	978-1-4201-0461-5	$6.99US/$8.99CAN
__Wild Conquest	978-1-4201-0464-6	$6.99US/$8.99CAN
__If He's Wicked	978-1-4201-0460-8	$6.99US/$8.49CAN
__My Lady Captor	978-0-8217-7430-4	$6.99US/$8.49CAN
__Highland Sinner	978-0-8217-8001-5	$6.99US/$8.49CAN
__Highland Captive	978-0-8217-8003-9	$6.99US/$8.49CAN
__Nature of the Beast	978-1-4201-0435-6	$6.99US/$8.49CAN
__Highland Fire	978-0-8217-7429-8	$6.99US/$8.49CAN
__Silver Flame	978-1-4201-0107-2	$6.99US/$8.49CAN
__Highland Wolf	978-0-8217-8000-8	$6.99US/$9.99CAN
__Highland Wedding	978-0-8217-8002-2	$4.99US/$6.99CAN
__Highland Destiny	978-1-4201-0259-8	$4.99US/$6.99CAN
__Only for You	978-0-8217-8151-7	$6.99US/$8.99CAN
__Highland Promise	978-1-4201-0261-1	$4.99US/$6.99CAN
__Highland Vow	978-1-4201-0260-4	$4.99US/$6.99CAN
__Highland Savage	978-0-8217-7999-6	$6.99US/$9.99CAN
__Beauty and the Beast	978-0-8217-8004-6	$4.99US/$6.99CAN
__Unconquered	978-0-8217-8088-6	$4.99US/$6.99CAN
__Highland Barbarian	978-0-8217-7998-9	$6.99US/$9.99CAN
__Highland Conqueror	978-0-8217-8148-7	$6.99US/$9.99CAN
__Conqueror's Kiss	978-0-8217-8005-3	$4.99US/$6.99CAN
__A Stockingful of Joy	978-1-4201-0018-1	$4.99US/$6.99CAN
__Highland Bride	978-0-8217-7995-8	$4.99US/$6.99CAN
__Highland Lover	978-0-8217-7759-6	$6.99US/$9.99CAN

Available Wherever Books Are Sold!

Check out our website at
http://www.kensingtonbooks.com